the
sleeping
father

a novel by
matthew
sharpe

soft skull press

The Sleeping Father
©2003 Matthew Sharpe

Soft Skull Press
New York, NY

www.softskull.com

Cover Photograph by Thomas Hopkins
Author Photograph © Carles Allende 2001
Book Design by David Janik

Printed in Canada

Library of Congress Cataloging-in-Publication Data

Sharpe, Matthew, 1962–
    The sleeping father / by Matthew Sharpe.—1st ed.
        p. cm.
    ISBN 1-932360-00-X (pbk.: alk. paper)
    1. Antidepressants—Side effects—Fiction. 2. Brain
damage—Patients—Fiction. 3. Parent and child—Fiction.
4. Divorced fathers—Fiction. 5. Jewish families—Fiction.
6. Teenagers—Fiction.
I. Title.
PS3569.H3444 S58 2003
813'.54--dc21
                                            2003013840

ISBN: 978-1-932360-00-4

For my mother,
Jacqueline Steiner,
and
for my father,
Myron Sharpe

the
sleeping
father

part one

1.

Chris Schwartz's father's Prozac dosage must have been incorrect, because he awoke one morning to discover that the right side of his face had gone numb. This was the second discovery on a journey Chris's father sensed would carry him miles from the makeshift haven of health. The first discovery had been, of course, the depression for which the Prozac was meant to be the cure, a discovery made not by Bernard Schwartz but by his son, Chris. Chris figured it out first because that was how things worked in this family. Soul of son and soul of dad were linked by analogy. No tic or mood swing in the one did not go unrepresented in the susceptible equipment of the other.

Bernie Schwartz leaned in close to the mirror in his bedroom and poked the right side of his face with the sharp bottom of the pocket-size silver crucifix his daughter, Cathy, had given him. Seventeen-year-old Chris, in his room, typed the following sentence into an e-mail he was about to send to his friend Frank Dial: "You know you're dead when . . . your friends throw dirt in your face." This was the newest addition to a group of aphorisms Chris and Frank were developing for a computer screensaver program that they hoped to sell one day soon for a huge amount of money or, failing that, a tiny amount of money.

Chris sent the sentence and went to the window and opened it and looked out. It was seven o'clock on a fine autumn morning in Bellwether, Connecticut. Chris looked at the trees and the grass, he looked at his own driveway, his wooden fence, the street beyond it, several houses within looking range, back to the fence, the roses by the fence, the cars, a crushed Coke can, a small unintelligible pile of dirt, a neighborhood squirrel, a fly, a dog. He looked at the street again, and the cars parked in the driveways, and he marveled at how each car had a driveway to park in and how every driveway in the world had a street at one end and a house at the other. Chris felt that if he'd been the guy they came to when they needed someone to invent the thing to convey the cars from the streets to the houses, he'd have choked, he'd have let down humanity.

Chris thought of his mom in California. Often when he thought of his mom in California, he thought of her standing tall and strong in a long white robe at the edge of the ocean, her arms aloft, her hands clenched in fists, watching a thirty-foot wave approach her. The wave breaks on top of her head, and when it has subsided, there she stands in the same position, fists high, face wet, eyes open, wet hair streaming down the back of her white robe. Chris had the same hair as his mother, though not literally of course.

Chris thought of his dad in the next room and felt the astonishing surge of affection and sadness that had accompanied his dad-related thoughts of the past year. Chris thought of his nervous, obsessive little sister, felt a discomfort he did not wish to explore, hurried on to the next thought, which was people all across Bellwether, Connecticut, waking up to classical music or a hangover, jogging with the dog, ironing a shirt, putting on aftershave or eyeliner, buying the paper, catching the train to the city: all the wretched conduct that made humanity God's chosen.

Chris made a stop at the mirror to study that miniature version of humanity, his own face, on which adolescent discomfort expressed itself through the medium of acne. Chris returned to his computer, where a reply from Frank Dial awaited him: "You know you're having a bad day when . . . you wake up naked and face-down on the sidewalk of an unfamiliar city to find a policeman beating the backs of your thighs with a billy club." Upon reading this latest of Frank's aphorisms, Chris felt so lucky to have a friend like Frank that he almost wept. He prevented himself from weeping by uttering the words "Don't weep, shithead."

2.

Chris entered the kitchen in time to hear his sister say, "Bless us, O Lord, and these thy gifts which we are about to receive from Thy bounty, through Christ our Lord. Amen."

"You've got to be kidding with that crap," Chris said.

Cathy's face reddened. "Please don't call it crap." She sat stiffly and correctly at the table with her hands clasped not in prayer but in the left hand's attempt to prevent the right hand from throwing her rosary beads at her brother.

"Did Mom and Dad forget to tell you we're Jewish?"

"No, they did not forget to tell me."

"So what's the problem?"

"There is no problem."

"The problem is that you're a Jew saying a Christian prayer."

"I have Jesus in my heart," Cathy said, believing for an instant that a simple declaration of truth would be understandable to her brother, or anyone.

"For all I care," he said, "you can have Jesus up your—"

"Chris, if I'm a Jew, that means you're a Jew too, right?"

"Yeah. You, me, Dad, Mom. It runs in the family."

"And how do you practice your Judaism?"

"Practice it? I don't practice it. That's the beauty of Judaism in this family and families like ours all across America. We're not the kind of Jews where you do anything. We're the kind where you just *are* it. Judaism isn't just a religion. It's a whole, like, thing."

"'Thing'?"

When did this twit get so good at arguing? "Religion is stupid, anyway," Chris said. "It's the crack cocaine of the masses."

Cathy made a gesture at her brother that was definitely not a sign of the cross.

Bernie Schwartz entered the kitchen and looked at his children as if he were bewildered to find them in his house. He sat at the kitchen table in front of a cup of coffee and tapped the right side of his face idly with the back of his spoon, unaware that light brown droplets of coffee were clinging to his cheek.

In the quiet kitchen, the tapping of the spoon against wet flesh made a liquid plop like big drops of water falling from a great height onto a pile of wet towels. "Dad, get a grip," Chris said.

Cathy gently took the spoon from her father and clasped his hand in her two. She wanted to communicate the compassion she felt for him in her heart through the look in her eyes. She tried to be careful in her actions. She focused on each gesture she made because she wanted Jesus to love her. She said, "What's wrong, Father?"

"'Father'?" Chris said. "His name is 'Father' now? Dad, what's wrong with you?"

"The right side of my face is numb."

"What do you mean, numb? You mean like it's not there?"

"Oh it's there, I just can't feel it."

"Yeah well don't tap it with a spoon, you're creeping me out, man."

Cathy removed her hands from her father's and wiped the coffee from his cheek with her napkin. The tremor in her hands wasn't the outward sign of some kind of saintly passion, it was the outward sign of the fear of a sixteen-year-old girl whose father was falling apart.

Bernie said, "I think my Prozac dosage may be off."

"You should call Dr. Moreau," Cathy said.

Bernie dutifully went to the phone on the wall by the dishwasher and punched in the number of his psychiatrist, Dr. Jacques Moreau. "Hello, this is Dr. Moreau speaking on a tape . . ." said the faintly French-accented recorded message of Dr. Moreau.

When it was Bernie's turn to speak, he said, "First, I wonder what idiot doesn't know you're speaking on a tape. Second, the

Prozac you're prescribing is making my face numb. Third, the Prozac is also giving me homicidal ideations that I'm unaware of, so unbeknownst to both of us I'm on my way over to your office to kill you. Listen, just call me back soon."

Chris said, "Look, Sister, Father's got his sense of humor back."

3.

Chris Schwartz met Frank Dial in the road. "Frank Dial" had become Chris's shorthand for joy itself; tough joy—Frank was acerbic and dark and quick. He had a word for everything, and often not a nice one; justly so, Chris thought, for the world was often not a nice place. But it was nice for Chris to have a good friend who was accurate in speech. Chris himself was not accurate or even truthful a lot of the time. He kidded a lot in a haphazard way—kidding without meaning it—and he lied a bit as well. He had a stern principle about accuracy and honesty in speech that he said he took pride in not living up to. Anyway he didn't have to live up to it because Frank Dial lived up to it for him.

In some half-secret place inside *his* heart, Frank wished Chris wasn't white. It was embarrassing for a young black man like Frank to have a white boy for a best friend, but the Negro pickings were slim in Bellwether, Connecticut, where Frank was one of five blacks matriculated at the Bellwether High School for Upper Middle Class Caucasians. Nevertheless, Chris was an excellent example of what white people could achieve when they set their minds to it. Chris listened closely and got most of the allusions. Chris could keep up with the pace of the patter and the pain.

The boys set out on the journey to school along Southridge Road. They saw many wondrous phenomena. They saw small children in their jackets, they saw schoolbuses and birds, they saw houses, they saw the paint jobs on houses. High up in the sky, they saw a cloud in the shape of their math teacher. They heard a distant siren and thought of death. They spoke of all and sundry.

The town's commercial center embraced them curtly as they passed through it. They entered a deli and came out with a pair of bright green electrolyte-replenishment sports beverages that God had not created nor intended to create. They passed the magazine store where they saw, on the cover of a well-known music magazine, a photograph of two middle aged rock stars imitating the famous pose they had struck for the same magazine twenty-five years earlier. Frank and Chris felt that both these rock stars and this magazine had used to mean something, but now merely made reference to the thing they used to mean without actually meaning it any more.

Frank reached into the wilderness of his backpack and came up with a frayed notebook. The words "EVERYTHING IN THE WORLD" were printed on the cover of the notebook in Frank's almost typographically neat hand. As the boys walked through the prosthetic heart of Bellwether, Frank flipped to the section entitled *Things that look like things that you already know what they look like*, stopped walking, and wrote a short description of the magazine cover. This section was getting very long. It took up more than half the notebook. That was because, in the estimation of Frank and Chris, the world was weary of itself—had trod, had trod, had trod, or whatever; now ground out shoddy reproductions of stuff it used to take pride in producing. Trees, shrubs, cats, people, clouds, and stars were now "trees," "shrubs," "cats," "people," "clouds," "stars." The world was just putting in the hours now, biding its time until retirement, when it would cast off its worldliness and return to being void and without form.

"Nigger!" a kid in a car going by shouted.

Frank said, "I'm so glad that gentleman reminded me that I am a nigger. I had forgotten."

Chris said, "I'll remind you next time if you want."

Frank stared at his friend, startled. Chris knew he'd misspoken. Whereas an instant before each boy had been half of a two-man friendship, the one now represented a group that would always commit indelicacies against the group represented by the other. Standing in the school parking lot, they continued to stare at one another, rendered speechless by the power of language.

"Sorry," Chris said.

"Ass," said Frank, and went inside the school.

Chris stayed outside, stunned. He had English but now would blow it off. He was supposed to be reading *Catcher in the Rye*, he thought, or some other *Catcher in the Rye*-type disservice to teenagers everywhere. Yes, it was *Catcher in the Rye*. It had to be. They'd long ago crammed *Catcher in the Rye* down his throat till he puked. Then they'd crammed *Catcher in the Rye* plus the puke back down his throat and he puked them up and then they crammed down *Catcher in the Rye* plus his puked puke and by now it was easier just to swallow. This wasn't *Catcher in the Rye*'s fault. It was probably a halfway decent book, if you were from someplace like Bulgaria and had never heard of it; decent for a book, that is, which wasn't saying much. There was no book that was good. There was no school that was good. There was no family that was good. There was no friend that was good. There was no life that was good.

4.

Chris Schwartz entered American History at 9:22 A.M. and sat in
the back corner where he hoped no one would see him.

He was still in his half-conscious youth. Sometimes he saw more
than he was able to feel; sometimes he felt more than he was able to
see; sometimes neither. During the course of any several minutes he
could think of something important, forget it, think of it again, forget it again, his memory a short-circuited strobe light in the dark
discothèque of his consciousness. So when his history teacher said,
"Mr. Schwartz will begin class today with his oral presentation on,
ah, Paul Robeson," Chris was both prepared and unprepared. He
had been, American History to one side, a casual Robeson hobby-
ist. He'd carried on an approach-avoidance relationship to the auto-
biography, *Here I Stand*; he'd rented and viewed *The Emperor Jones*
and a few other Robeson cinematic vehicles; of an afternoon, he'd
worried his Smithsonian *Paul Robeson Anthology* CD which, as luck
would have it, was in his backpack right now. Chris fell into a reverie about the Robeson CD. The reverie, during which everyone in
the class was waiting for Chris to talk or stand up, was interrupted
by someone called Richard Stone, who said "Schwartz!" Chris
jumped out of his chair.

Stone was a psychopath who had it in for Chris. He'd moved to
town the previous year. Rumor had it that his enormously wealthy
parents were bringing him up without love, that in the town in New
York where he'd lived before moving to Bellwether, Stone had killed
a kid by punching him in the face again and again, and that the
Stones had purchased their son's nonincarceration, thus proving
once again the terrible injustice of American so-called democracy
and encouraging in Chris a fervent belief in the life and good works

of Paul Robeson.

Tall, thin, stoop-shouldered, trembling slightly, Chris stood at the front of the room, facing his classmates. Fear mixed with passion and rendered Chris's mind—like the 3 by 5 cards on which he was meant to have written notes for his report—a perfect blank. Frank Dial entered the classroom, stared at Chris, and sat in the back. Chris said, "I'd like to begin by playing a selection from the *Paul Robeson Anthology* CD, available from Smithsonian records for $11.99 plus shipping and handling." Chris removed the CD from his backpack and took the portable CD player down from the metal filing cabinet behind his teacher's desk. He fumbled endlessly with the CD player's electric cord. "Excuse me, folks, I've never worked with a CD player before."

Richard Stone muttered a violent imprecation.

Chris said, "Hook up, hook up, the Zen thing always works for me." Not most, but a few of his classmates—the ones with divorced parents, or a live-in, senile grandparent, or a younger brother with leukemia—admired Chris's self-effacing irony.

Chris popped his Robeson CD into the player and programmed it for number 4, "No More Auction Block for Me." He figured that while the song was playing he could mentally assemble things to say about Robeson. What he didn't figure was that yesterday he had mistakenly put his Nirvana *In Utero* CD inside the *Paul Robeson Anthology* CD case, so when he pressed the play button, instead of Robeson's monumental bass-baritone, Kurt Cobain's plaintive, searing tenor emerged:

> Rape me.
> Rape me again.
> Rape me.
> Rape me my friend.
> I'm not the only one.
> Aaaaaahm not the only one.
> Aaaaaahm not the only one.
> Aaaaaahm not the only one.

"Oops, wrong CD. Which brings up an interesting point. We're all human, you know?" Chris asked, inadvertently looking into those little portals of hatred, Richard Stone's eyes. "Which was the main point of Paul Robeson's valedictory speech before the graduating class of Rutgers University, 1919, which meant he had the highest grade point average—a 97.5—of anyone graduating from Rutgers at that time.

"Paul Robeson was a great black American football player, actor, singer, orator, and political activist who, throughout his adult life, enjoyed sexual relations with many women, including many white women. This is a type of activity he shared in common with that other great prominent African-American political figure, Martin Luther King, Jr., though I don't think it's fair that we speak of only African-American political figures who were cockswains—I mean, uh, yeah that's not a curseword—cockswains, because a lot of white men did it too, like Thomas Jefferson and John F. Kennedy Jr. Plus Robeson had a high degree of sophistication and athletic physique which women would definitely like, which is only my opinion.

"Another point I would like to point out about Paul Robeson is his Communism. Robeson was admirer and friend to the great Russian revolutionary Leon Trotsky. After a falling out with Vladimir Lenin, Trotsky fled the Soviet Union and took up residence in Princeton, New Jersey, Paul Robeson's hometown. One summer day, while Trotsky was bathing in his wooded backyard in Princeton, New Jersey, Richard Nixon, who was then the head of the House Un-American Activities Committee, snuck up behind Trotsky and, just when Trotsky was giving himself a nice shampoo, Nixon forcefully inserted an ice pick into the back of Trotsky's brain."

Chris Schwartz paused. He was troubled by the violent death of Trotsky and had to quell the turmoil inside himself in order to continue his speech.

"When Robeson heard of Trotsky's death, he suddenly converted to Judaism, in solidarity with his martyred hero. At this time in American history, Congress considered all Jews to be Communists. They were wrong. Only some Jews were Communists: the smart ones. Like Paul Robeson, who cherished freedom and decency and respect for mankind and the dignity and decency of the common man."

Chris Schwartz was experiencing a deep kind of truth that transcended mere facts. Frank Dial was smirking. Richard Stone was restrained from murdering Chris Schwartz with his hands and teeth only by the force of social custom.

"Paul Robeson, though never allowed to set foot on American soil after his conversion, toured the world giving concerts. No matter what song he was singing—a Negro spiritual, a European peasant song, an opera, a child's nursery rhyme—he always changed the lyrics to include diatribes against America as well as biographical facts about Leon Trotsky.

"Recently, *Ebony* magazine honored Paul Robeson by naming him one of the ten greatest African-Americans of all time. Not long after, the *Jewish Daily Forward* put Robeson on its all-time top-ten list of American Jews. Regrettably, Leon Trotsky's name was absent from both lists.

"In conclusion, Paul Robeson was the greatest man who ever lived. We should all try to be more like him. Now I will play 'Serve the Servants,' by Nirvana, a song Paul Robeson would have sung about Leon Trotsky if he were alive today. Thank you."

At the end of "Serve the Servants," a few people clapped faintly. Frank Dial made a teetering gesture with his right hand that meant something along the lines of *comme çi, comme ça.* Inside the mind of Richard Stone, a place inaccessible to Communism or God, violent thoughts gathered and swarmed.

5.

At lunchtime, Chris Schwartz and Frank Dial walked across the school parking lot. "You're cute when you're panicking," Frank said.

"You got any more screensaver apothegms?" Chris asked.

"How about this: 'To err is Caucasian.'"

"What's the rest?"

"There is no rest for the wicked."

"That's it? 'To err is Caucasian'? I don't get it."

"That's the point."

"I thought the point was you and I collaborate on a business venture, not you use the business venture as a vehicle to make oblique remarks that would probably be insulting to me if I understood them."

"Kill two birds with one stone."

"Speaking of Stone, *hello*, is that guy a freakshow?"

They stepped off the blacktop of the parking lot onto the packed dirt of the path that led down into the woods behind it. The woods were like a mustache of wilderness between the gelid nose of the high school and the hot maw of the adult world. *Pace* Robeson, Chris and Frank walked along the path discussing their modest capitalist project. It was possible for a young man in Bellwether, Connecticut, to have accomplished the larger part of his life's serious drug abuse by the age of seventeen. So it was with Chris and Frank, who beginning at twelve had put themselves on a rigorous schedule of beer; following that, whiskey; then codeine, then nitrous from whipped cream spray cans, then pot, then speed, then valium, then coke, then crack, then acid. After a thorough empirical survey of each, plus the briefest of dalliances with heroin, they lost interest in all. Following this, a vague and formless period of anxiety corresponding with the year they were sixteen, and culminating in the capitalist impulse.

They found a flat, soft, mossy patch of forest floor and sat down on it. They leaned and loafed, they lay on their backs and observed a brown spear of autumn grass. They gazed at the pattern of negative space created in the sky by the semidenuded branches of deciduous trees. They soothed themselves with the narcotic of nature.

Chris said, "Sorry about what I said before when that guy called you that name out of the car window."

Frank said, "You managed to climb back up the Negrometer with that Robeson bizarreness. Let it go."

"No really, I was making a stupid—"

"Let it go, my man. Let it go. Let it all go."

Chris took Frank's excellent point and did a kind of uptight middle-class suburban Jewish version of letting it all go, which to the casual observer might resemble not letting any of it go. Chris felt a surge of brotherly love for Frank. Frank felt something similar and they rolled toward one another in the moss. Their faces were suddenly an inch apart. Hard to say what happened next. Possibly their lips touched, maybe for a couple seconds, maybe a little bit on purpose, but neither could tell for sure because it was such a crazy event. They sat up and looked at each other.

Chris said, "Huh, that was weird."

"Not so weird, really."

"Kind of like kissing a girl."

"Or so one would imagine," Frank said.

Chris said, "We don't have to do it again, do we?"

Frank said, "I don't think so but I'm not sure."

"It would make our lives so much more complicated than they already are. We just pursue girls from now on. Right?"

"Oh, you mean the noncomplicated pursuit of girls." Frank felt rejected by Chris. Chris was sad but he didn't know why. They sat side by side, looking away from one another, not speaking or knowing what to do.

"Wow," said Richard Stone, their high school classmate who

was hatred made flesh. "I'm just minding my own business jogging through the woods when I practically trip over a Jew, a commie, a nigger, a nigger-lover, and two fags, and the amazing thing is, there's only two of you."

Richard Stone was on the Bellwether High School football team and a couple of his teammates came jogging up behind him. Chris and Frank stood up. Stone was like a six-foot-tall fire hydrant: wide and cylindrical and hard, with hard geometrical protuberances.

"What's that book?" Stone said, referring to Frank's notebook, *Everything in the World*. "Is that *The Communist Manifesto*, or is it *How to be a Homo?*"

Frank said, "It's *White Football-Playing Idiots*. I was just reading aloud from chapter one, entitled 'Richard Stone.'"

Chris was trying to get Frank to look at him so he could communicate with facial gestures a *What the hell are you doing?* type of sentiment. Chris was thinking what a no man's land the woods behind the school was, a little unpopulated area of earth surface not devised by human thought and beyond the rule of law. Anyone could do anything to anyone out here as often and as long and as hard as they wanted to.

"Tough guy, eh?" Stone asked Frank.

"Did you just say 'Tough guy, eh' to me? What a walking fucking cliché you are," Frank said.

"I gotta hand it to you niggers. You guys got balls. Look at the Jew. Too scared to say a word."

"Too dignified to respond to your taunts, you mean."

Stone said, "Look guys, he's defending his boyfriend."

Frank said, "Hey guys, at least we're open about our homosexuality. You football players have to disguise yours. You're too scared to kiss the other boys, so you hit them instead."

Frank Dial was a short, thin, elegant young man. Richard Stone hit him in the belly with his fist. Then he smashed the bridge of his nose with his forehead. Frank fell onto his back and blood poured from his nose. Chris Schwartz stood there paralyzed. Stone bent over and picked up *Everything in the World*. "I'm taking this, and if you try to stop me I'll kill you."

After Stone and his companions had rounded the corner of the wooded path with Frank's notebook in their possession, Chris squatted next to his fallen friend. "Can you hear me?" he asked.

Frank Dial thought he would die. The one weapon he had against the terrible onslaught of life—his brain—was now dislodged and floating free inside the flimsy casing of his skull. The head-butt kept on giving. With each beat of his heart he felt as if another Stone head was smashing him in the face. The blood was all over his neck and arms and hands. The pain radiated around to the back of his head, down through his jaw, his neck, his shoulders, his upper back. "Can you take me home?" he asked Chris.

Chris helped Frank walk to the parking lot and called a cab, which dropped the boys off in the middle of the cluster of two dozen identical and ugly single-story houses where most of the black families in town lived: Bellwether's ghetto.

Frank Dial lay on his back in his bloodied T-shirt on the couch in his dark living room pressing a bag of ice to the bridge of his nose. "It is imperative that I create a description of this event in the notebook as soon as humanly possible," he said, attempting to counterbalance the chaos of the universe with an achy grandiloquence. "I believe this inaugurates a new category. 'Head-butts My Face Has Received,' or perhaps 'Senseless Acts of Violence I Have Known.'"

"Um, the thing about your notebook," Chris said.

"You didn't leave it in the woods, did you?"

"No."

"So bring it to me."

"Stone took it."

"Oh no."

"I didn't try to stop him," Chris said, trying to make up for his own cowardice with a bald and accurate description of the unhappy event.

"I take a head-butt for you—"

"Oh, I didn't realize you took it for me. I thought you took it because you had to keep talking smart to Stone because you have no instinct for self-preservation."

"You're amazing," Frank said. "You let me take all the pain. You let some asshole walk off with my most valuable possession—no, more than that, the only thing that makes the world tolerable to me—and then you take the opportunity to impugn my instinct for self-preservation?"

Chris was feeling lousy but also impressed that Frank could be practically on his deathbed and still come up with 'impugn.' "I'm just saying," he said.

"Get out of my house and don't come back."

"What?"

"You heard me."

"Why?"

"I just told you why and I don't even have to tell you why. I can do anything I want. Get."

Chris walked out the door of Frank's house, dejected. At that same moment, in the special section of the boys' locker room of Bellwether High School reserved for the football team, Richard Stone was holding a butane lighter to *Everything in the World*. Small blue and orange flames darkened and consumed the contents of *Everything in the World*. Chris Schwartz pressed his forehead against a stop sign at the corner of Frank Dial's street. As all the little flames ate away at the notebook and then joined in its center to make one large flame, turning *Everything in the World* to fire and smoke, Chris wept.

6.

Bernard Schwartz had been a publicist and a corporate speech writer but now worked at home, writing, editing, and producing high-quality newsletters for professional organizations as well as unprofessional organizations. He'd made the transition to the home office shortly before the breakup of his marriage. The words *low overhead,* toward the end of the marriage, produced a pain in the heart of the person who had then been called Lila Schwartz, a person who, as such, no longer existed. *Bernie's job change killed the marriage* was the conventional wisdom of the two people who had been the marriage's most direct participants. To say *Bernie's job change killed the marriage* was soothingly irrefutable. *Bernie's job change killed the marriage* held in abeyance densely clustered groups of painful memories, inchoate feelings, the disappointments of personality and love, the unrelenting dullness and shallowness of deep intimacy, a shallow sea stretching to the horizon in every direction. *Bernie's job change killed the marriage* was a tame little restaurant watercolor of that sea, each dot of white paint standing in for the legendary tablespoonful of water it takes to drown a full-grown adult.

This week Bernie was on deadline for *Gates of Horn* (newsletter of the American Association of Ophthalmologists), *Indefinite Horizon* (travel newsletter for senior citizens), and *Soft Shoe* (newsletter for podiatrists specializing in osteoporosis). Working out of a home office may be fine for obsessive-compulsives or borderline personalities, but it's the kiss of death for the chronic depressive. Bernie had done no work the entire morning, and facial hypesthesia is only one of many excuses the conscience of the depressed home office worker cannot bear to accept.

After a lunch consisting of the sort of sandwich a man would not eat in polite company, Bernie left the house to pick up the dosage of Prozac his psychiatrist had adjusted for him that morning. Driving toward town, he felt confused and disoriented. This particular bout of confusion and disorientation may have differed little from any of the others in his life, but now that he was taking an antidepressant, he wondered where the drug ended and he began. The thought that his every thought was contingent upon the amount of serum serotonin the drug allowed into his bloodstream disturbed Bernie. He experienced Prozac as an oppressive presence in his body that bound his mind too tightly to the causal/scientific worldview, making him doubt the mystery of his own soul.

Bernie ducked his head and lifted his hand in greeting to the pharmacist and a man standing at the counter. The pharmacist returned the greeting warily, and the man ignored him. There was something deferential or even submissive in Bernie's greeting that rankled not everyone but these two men in particular. The pharmacist, Bill Yardley, had used to greet Bernie warmly, but had turned cooler once he began self-prescribing Paxil. Bill Yardley took Paxil because he'd been afraid of his customers. The fear was painful, resisted all of his efforts to understand it, and depressed him. The Paxil cured the fear and depression, but had a peculiar side effect: Yardley found himself less kind and helpful to his customers now that he was no longer afraid of them. The absence of fear helped him to prepare prescriptions and do his paperwork more efficiently, and made his advice to his customers clearer and more coherent. But this excellent advice left the customers unsatisfied and bewildered. Previously, when his advice had been oblique, groping, and delivered in a shaky voice, his customers had seemed comforted; he had felt emanating from them a soft, vulnerable gratitude that he did not feel any more and did not care to feel. Thus Paxil made Yardley less depressed and more efficient, but also less happy and not as good at his job, his own unbearable fear having been his most sensitive and useful instrument of community relations.

Bernie gave Yardley his new Prozac prescription and proceeded to wander around the store, still touching and tapping and massaging his face in response to the numbness. Yardley handed his other customer a bottle of Nardil, a monoamine oxidase inhibitor that was sometimes prescribed for patients whose depressions resisted Prozac or Paxil. Yardley said, "If this doesn't help, maybe you should kill yourself." The customer was so hurt by this joke that he left the pharmacy without his prescription. Yardley's customers used to love this joke and respond to it with knowing, deep-body laughter, before Yardley had cured his own depression with Paxil. Now they all got offended. Perhaps out of cruelty, Yardley continued to make the joke anyway, though he feared that for doing so he would be repaid later in life with some crippling psychosomatic illness.

While Yardley bottled his Prozac, Bernard Schwartz found his way to the new self-service heart rate and blood pressure machine at the back of the pharmacy. For a dollar, he discovered that his pulse was 75 and his bp was 120/80. He dutifully wrote these numbers on a piece of scratch paper and stuck them in his wallet, though he had absolutely no idea what they meant. He returned to the front of the store. Yardley emerged from pharmaceutical backstage and placed Bernie's bottle of Prozac on the counter next to the previous customer's bottle of Nardil. Bernie made his copayment of $10—the remainder of the cost being covered by his HMO—and neither man noticed him pick up the wrong bottle.

7

Pill-taking time came. Driving in the late-afternoon traffic on Southridge Road, Bernie leaned down and to the right, opened the glove compartment, removed the brown cylindrical bottle, opened it, shook out a pill, placed it in his mouth, swallowed. While the pill was in his hand, Bernie's fingers half-noticed that the pill was not the usual Prozac shape, but by the time it was in his mouth, Bernie had already caught sight of the distinct shape of his son, Chris, moving along the shoulder of Southridge Road a hundred yards ahead·of him, and thus his brain was distracted from processing the pill shape discrepancy.

Bernie knew much more about the shape of his son than he did about the shape of his pill. He could have picked out the form and gait of his son from up to a mile away in a dense crowd. The visual stimulus of his son set off a series of systemic reactions within Bernie. When either of his children's bodies entered his perceptual field, Bernie's own body made subtle cardiovascular, autonomic, gastrointestinal, neurologic, respiratory, and endocrine accommodations which, taken together, constituted the feeling a layman would call love.

He slowed the car and watched his son increase in size and definition. Bernie thought Chris's walk showed signs of fierce contemplation. The peaks and valleys of the usual junior-Schwartzean up-and-down walking motion were diminished, the typical wild arm swing contained. Yes, Chris must have been thinking hard and well. What was he thinking? No, not thinking, dreaming: Chris was dreaming of a more heroic adulthood for himself than either of his parents had been able to model for him, especially his father. Bernie pictured Chris picturing a life for himself *sans* the distressed Damsel of Depression and the Lone Ranger of Prozac. Chris was no doubt dreaming of his future as an uncompromising screenwriter or beloved professor of political science. While Chris often generously gave away his sweet boyish comic energy to the world, he was at this moment containing it, saving it for something special: a dignified adulthood, Bernie thought. Chris was gathering all the facts and memories and wishes at his disposal and pointing them toward the future.

Chris was thinking of suicide. Walking westward on Southridge at the end of a miserable day that wasn't half over yet, Chris hunkered in tight to his own body, prepared to have as many suicidal goddamn ideations as it would take to cheer him up. He wasn't committed to suicide, but the thought of it comforted him. Suicidal thoughts as entertainment. Chris was creating an annotated mental list of suicide's well-known practitioners, beginning with those honorary suicides, the drug overdose stylists. Chief among them was Jimi Hendrix, a man who had brought choking on one's own vomit the honorary status of famous last words. He had a lot of admiration for Sylvia Plath as well. He actually liked the few Plath poems he'd been exhorted to read by his lady English teachers. "Oh Daddy, Daddy, Daddy" was a line of poetry that made a lot of sense to Chris. As for Plath's most famous poem, her suicide itself, Chris had found it confusing at first. That was because he misconstrued the technical details of the head-in-the-oven method. Before he figured it out, Chris thought Plath and other head-in-the-oven aficionados had *turned on* the oven—okay, preheated the oven to 450 degrees Fahrenheit—and then stuck their heads inside the scalding hot oven and roasted their own heads. Which seemed to Chris like an act of untenable self-discipline. It wasn't until he had ceased to misapprehend the head-in-the-oven suicide as *The Joy of Cooking Your Own Head* that he could abide it as a realistic approach to self-murder.

The suicide *pact* was a form of problem-solving that Chris was still grappling with. A suicide pact required a lot of trust, and Chris figured if you were killing yourself, trust of other human beings was probably not real high on your list of values, attributes, and achievements. Frank had told him that the famous Abstract Expressionist painter Mark Rothko and his wife—Mary Rothko, Chris wanted her name to be—had killed themselves together. Frank said they'd slit their wrists. Chris would rather roast his head or even pan-fry his fucking head than slit his wrists. They supposedly did it in the bathroom, and Chris pictured the bathroom floor as looking a lot like one of Mark Rothko's big red paintings.

Chris really couldn't get past the whole *pact* aspect of the suicide pact. How did *that* work? Was it like, "Mark honey, want to go see that new movie about Picasso tonight?" "How about let's slit our wrists instead?" "Okay hon." Really, what was in it for the missus? Did she love Mark so much that if he died, she would die? Was that the ultimate expression of love? Chris hoped not. In fact, he hoped that a lot of what went by the name of love in this world was not what love was.

The sound of Chris's father's Honda Civic's horn intruded upon Chris's morbid thoughts. Bernie let the car drift toward the shoulder of the road. Chris saw it and opened the door and got in. "You looked like you were lost in thought," Bernie said.

"I guess."

"What were you thinking about?"

"What I'll be when I'm older."

"I knew it! What will you be?"

"Dead."

"That's nice, Son."

"How's your face, Dad?"

"Okay. Better, maybe. Any thoughts about what you're going to be for the Halloween party tonight?"

"A giant penis."

"That's funny, because I was thinking of going as a pair of testicles."

"Oh Dad, I love your special boyish sense of humor. I guess that's why I was conceived by you instead of someone else's dad. Do you think our family's fucked up?"

"In what sense?"

"I don't know."

"Like your mother and I are divorced, your sister's a religious fanatic, your father's depressed and his face is numb, sort of thing?"

"Yeah."

"Did something happen today? Something happened today, didn't it? Do you want to tell me about it?"

"No."

Chris wished his dad were one of those dads who gave advice. He wished the advice came in numbered lists and started with words like "Always," or "Never," or "Remember," or "Son." "Son, now that you're leaving home, I want you to remember three important things. One, always bring a woman a bouquet of lilies before you make love to her. Two, look a man in the eye when you shake his hand. Three, never buy a house that doesn't have a basement."

"Anything I can do?" Bernie said.

"Couldn't you be more dadlike?"

"In what sense?"

"Like when I say the word *fuck*, hit me across the face."

"So, be more authoritative?"

"Yeah."

"I'll try."

"Oh, you'll have to do better than that."

"Don't you talk to me that way, young man. I've had just about enough of your backsass."

"Yeah, good. Like that."

"I mean it. Shut up or you'll be sorry you were ever born."

Chris pressed his head against his father's shoulder, wrapped the fingers of both hands around his father's upper arm, and was overcome by a great, intense, sorrowful feeling of loving affection that would last for the rest of his life.

8.

It was Friday evening at the end of October in Bellwether, Connecticut. The three Schwartzes prepared to leave the house as one diminished nuclear unit. Bernie was making them go to the annual Bellwether High School Halloween Dance in costume, though none of them wanted to, including Bernie. As unconventional and irreverent and benighted as he was, Bernard Schwartz was a family values parent, and he'd be damned if he was going to let a divorce or a chronic depression put a crimp in his sincere belief in or rich enjoyment of family life.

The efforts that Bernie and Chris had made to come up with costumes for the party consisted mainly in hat choice. Bernie, having decided to go to the party dressed as Someone's Dad, had chosen a brown fedora. This he accompanied with brown tweed blazer, blue Oxford shirt open at the collar, gray wool slacks, and brown nautical slip-on loafers. Chris chose a standard red Santa Claus hat with fluffy white pom-pom and trim. The rest of his outfit was his usual outfit: blue jeans, monochrome flannel shirt of a shade of blue almost identical to that of the jeans. It was a costume whose intentional ambiguity—if something that barely existed could be said to be ambiguous—was meant to elicit the question "What are you supposed to be?" so that Chris could respond, "I'm a ho." "I'm a ho" was not even a mediocre pun, it was a non-pun, Chris knew. He was secretly happy that his father was forcing them all to go to the costume party and felt the least he could do in return was to express his filial resistance with a slapdash costume.

Cathy, on the other hand, threw herself into the preparation of her costume. She'd researched it for weeks. She was going to the party as Edith Stein, aka Theresa Blessed of the Cross, a twentieth-century Polish Jew and brilliant Husserlian phenomenologist who converted to Catholicism and was martyred at Auschwitz in 1942. Pope Pius beatified her in 1987, when Cathy was a small child. Cathy was moved by the word *Husserlian*. She was moved by the word *phenomenologist*. She did not know what they meant. She felt that each was a mystery like the mystery of God, waiting to open itself to her. She could have gone to a store where they sold nun's uniforms but she thought that would be disrespectful. She had sewn each part of her nun's habit: the surplice, the wimple, looking all the while at a color reproduction of a painting of Edith Stein she had found on the internet. She made all of the garments in white or pale blue, the colors of the Carmelite order to which Edith Stein had belonged. The cattle car on which Edith Stein and her sister Rosa were transported from Holland to Auschwitz stopped in their hometown of Breslau, Poland. Stein emerged from the crowd on the train, still wearing her habit, and said, "This is my beloved home-town, I will never see it again. We are riding to our death." Cathy spent hours staring out the window of her room contemplating the meaning of Edith Stein's death. These long bouts of contemplation pained her, and she resisted them, but she knew she had to carry on with them. The fate of Edith Stein was the central problem of her seventeenth year, or so she thought at the time. When she had solved this problem, or when it had ceased to cause her such vexa-tion and pain, she would be ready for the next problem. She breathed deeply and thought of a lifetime of one problem after another, each more difficult than the one before it, or so she hoped. She silently recited these few lines written by Edith Stein:

> To suffer and to be happy although suffering,
> To have one's feet on the earth,
> To walk on the dirty and rough paths of this earth and yet
> To be enthroned with Christ at the Father's right hand . . .

Cathy appeared to her father and brother in the living room. Without knowing it, she had set her face in the shape of the face of Edith Stein in the painting; she bore into them with the irradiating stare of this twentieth century Middle European Jewish saint.

"Nice costume."

"Thank you, Chris."

"Dad, maybe on the way to the dance we could stop off and buy Cathy a sense of humor."

In addition to the mystery of the life and death of Edith Stein, the anger caused in her by her brother was the ongoing challenge in Cathy's spiritual development. She recognized in him the triviality and meanness of a lost soul, and it troubled her that this meanness could penetrate her heart again and again.

"My sister the sister, ladies and gentlemen." Chris looked at Cathy, saw her wince, and regretted his joke. She'd always been fragile and overly serious. Chris remembered a Halloween of a half dozen years ago, back when the family was intact, in a manner of speaking. Cathy was in her ornithology phase then, carrying around her birding binoculars and guidebook as she now carried around her rosary and cross. She had spent hours in her room listening to her *Bird Calls of the Northeastern United States* CD as she now spent hours in her room praying and meditating or whatever the hell she did in there. That Halloween six years ago, their mom had made the mistake of bringing home a store-bought Big Bird costume for her. Big Bird was the giant yellow flightless walking talking gentle stupid bird from the children's television show. The costume was Lila Schwartz's way of trying to welcome her lonely ornithological daughter into the human community of jokemaking. She should have known that Cathy was just not someone you made bird jokes with. The costume was a humiliating insult to Cathy, a violent travesty of avian dignity. She had a fit, as she had been prone to do during the first twelve years of her life: her face grew red, she stamped around in tiny circles on the floor and patted her thighs fiercely with her open palms.

Chris looked at his sister and had to look away—that gaze was too much for him. As happened every once in a while, Chris realized his sister was not a cartoon, and it shocked him. Not only was she not a cartoon, she was becoming an intense, purposeful, almost scary little person, and it wasn't fair. How come Chris didn't get to become anything? Why did he have to go on being Chris until death rent him asunder from himself?

9.

The motley trio of Schwartzes arrived at the Bellwether High School gymnasium. They were fearful, as befits a Halloween party or other type of party. Cathy knew that her few eccentric friends were having a hard time coping with her Catholicism, but she forgave them. It was not her friends' misunderstanding she was afraid of. She knew that parties were places where people suffered, and that was what frightened her. To be more precise, her interest in suffering and her inability to give genuine succor to a suffering soul frightened her. Her interest in suffering: she would not allow herself to fear for her own soul because that would have been grandiose, but in an ordinary secular way, she wondered if she would ever be happy.

Chris Schwartz was distraught about Frank Dial. He knew he wouldn't be at the party. He longed to see the costume Frank would have come up with. He hungered for Frank's ironic remarks about the goings on. He was afraid Frank was seriously injured and yet he felt he could not go to him to find out. He saw Richard Stone on the other side of the enormous, high-ceilinged room. Stone was not wearing a shirt. His face and Volvo-size torso were painted green. Chris felt sick with fear and anger; no, not anger—anger implied hope; hatred.

Bernard Schwartz was enjoying himself, except he was sweaty and his heart was beating more than a hundred times a minute and his limbs were jerking involuntarily once in a while. He wanted to sleep. He went in search of a bottle of beer to wake himself up. He wandered the perimeter of the party. He saw his two children stagger tentatively through its center. He saw a werewolf and a Frankenstein monster, a group of bumblebees, three Lone Rangers huddled together, a human-size carton of milk, characters from space movies clad in black and carrying plastic futuristic-istic weapons, the current President of the United States, Tonto, Elvis, Hitler, Jesus. He saw a universally known basketball star, the Incredible Hulk, Superman, an aardvark, a leprechaun, a wolf, a bear, a giant ice cream cone, Little Red Riding Hood, Nixon, Death. The music was loud. People flailed their arms to it and shouted above it. Again he saw his Carmelite nun and his partial Santa, not blending in, not having a good time. He worried about them. He found a beer but he couldn't drink it. His heart must have been going 110 beats a minute. He saw the Incredible Hulk speaking with his son in what looked like a hostile manner but he thought that was play acting as befits a Halloween party.

"You got off easy today," the Hulk was saying to the sad, thin half-Santa. His thick bulbous arms did not hang straight down but out to the side to accommodate the bulk of his torso. His four fingers hung off his hands like a single solid mass, and his thumbs arched away from them as if to show their owner had achieved hominid status.

"You hurt my friend," Chris said.

"Isn't that sweet. You sound like a fairy."

"You're a simple boy, Dickie Stone. There's fairies and there's real men and that's all ye know and all ye need to know."

"That's right."

"You'll never know how interesting and complicated life is because you're a simpleton with a brain the size of an eyelash." Chris spoke out of some intelligent and calm place in himself that he wasn't familiar with. Richard Stone shoved Chris and he fell backward onto the gym floor.

Stone kicked Chris once hard in the thigh. Bernie Schwartz put a hand on Stone's shoulder. "Don't, kid."

Stone turned to Bernie Schwartz. Chris got to his feet. "Who the fuck are you?"

"I'm his father."

"And what are you gonna do if I beat the crap out of your son?"

"I'll rip your heart out." Bernie's heart was going two beats per second, his head hurt, his limbs were twitching, his skin was clammy under his tweed blazer and shirt, and he was so angry that he almost bit this kid's nose off. "You need to leave this building now and cool off outside before you do something stupid."

Stone stared at Bernie for a few seconds. He glanced briefly at Chris. He turned and walked out of the gymnasium.

Chris said, "Whoa, Dad, that was amazing."

Bernie said, "This beer isn't agreeing with me. I have to go home. You stay at the party if you want to. I'll go get a glass of punch and come back and say goodbye to you and Cathy."

"Dad, you're sweating like a freak."

Bernie walked toward the punch bowl. The music was louder now. He walked through a thick mass of dancers. Someone turned off all the lights except a strobe, which illuminated the costumed dancers in a quick nauseating series of still poses. In momentary, garish close-ups, Bernie saw the fangs and red tongue of a werewolf, the mucouslike goo clinging to the reptilian face of a space alien, the powdered complexion of a ghoul, the coppery crown of the Statue of Liberty, Hitler's beer-drenched mustache, the sorrowful and beatific face of his daughter. He reached the punchbowl as he felt his feet slipping out from under him. He tried to grab the edge of the table as the gymnasium floor approached his face. He upended the punch bowl. It shattered next to his legs. Its red contents spread and drenched his Dad costume as he lost consciousness.

part two

10.

Chris sat on the hard molded metal bench in the emergency room of Port Town General Hospital. His sister sat next to him saying, "Holy Mary, Mother of God, pray for us sinners, now and at the hour of our death . . . " This annoyed Chris, who was trying to remember word for word each excellent thing he had said to Richard Stone. He pictured his father's legs and face twitching, and all the red fluid that dripped off of him as the paramedics lifted him onto the stretcher at the gym.

Chris stood up and paced the hard green floor. Port Town was a small industrial city, and the medical emergencies of its denizens this Halloween night were not genteel. A drunken man came in and wavered under the fluorescent lights, bits of clear broken glass sparkling inside the gouged-out portion of his cheek. Another man came in clutching his side while blood leaked out around his hands. A pregnant woman with black cat whiskers drawn onto her face was brought in shrieking and cursing on a wheelchair. Cathy made the sign of the cross as each patient passed her.

A whimpering, moaning twenty-year-old Count Dracula entered the emergency room. He'd broken his elbow. A woman with a bruised face and God knew what other maladies was brought in on a stretcher amid the clinical shouts of paramedics. A tipsy clown limped in supported by two friends, the big toe of his right foot wrapped in an ice pack. He held a huge fake red carnation. "What island am I?" he said to the room. "Krakatoa!"

Cathy tried to start conversations with the other waiting friends and relatives of patients. They dismissed her with minimal politeness. The clown gave his flower to a worried-looking middle-age woman, bowed, and grabbed the flower away from her with exag-

gerated irritability. The woman laughed gratefully. The clown per-
formed variations on this routine with other emergency room sup-
plicants, delighting them. Cathy wished she had the ability to
relieve suffering, even momentarily, as the clown did. She tried to
suppress her envy of the clown. She continued to try to speak to
people soothingly and they continued to rebuff her. They thought
they were being mocked by the overly solemn ministrations of this
teenager in a nun's habit, and they didn't want to be mocked by a
nun; they wanted to be mocked by a clown.

At 3 A.M., five hours after they'd arrived, Chris and Cathy were
approached by a doctor they hadn't seen or spoken to. This one was
young and had luxuriant, tousled brown hair and deep green eyes.
In her wrinkled cotton surgical scrubs, she looked as if she were in
her own messy living room late on a Sunday morning, about to put
a workout tape in the VCR. "Your father is still unconscious," she
said to them quietly, almost tenderly. "His heart rate is stabilized
and we've intubated him to help him breathe."

"He can't breathe on his own?" Cathy said.

"He can, but he's unconscious and we don't want him to
inhale any fluid inadvertently. Tell me, is your mother available to
be contacted?"

Chris, who felt that this young lady doctor was telling them
something very intimate not only about her father but about herself, explained, "She divorced him. You know how these things are.
Nobody was really in the wrong per se. People grow apart. Their
needs change."

"Do you have a phone number for her?" the doctor said. Her
name was Lisa Danmeyer. She smelled of lilacs and competent sweat.

Cathy said, "I tried her twenty minutes ago. She wasn't home.
She lives in California."

"All right, then let me tell you what we've found. Thanks to
your answers to the doctors' questions earlier, we have discovered
that your father has what's known as serotonin syndrome. This can
happen when a patient ingests a serotonin reuptake inhibitor like
Prozac, but it seems your father also ingested a monoamine oxidase

inhibitor, and the combination of these two often has traumatic side effects. It caused the sweatiness you noticed in your father and the muscle twitches. In rare cases, the combination of the two medications also interferes with higher brain function and the patient enters a coma. This seems to be what has happened to your father. We've given him a CAT scan and we don't detect a stroke, but we'll continue to monitor him. Do you happen to have the numbers of his psychiatrist and his pharmacist?"

At the word *coma*, Chris and Cathy looked at each other. In an instant they came to a silent mutual realization, if not an actual agreement. *Coma* was the scientific conclusion of their father's unhappiness. They had become the son and daughter of an aging, infirm man. They were adults now; unprepared in the extreme, but adults nonetheless.

Cathy told the doctor she'd get the numbers of his psychiatrist and pharmacist when she got home.

Chris said, "Let me get this straight, Dr. Danmeyer. Our father's in a coma?"

"His vital signs are stable. He will probably wake up soon. We'll monitor him closely and provide him with excellent care. We will contact his psychiatrist and pharmacist when you give us the numbers. In the meantime, I strongly urge you to contact your mother."

"So you're saying he could die."

"Most patients with serotonin syndrome recover."

"But some die," Chris said.

"Very few die," said the doctor. She guided the children down the hall to the intensive care unit. They peered through a picture window at their pale little father on a metal bed, a ghastly-looking tube in his nose and a more acceptable-looking tube in his arm. Cathy kissed her cross and pressed her healing palms to the window.

Dr. Lisa Danmeyer walked them to the exit of the hospital. She was grave and cool and a little bit delicious, in the estimation of Chris Schwartz, who felt the urge to embrace her. He did so fervently, but also cannily, knowing she'd perceive the embrace as the act of a boy in the hour of his need. The doctor found the embrace inappropriate, but as Chris had guessed, allowed him to hold her. It was probably his erection that made her pull away, finally. "I—"

"I know," Chris said, "you suggest we contact our mother immediately. Our father's in a coma. Gotcha." Chris gave her the thumbs up. He felt loose and angry and alert and elated and panicked.

They climbed into their father's car, which Chris had driven to the hospital *sans* license. In the passenger seat, Cathy relaxed the muscles of her neck and back and arms, and sobbed. Chris's elation disappeared, as did the clarity of his thinking. He was left with the panic, some stray anger, and crippling fatigue.

On the living room couch at 5 A.M., Chris dreamt of his mother's hair. In the dream, his mother was lying on the couch that Chris was in reality sleeping on. Chris himself, in the dream, was lying on the floor next to her, taking the place occupied in reality by the glass-top coffee table. He was listening to Franz Schubert's String Quintet on headphones, and so was his mother. No, they were not headphones. The Schubert String Quintet was entering Chris's brain via his mother's hair. His mother's thick hair came in five different colors: blonde, deep blonde, auburn, coffee-and-cream, deep brown. The hair was not the vehicle for the music, the hair *was* the music, and vice versa. Also, Chris's hair was the same hair as his mother's hair. Each hair that began beneath the surface of his mother's head ended beneath the surface of his own. They were Siamese mother and son, connected by the hair. Chris's mother used their mutual hair to think the music into Chris's mind. Chris had a perfect understanding of the music, each phrase of which he experienced as if it were a part of his body. Then he woke up, and could not hum even a single bar of the quintet. He felt he had lost something vital to his happiness.

11

Lila Munroe—who had been Lila Schwartz for the largely unhappy period of her life in which she was married to Bernard—arrived in New York on the red-eye at 6 A.M. the following morning and went directly to the hospital. Six years ago she had applied to law school at U.C. Berkeley, had been accepted on early admission, told Bernie and the kids about it, and moved to Oakland a week later. She'd already completed two years of law school before the marriage. After the marriage, she finished in a year and a half and became a successful litigator. Living alone and having an important job gave her the confidence to do what she felt like doing and get what she wanted. She wore a dark, soft green silk suit, arrived at the hospital before visiting hours began, overcame the objections of the nurses, and strode into the room where they were keeping her comatose ex-husband.

"Hiya Bernie," she said. His eyes opened. He watched her walk to the corner of the room, pick up a chair, and carry it toward his bed. She sat down beside him and touched his hand. "Are you awake now?" she said. He looked at her for a moment longer, gazed at the ceiling, and closed his eyes again. The computer screen on which his heartbeat was represented did not show any fluctuation. "How are you, anyway? I'm sorry I haven't called in the last few months. I meant to. No, the truth is I didn't mean to. The kids give me regular updates about you, though I know they don't like to. You're their special one. They adore you. You're the one they count on. They want to protect you from me. They want to protect even regular old facts about you from me. They can't bear when I make the slightest negative comment about anything. Aw, what am I saying? Why did I say that?" She cried a little. "Listen, Bernie, you are going to wake up eventually, yes? Don't fall apart on me, pal. I suppose I don't have a right to say that, but you are necessary to me. You are necessary to the life I have in California. I don't mean just that you are raising our kids—oh, don't think I don't think about that, toots. No, I mean the idea of you back here in Connecticut bolsters me. Every day I think of your sweetness existing somewhere in the world. I have a mental map of the eastern United States and it's got your sweetness and goofiness on it. I carry a small Bernie around in my mind. It's like a precious little doll that someone I cherished gave me in childhood. I need it. I need you alive over here. Do whatever you want but you mustn't die, I forbid it. We're not even fifty yet, for Christ's sake. This is the halfway point. Modern medicine is supposed to keep us all going till at least a hundred—haven't you been reading the newspaper? Come on, Bernie, I'm pleading with you here."

"Do me a favor and page Dr. Lisa Danmeyer," Chris said gravely to the tough front desk receptionist who had been in the bathroom when Lila passed through, and who was not allowing Chris and Cathy to visit their father in the ICU.

"Sure, I'll page her," the woman said, "but she probably won't come and you definitely won't see your father until the big hand reaches the twelve and the little hand's on the ten." The woman proceeded not to page Dr. Danmeyer.

"My father's up there in a coma and you're like a low-level Nazi down here following orders. What a charming idiot you are," Chris said.

The woman laughed and told him if he sat down and could contain himself she'd let him go up fifteen minutes early. That was a most unsatisfactory result for Chris. This woman wouldn't even pay him the respect of being offended by his impudent remark. Walking so lightly in the world was a source of intense frustration for Chris. If having a father in a coma wasn't going to bestow upon him at least a little of the gravitas he craved, what the hell good was it? Chris tried to loom in front of the reception desk, and considered how best to offend the officious crapdog who was thwarting him. Cathy took his hand in hers and tried to guide him toward a chair in the waiting area. "Get off me. What is *wrong* with you?"

"Yes, that's it, be impatient with me, that's the spirit," Cathy said, and regretted her anger, and continued: "What a fine young man you are. How proud Dad would be of you."

Cathy entered the room first. Lila was sitting next to where the bed had been before they wheeled Bernie out for his morning constitutional CAT scan. She hadn't seen her daughter since June and was momentarily paralyzed by the sight of her. Lila was a big light pale WASP-y looking Jew. Cathy was dark and fine and Russian-looking like her father. The meeting of mother and daughter had about it the undertone of a meeting between the wary representatives of two hostile tribes. Cathy's mouth was closed and relaxed. She bent forward and kissed her mother's forehead. She put her hands on her mother's shoulders and asked, as if Lila were an emotionally weak friend suffering a loss, "How are you?" Cathy had circles under her eyes. She looked as if she had borne her fatigue for a long time, accepted it, was strengthened by it, had baked the fatigue in the fire of her burning soul and returned it to the world as wisdom.

Chris entered. He looked at his mother and smiled and looked away. He was embarrassed about the dream. He needed to check her hair to see if it was the same as in the dream. He looked at her hair. It was neater and a little thinner than what he'd dreamt of. A barrette was holding most of it behind her head. She had put one of those gels or creams or fluids in her hair which made her whole head look more efficient and her face look hard and unsusceptible to filial affection. She beckoned him. He bent to receive a kiss on the cheek. "Ah kid," she said.

An orderly wheeled Bernie back into the room on his metal sick bed and walked out. The three waking members of the family were stunned and could think of nothing to say. They all half expected Bernie to sit up and make a joke. To dissolve her own panic, Lila had to say to herself again and again that she was not a thirty-five-

year-old housewife, they were not in a cheap motel room, they were
not at the beginning of a nightmare vacation in an overcrowded
beach town on the Jersey shore, she would not have to eat every
meal with these people, she would not have to return every noon
and night to this room occupied by these same three people for the
next several weeks, months, years, or decades. And then, of course,
she wished she'd been able to do just that.

The doctor came in. "Ms. Schwartz? I'm Dr. Danmeyer."

"Not Schwartz, Munroe. You're so young!"

"Your husband has had a stroke."

"Ex-husband."

"Mom!"

"When?"

"The CAT scan picked it up today," the doctor said, "but it may
have happened yesterday or even the night before. The serotonin
syndrome caused a temporary arrhythmia in his heart, which in
turn caused a small thrombus or clot to form in one of the major
blood vessels near his heart, or released an already existing clot into
his blood stream. The clot traveled to his brain and temporarily cut
off circulation to an area of his brain's left hemisphere. That's what
a stroke is, or at least that's one kind of stroke." Dr. Danmeyer continued to talk about her patient Bernard Schwartz. She added
details with loving precision. In the room where Bernie lay inert,
Lisa Danmeyer created a second Bernie made of test results and
drug names and names of parts of the brain and biochemical causality and possible outcomes. Lila and Cathy and Chris all felt the
power and danger of what Lisa Danmeyer was doing. This second
Bernie she was creating out of science threatened to supersede the
real Bernie who was lying there in the room with them. Already,
none of his family could think of "the real Bernie" without including in their thoughts some of the words Lisa Danmeyer had spoken
about him. Lisa Danmeyer's Bernie was the opposite of Jesus: flesh
made words.

Lila Munroe asked the doctor questions about serotonin syndrome. The doctor explained it, with Chris periodically interrupt-

ing to add his own details where he thought hers were lacking: "Fluoxetine is commonly known as Prozac, and vice versa." At some moment yesterday or this morning, Chris had begun cultivating disdain for Dr. Danmeyer. He liked to think of her as just Lisa, or ironically as "Doctor" Lisa Danmeyer. She was really no more than an older version of the goody-two-shoes math and science girls at his high school, the girls who dressed neatly and had neat hair and did all their homework and let you know it, the girls who won all the awards in the spring. They had no sense of humor and they used their diligence as a weapon to crush anyone with a sense of irony, like Chris. Ah but little did they know that irony operates best when crushed; little did practically anyone know, except Chris's dad, Bernie, who was now almost dead. If he ever came back to life he'd be the King of World Irony. By uttering three words, or maybe two excellently chosen ironic words, the lean, essential, post-crushed Bernie would have Lisa Danmeyer and Cathy and all the prissy presumptive Ivy League twits of Bellwether High School weeping for mercy.

When she finished her explanation, Dr. Danmeyer asked Lila if she had any more questions. Lila said, "No, but I have a request. Understand that this man is not my husband. These two people here, however, are his children. They are intelligent and mature and I encourage you to tell them everything. I live in California. These two are the ones to be kept informed about the prognosis of their father. They will convey the information to me and we will do what is necessary. I don't mean to be cold, I merely mean to make a special plea that you treat Chris and Cathy as adults. I think that will be quite helpful to them now, actually."

Cathy wondered if Lisa Danmeyer was a whole woman, which was what Cathy longed to be. Cathy looked up and down the world for such women. She needed to borrow from their lives, even as she knew she had to complete herself in her own way, if she had the strength, the courage, the intelligence. She did not regard her own mother as a whole woman because, in order to remake herself as an effective woman and possibly even a happy woman (though on this point Cathy had her doubts), Lila Munroe had to pay the price of being a hard and impermeable woman. Cathy felt her mother did not and would not ever know surrender. Surrender was necessary for wholeness. Surrender and strength. These were Cathy's thoughts and she didn't know where they came from or whether they were true.

Lila took Chris and Cathy to lunch at a new gourmet sandwich shop in Bellwether. She asked Cathy if she was going to convert to Catholicism. "That's something I need to think about. I'll let you know when the time is right. For now the decision is something I must work out alone with God."

Lila could not entirely suppress a snort of dismay, which Cathy understood as derision.

"Don't make fun of me, Mother. You tell the doctor to treat us like adults and then you turn around and condescend to me and laugh at me."

"No, honey, I—"

"Christianity is a serious, age-old religion. It existed on this earth before science came along and fooled everyone into thinking they could understand everything with their intellect. Christianity definitely was here long before the U.S. Constitution, which is what you have faith in. I'm trying to have faith in the highest possible thing in the universe, God, which is extremely difficult, especially nowadays. You can mock me but I think it's important. I have to try to understand the meaning of faith. I have to." Cathy's heart was so full now that she thought it would burst. She wouldn't be sorry if it did. She wouldn't be sorry if she died reaching out in the direction of faith.

"Cathy, please forgive me for not entirely understanding your interest in religion, especially Catholicism. I admire you. If we're lucky, we find a person or a kind of work or a belief system that will help quiet the terrible restlessness of being alive. If we're lucky *and* determined *and* strong, as I think you are, then we don't have to depend on another person to make us quiet. We find the quiet in some symmetry between the world and our hearts. I'm baffled but also proud, sweetheart."

"Well Mother, thank you for your support, but also you don't get it at all. First, I don't have a 'belief system.' God exists. I just need to find out how to honor His existence with my whole life, my every thought, my every gesture. Second, I don't want quiet. Grace is not achieved in quietness and stillness. Grace is achieved in motion, in action, in active service of God. I'll be very quiet when I die—I won't move a muscle."

"What is the matter with you people?" Chris said. "Dad's the quietest guy on earth right now, and you two are talking about—I don't even know what you're talking about. Mom, you fly in once a year to boss us around like you still have the right to. Cathy, you talk like you're reading aloud from some fanatical religious tract. I know something about Christianity. I had to read the New Testament for school. At least when the Holy Spirit went into Mary she ended up pregnant. You just ended up brainwashed."

Chris hated himself. He wished he would die right now. No, he wished he would levitate out of his chair and leave the planet, not like a soul ascending to heaven but like a helicopter ascending to do a shadow traffic report. He would gaze down on all the little tantrums people work themselves up into and not care. He looked over at his mother and felt he was seeing her clearly for an instant. She was beautiful, she was not nice, she was not generous. He wanted to hug her and he wanted her to hug him. He wanted her to urgently wish to hug him. How tremendously satisfying it would be to be the one sought after and hugged and loved by the beautiful, selfish, domineering bitch. What a triumph. As for his sister, he didn't see her clearly now or ever and he didn't want to. Her capacity to make him angry made him furious. Her he longed not to notice at all.

Each of the three of them wanted to get up and leave the table, but each needed to stay. For the next two hours, mostly silent, dazed by the force of familial love, they remained seated at the glass-top table in the cast iron, white-painted, bohemianly uncomfortable chairs.

12.

Frank Dial sat on a couch in the dark of his living room. On his lap lay a new notebook. This one was called *Everything I Hate*. So far he had written:

> Chris Schwartz
> Richard Stone
> Football players
> Theft of previous notebook
> This couch
> This room
> This house
> This town
> This state
> This earth
> This list

The new book was preliminary and crude, to be sure. The intellectual energy Frank might have used to organize or annotate it or consider its meaning in relation to the disappeared notebook had not yet returned to him. A livid bruise blossomed across the bridge of his nose. It swelled and distorted the flesh beneath his eyes. He took aspirin as often as legally allowed in the state of Connecticut; the pain hardly abated.

On Halloween night, his mother had questioned him closely about the injury and he had told her everything, or at least everything she needed to know. She was disturbed. In the very room where he sat now—the same room from which he had banished Chris Schwartz—she had sat across from him in silence for several minutes after his description of the fight, if that was what you would call it, with Richard Stone. "I'm not going to fight your battles for you, Francis," she'd concluded. She was a tough mother, but he was glad she was not the sort of tough mother who marched right in or marched right down. He was glad she was not a mother who said, "Well then I just marched right into that boy's father's house and I gave that man a piece of my mind. I told him how it was going to be between his son and my son in this town or anywhere else from now on. And I'll tell you one thing, Francis: that man listened to me and life is going to change for that Stone boy in ways he never dreamed." No, that sort of mother would not do at all.

Not that Frank had always preferred or understood his mother's laissez faire policy. In the Philadelphia neighborhood where he'd grown up, Renata Dial had watched her son fight. That's right. At age six, age eight, age ten, he had fought other boys not ten yards from the stoop on which his mother sat looking on. That was difficult for his young mind to comprehend. That made the fights harder; harder to win because he'd glance over at her, not see a crucial fist moving toward his face, and get bloodied by it; harder to lose because there would be his mother watching him be weak and girlily defeated by a boy he should have been able to beat, if only by virtue of his mother's quiet, passive, loving confidence in him. Loving confidence was what it had to be. Loving confidence was what made her sit there and not lift a finger to defend or help her son. If not loving confidence, what else could it be?

Frank made a new entry in his *Everything I Hate* notebook: "Mom's loving confidence."

He wondered why Chris Schwartz didn't call. He hoped Schwartz would call so that he could hang up on him so that Schwartz could call again so that he could hang up on him again so that he could call a third time so that Frank could tell him how much he hated him so that they could start being friends again.

13.

Lila Munroe flew back to California. Bernie Schwartz remained unconscious. Dr. Lisa Danmeyer honored Lila's plea by speaking frankly not quite with but to Chris and Cathy about their father. She suggested they prepare themselves for a Bernie who might wake up different from the Bernie who had gone to sleep. She remained cautiously optimistic about his waking up, an event Chris and Cathy looked forward to with anxiety and wonder. Who *would* their father be when he woke up? Maybe he'd be a millionaire. Maybe he'd be Fred Astaire. Maybe he'd be cruel and violent. If one were to believe Lisa Danmeyer, he'd have mild to severe brain damage, mild to severe difficulty moving his limbs, a mild to severe speech disorder, and mild to severe psychological problems if, that is, one believed Lisa Danmeyer. But who wanted to believe Lisa Danmeyer? Not Chris, not Cathy.

Chris did not only not want to believe Lisa Danmeyer, he continued to disdain her openly. He knew all about the Hippocratic Oath, and therefore felt free if not completely justified to say what he wanted to Lisa Danmeyer. He treated Lisa Danmeyer like shit and she had to take it while continuing to care for his father to the best of her ability. It was a special thrill for Chris to treat Lisa Danmeyer like shit because it was so unlikely that he would do so because she was a doctor and he was merely a schmuck seventeen-year-old with an unconscious father and two dozen pimples. She was a doctor, yes, but she was also a former girl, just like the training-bra-wearing homework-doing scholarship-winning but essentially ignorant and idiotic girls in his school. And that was the chink in Danmeyer's armor. That was why he didn't believe her prognosis re the paternal coma. He believed the coma was all his father needed to turn his life around, get the job and the income he wanted, walk with his chin up once again across the face of the earth, though he'd never before walked with his chin up across the face of the earth. No. Chris didn't believe that. He believed his father would wake up and have roughly the same life he had before. He'd come out of his long, self-indulgent nap and carry on with his mediocre life just like before. Which meant that it would be entirely up to Chris to have anything other than the stupid and degraded life *he'd* been having up to now.

Cathy also did not want to believe Lisa Danmeyer's dire portrait of her father's recovery, if recovery was what you would call what Lisa Danmeyer was predicting. What she wanted to believe was that her father's coma was the necessary slumber that preceded a spiritual awakening. That was what she wanted to believe but that was not what she believed. She did not believe that because she was all too aware that by devoting herself rigorously to the sacred, she incurred the danger of becoming a narrow-minded idiot. Ah, how much easier her life would be as a narrow-minded idiot. Becoming a narrow-minded idiot was one of the central temptations of Cathy's life. She knew that the essence of temptation was that one had already succumbed to it; to resist temptation therefore consisted not in banishing it from one's heart, but in not letting it seize control of that organ. That was why Cathy wasn't so inspired by the desert temptations of Jesus: they were not realistic; His resistance to them was too easy for Him, too assured and complete—He wasn't *seriously* tempted. In this way, the Gospels were a disappointment to her: she couldn't use them as a how-to manual. On the bright side, her disappointment in the Gospels made it easier for her not to become a narrow-minded idiot. On the not-too-bright side, maybe what she was calling narrow-minded idiocy was really faith, and maybe her real sin was her disappointment in the Gospels, and in every other damn thing. Which meant she was not merely tempted by sin, but covered by it and imbued with it; which meant she looked upon sin and called it virtue; which meant she was lost.

14

Chris and Cathy returned to school five days after their father was brought to the hospital. School was worse than ever for Chris, if that was possible. Nobody was making him go but he knew he had to. It outraged him that he had to. Shouldn't his father's coma have exempted him from ordinary life? Shouldn't he be the Crown Prince of the Medical Trauma of which his father was the King? No. He went back to his B-minus-to-B-plus school life, his same old awkwardness and shyness with girls and boys and women and men. He saw garish-faced Frank Dial but would not look at him. Frank saw Chris and looked at Chris and scalded him with his looking. How grotesque to be hated by Frank Dial.

After school, Chris went to commune alone with his father at Port Town General. Lisa Danmeyer was in the room when he arrived. She was leaning seductively (Chris thought) over the bed and pressing the palm of her right hand to Bernie's forehead.

"What sort of medical procedure is *that*?" Chris said.

"Hello Chris."

"You like touching my father? When he comes out of his coma he'll be eligible for marriage."

"I see," the doctor said without conveying what she thought or felt.

"But you probably have a boyfriend. He's probably a doctor too. He's probably a podiatrist. But he'll break up with you because you think you're better than him because he's only a podiatrist. And you know what? You are better than him, intelligence-wise. On the other hand, your podiatrist boyfriend knows how to have fun. On the *other* other hand, you *don't* know how to have fun. You haven't cracked a smile since day one of medical school. It's just work work

work for you. My father's isn't going to wake up and marry you. He's going to wake up and get the hell away from you as fast as he can. You'll do your self-assured medical jargon routine for him and he'll say, 'Chris, get me away from this amazingly intelligent doctor before she bores me to death.'"

Lisa Danmeyer had made a professional decision to take Chris's shit. She knew the shit he gave had nothing to do with her. He was furious at his father for being in a coma, and since his fury would have been unbearable to him if he admitted it to himself, he transferred it to his father's doctor. Not, that is, to Lisa herself, but to the straw woman called "Doctor Lisa Danmeyer." She had been warned about this type of patient behavior in Empathy class. Perfectly understandable. No one had ever spoken to her like this. She didn't care what he said. He was a wounded child. But his irreverence and his insults were a shock to her system. Not even the senior neurosurgeons during her surgical rotation had been this disrespectful. She was an overly serious person, it was true. Not terribly at ease outside work, true. However, this son of her patient was wrong about the podiatrist boyfriend. She didn't have a boyfriend. Zero boyfriend. Boyfriend. Boyfriend. *Boyfriend* was a word that compensated in oppressiveness for what it lacked in charm. She had been about to massage the patient's legs to prevent permanent muscle contractions, but now she decided to get a nurse to do it. She made a few neutral remarks to the boy about his father's condition—she *pulled* a few neutral remarks *out of her ass* is how she unmedically thought of it—and left the room.

Chris sat in the chair by the bed, alone with his father. "Half the stuff she says I think she just pulls out of her ass," he said. Bernie lay inert and pale and did not open his eyes. "You have to understand, Bernie, she's doing a good job, it's just someone has to remind her that she's only a doctor on the surface, on a very thin layer on the surface which makes up five percent or less of her being, and underneath the surface she's just a mortal like the rest of us. They're good for her, these little talks I give her." Chris called his father Bernie now because he felt the coma put them on a level playing field. "You are in there, right Bernie?" He pantomimed putting a microphone to his mouth. "Hello? Is this thing working? Is this thing on?" He dropped the microphone. "By the way I thought you should know, I'm the one who switched the pills. I didn't mean anything by it, I was just a little sick of you being *awake* so often. You know? Every morning you wake up and you're *awake* all day. That's really tiring for me. Hey calm down, I'm kidding, relax. It—was—a—joke. Seriously, take it easy, let's not get crazy with, you know, eye opening, or *movement* of any kind. Settle down and shut up. No back talk. That's a good boy.

"I see they've been shaving you. They do an excellent job. They do a better job than you ever did. I've been meaning to tell you that you ought to shave more carefully. Those little patches of short graying hair under your jaw make you look like a mental patient. I know, I know, you're divorced, you're depressed, blah, blah, blah. Whatever. Spend the extra thirty seconds to check for spots you missed, is all I'm saying. No, they do a really good job of shaving you here which eases my mind a *lot*. I bet Danmeyer does it personally. Danmeyer's a full-service doctor. How full I can only imagine. I wouldn't be surprised if she gets a pregnancy out of this coma of yours. You know what I'm saying, right? I don't have to spell it out for you, do I? You may be unconscious, but you're not stupid. If I were them, I think I'd experiment with different types of facial hair patterning. Now'd be a good time to try out sideburns or a mustache or a goatee. If they don't look good, no big deal. It's not like you're about to go on a job interview or a date or anything, unless you count those intimate sessions with Danmeyer as a kind of really low-pressure date. That's the kind of date I want to go on, where I can just lie there unconscious the whole time. Hold on, I have an idea." Chris thrust his hand into the chaos of his backpack and came up with an indelible black marker. "Let's begin by extending the sideburns an inch on either side." He leaned over his father's body and drew a crude trapezoid below and adjacent to the conservative rectangle of short dark hair in front of his father's left ear. By the time Chris was done evening it out, the base of the trapezoid was flush with the bottom of Bernie's earlobe. As best he could, he made an identical design on the right side of his father's face. He stepped back to assess his work.

"I tell you Bernie, that's not half bad. It's three-quarters bad. Kidding, kidding. No really, you were looking very pale before, and this darkens the facial features. What's that you say? Less is not necessarily more when it comes to fake, drawn-on facial hair? You're sure now? You're not pulling my leg, are you? I can't always tell when you're joking with me. I'm just saying it's going to look very artificial is all. All right. Don't say I didn't warn you." Chris brought the thick black tip of the marker to the narrow place between the two small vertical ridges of flesh under his father's nose, being careful to avoid the breathing tube. "I know this is going to sound a little crazy, but I've always—I don't know why this is—I've always wanted to see how you'd look in a Hitler mustache." While drawing a half-inch square in the middle of the space between his father's nose and lip, and then vigorously inking it in, Chris commented, "Anyway we've got to do something to make you more, I don't know, let's call it *effective* in the world. A little self-esteem, a little authority, a little charisma. The Hitler look is one obvious way to work toward achieving these goals. I'm not saying you're not going to offend some people, but you knew that from the moment we started this Hitler thing fifteen seconds ago. People will notice you is the thing. Men, women, it couldn't hurt."

Chris stepped back again for objective consideration of his work. "It looks a little funny with the sideburns. I'm going to admit my mistake here: I should've done the Hitler part *before* I did the sideburns. That error is all me and I take full responsibility for it. Don't worry, I'm not going to leave you with that Disco-Führer look. The only thing I can figure to do at this point is extend the mustache. I can see now a thin Clark Gable mustache was what was needed but that's no longer an option, we can't exactly go back to that now. This is going to be more of a Saddam Hussein-cum-Elliot Gould-in-M*A*S*H affair." He stepped forward again and added wings to the black square under his father's nose. Again, perhaps because of poor drafting skills, he kept having to even them out, and ended up with a thick black bar which horizontally bisected his father's face. "Oops. Wow. But I'm not thickening your eyebrows no matter what you say—I'm not interested in turning you into a buffoon. I guess while I've got the cap off the black magic marker though, let me give you back some of the hair you've lost in the last ten years." Bernie still had hair on top of his head but some of it had gone gray and it was certainly not what anyone would call a *thick* head of hair. Chris extended the hairline forward by about an inch, and spent a few minutes coloring in a several-square-inch area of barish scalp that could be seen between the strands of hair on top of his head. For a third time he stepped back to see what he'd accomplished.

"Oh God, it's still the paleness that's killing me more than anything. Nothing I do, it seems . . . wait a minute. Oh no, this is a terrible idea. All right I'll just say it, but one word of objection from you and I forget the whole thing. Makeup. Well, on a woman it would be called makeup. On you we'll call it returning you to flesh tone. And anyway I haven't got actual makeup on me. I've got some colored markers. Well, one colored marker. A red marker. You won't even notice this. Nobody'll notice this, they'll just go, 'Hey, Bernie's looking a little healthier today.'" Chris found the red marker in his bag and removed the cap. "What I'm going to do is I'm going to put a little color in your cheeks. I'll do this with the lightest of touches." Chris made a big red dot just below each of his father's cheekbones. He went to the bathroom in his father's private room and came back with a wet paper towel to "blend" the dot of red. It didn't blend. A fact he'd forgotten: the red marker was indelible. "Okay I'm just going to have to make a color gradation here by expanding the circle while pressing very very lightly with the pen. In-pen blending, we'll call this." It didn't work. "I'm not getting a lot of subtlety with these tools, I have to say." Now there were two large circles of deep, saturated red, one on each side of Bernie's face, connected to one another by the thick black bar that Chris had intended to resemble a mustache. "That looks just plain weird. That is totally unbalanced. I think it'd be less . . . less, just, *odd* if we bring the lips forward a bit. Chris was exceedingly cautious about coloring in his father's lips, and not only because of the breathing tube. By the time he was finished, there was just one tiny accidental betrayal of his father's natural lip line: he did an excellent job with this part of the project by almost any standards, the garish and inappropriate color of the "lipstick" notwithstanding.

"Hold on a sec, Bernie, nature calls." Chris went into the bathroom and had a leisurely, blank-minded urination. He washed his hands and, when he was done, gazed at the reversed version of his own face in the mirror above the sink with almost no inner commentary on what he was seeing; just some good old-fashioned low-level calming unthinking self-composition before the altar of the household god of physiognomy.

He came back out and caught sight of his March-of-the-Wooden-Soldiers father. His skin got clammy and he felt sick. He returned to the bathroom and tried to escape the consequences of his actions through vomiting. He couldn't vomit. He hid behind the door of the bathroom and peered out hoping his marked up father wouldn't be there any more. His father was not only there, he was lying in a stupor with a child's thick and angry scribbles covering his face. Chris was exhausted by the reconstitution of his father's face as a work of idiot modern art. He gathered up his backpack and went around to the side of the bed away from the door of the room. He lay down on the floor parallel to the bed on which his tarted-up father lay. He was practically under his father's bed. He curled up on his side, put his head on his backpack, and fell asleep.

15.

After a difficult hour of prayer at the Church of Saint Francis Xavier in Bellwether, Cathy made her way by bus to Port Town General. Prayer was still new to Cathy. She didn't know how to do it yet. She'd memorized the Our Father, the Hail Mary, the mealtime prayers, the Act of Faith, the Act of Hope, the Act of Love, and—though she had not been to Mass, let alone confession—the Confiteor, finding herself in the line "I have sinned exceedingly in thought, in word, in deed, through my fault, through my fault, through my most grievous fault," as if it had been composed not by the Holy Spirit but by a sixteen-year-old girl looking in the mirror.

Cathy also knew that prayers could be customized. She figured God might appreciate hearing something she hadn't learned by rote. But she didn't know what a personal prayer should sound like. She thought of asking a priest, but she didn't see any priests around that afternoon in Saint Francis Xavier, and she didn't want to go backstage, or to the back office, or whatever they called that closed-off area behind the altar. Jesus had said, "Your father knows what you need before you ask him." So why ask? For whose benefit was she praying? Certainly not God's. God did not need Cathy. Cathy needed God, and she didn't want God to get sick of her because of it. What she ended up praying for first, in terms of her own needs, was for God to strengthen her faith. That seemed non-naggy. She then asked God to heal her father, and added that she knew He was basically going to do what He thought best anyway but would He at least consider this option. Then she prayed for Him to soften her mother's heart. Then she prayed for Him to give her brother strep throat—that is, if it was His will to do so. She knew she'd erred on that one. That one just slipped out. She added a couple of

Confiteors after it, but left the house of God feeling like she'd really screwed up in there.

She rode the bus from Bellwether to Port Town. Outside the window, things were getting less lovely by the minute. Fewer trees, less well-paved roads, houses smaller and shabbier and closer together, greater number of people per square foot, greater per capita personal dissatisfaction. The dissatisfaction Cathy detected in facial expressions, positioning of torsos, angling of limbs. The bus ride became a kind of parable for her. In her Parable of the Bus Ride, the passenger—Cathy—was like a divine thought taking a trip through the mortal mind. Like a passenger boarding the bus in Bellwether, the divine thought entered the human mind at the mind's most purely spiritual moment, like when Cathy took a hot bath at the end of the day and could feel all her base and sinful thoughts float up away from her mind like steam. In order to be tested, the thought then encountered the temptation every mortal mind contained, which was like when the bus passenger went from Bellwether to Port Town. A thought or passenger that felt good and correct in the Bellwether of the mind would begin to feel out of place and wrong as it moved into the mind's Port Town. No. This was a bad parable. She had made the obvious mistake of equating spiritual poverty with poverty poverty, which was the total opposite of what Jesus taught, for a rich boy had come to Jesus and asked him what he had to do to get into heaven, and Jesus had replied, "It is easier for a camel to go through the eye of a needle than it is for a rich man to enter the kingdom of heaven." She wondered how someone who lived on the shabby, desolate street that the bus now carried her safely through would feel about that remark. The people who lived on this street had probably not given away a lot of money to get here. Maybe the poverty-is-holy aspect of Christianity was written into the scriptures by rich people as a kind of trick on poor people so the poor people wouldn't start to want to take the rich people's money away from them. Cathy was confused now and she felt gross inside, like either something was really wrong with her or something was really wrong with the world, or both. It turned out to be not such a great bus ride.

Cathy entered the hospital room where both her father and her brother lay sleeping. She saw her father's face and cried out. She went to the bathroom, wet some paper towels, soaped them up, stood exactly where Chris had stood while defacing his father, and began to scrub. She didn't know her brother was in the room. "Chris, you asshole," she said. She'd have to put piety aside for long enough to call Chris by the name he deserved. What Chris had done to her father's mouth offended her the most, and that was where she concentrated her scrubbing, working around his breathing apparatus as best she could. Her father gagged on the soapy water that ran into his mouth. She squeezed the excess water from the paper towel and continued scrubbing. "Asshole," she said again. The scrubbing removed some but not all of the red marker. A morning-after redness remained no matter how hard she scrubbed. She stopped scrubbing when some darker red appeared—blood from the inside of his lips, which had been scraped roughly along his teeth as Cathy scrubbed. "Asshole!" she said again, waking Chris this time. He sat up quickly and bumped his head on the railing of his father's bed. "Ow!" He stood up and saw Cathy.

"How could you do this?"

Chris didn't know how.

"What were you thinking?" Cathy said to Chris across her father's supine body. "Please tell me because I can't imagine what thought went along with this."

"I don't know."

"Did you go into a little coma of your own?"

"I guess so."

"You guess so? You *guess* so? Look what you've done."

"Hey, you're not my mother."

"Yeah? Well then why is it me who's scrubbing him off, cleaning up after little baby Chris's mess?"

"So? Stop. Nobody's making you. Let *Lisa* do it. I'm sure *Lisa* would love to do it."

"You're about as responsible as a– as a– snake."

"Ooh, a snake. Bible imagery from the bible bitch. Well listen, you moralistic little twit, I don't have to take this crap from you. I'm outta here." Chris grabbed his backpack and left the room.

Cathy paced the room a dozen times in a rage. She managed to calm herself enough to sit down again. She resumed washing her father. She washed his rose-red cheeks more gently than she'd washed his lips. She spoke as she washed. "Dad– um, Father– um, Dad? B– Bernard Schwartz? It's your daughter, Cathy. I don't know what I'm about to say to you, and I don't know for sure that you'll hear me. I don't expect any visible sign from you that you've heard me. But I'm going to try to have faith that my words are reaching you. I want you to get well. I even want Chris to help you get well. Can you reach Chris? Can you forgive him? Can you help him to help you? I know you have a way into his heart. I know you two can kind of reach each other without talking, through each other's hearts. I don't know how I know it but I do. It's okay, Dad, that you and I don't have that. And it's okay that I don't have it with Mom, or anybody. God can reach my heart. I feel that and I know that." Cathy neither felt it nor knew it, but thought it might become true if she said it was true. "So I might seem like I'm alone with no one to really comfort me or take care of me, but I'm not, because God does. So you don't have to worry about me. I wish I could somehow bring Jesus into this hospital room to heal you. You know how He's always healing people in the Bible? You're like those people. You're like that dead girl who He made come back to life. Oh no I didn't mean that. I mean I didn't mean you're like a dead person, like dead. I know you're alive. I see it on the monitor and if I watch carefully I can see you breathe, and I also know, know, know it inside. I sense your soul inside your body. I know my faith isn't that pure yet. It's like faith-in-progress, and I want you to have it all and use it all and I hope it's enough to heal you."

Bernie opened his eyes, or at least his eyes opened. Perhaps it was the air against Bernie's bare eyeballs that caused his body to produce tears. The tears dripped down his cheeks and mingled with the soapy red water on them. It looked to Cathy as if her father were crying tears of blood. She could not contain herself. She took Bernie's hand in her two hands. Her father was weeping tears of blood, and Cathy knelt and wept for the miracle she thought it might be, and for the miracle she knew it wasn't.

16

Lila Munroe walked the immediate result of her latest bout of promiscuity to the door of her house in Heart Valley, California. He was a handsome, dark-haired computer repair person named Mark or Mike who was fifteen years younger than Lila and wore his sunglasses on the top of his head. Maybe he wasn't a computer repair person. He was, at the very least, a computer person. That morning he'd done something to Lila's computer at her law firm. It was still possible that he'd repaired it, but he may also have diagnosed it or inspected it or upgraded it or installed something in it or attached something to it or it to some thing. The point was she'd offered to buy him dinner in exchange for a consultation about her personal laptop at her house, and during the dinner had made clear in about nineteen different ways that the laptop she'd had in mind all along was the one that disappeared when she stood up.

They lingered in her doorway at 2 A.M. Heart Valley time. Mike or Mark was shy and tender and proud. Lila was pleased and amused, looking forward to a sweet hour of wakeful assessment before a good night's sleep.

"You're so lovely, but I can't remember if your name is Lila or Layla."

"That all depends."

"On what?"

"On whether I'm having sex with someone or having sex with myself."

"What?"

"It's a joke."

"It is?"

"About transitive and intransitive verbs."

"Which verbs?"

"Lay and lie."

"Oh, yeah. I sort of get it. I don't think it's that funny."

In the doorway, Mark kissed Lila for a long time. She enjoyed it, but she didn't know why men kissed her for a long time after this sort of sex. She didn't know why she had this sort of sex. She didn't do it that often. Once a year, in the fall, when the rain began in California, but before that as well, in Connecticut, when the leaves instead of the rain fell, Lila found herself standing naked before a full-length mirror noticing all at once the changes that her body had undergone in the previous fifty-two weeks—the slight downward shift of bulk, the marginal loss of elasticity of skin—and in those changes plainly foresaw her own death. Not so much causally as ritualistically, this annual moment in the mirror was followed by two or three or four sexual encounters with men, each lasting no more than a week. She had begun this yearly tradition a year before leaving Bernie. Just as the trees' loss of their leaves signaled the onset of the death of another year, so Lila's first annual round of sexual adventuring had signaled the death of her marriage to Bernard Schwartz. The signal had not been the extramarital sex per se, but Lila's realization that thoughts of Bernie did not enter her mind in relation to the sex; not before, not during, not after. So attenuated was her connection to her husband—or, more accurately, to the institution of marriage—that Lila hardly experienced sex with other men as adultery. Thus, during her second yearly season of adulterous sex, she'd applied to law school, and by the following fall, she was fucking California boys.

A terrible thought came to her, a mental picture of her daughter's face. Not Cathy's face as it looked now, but as it had looked a half a dozen years ago; as it had looked, to be precise, at the moment when Cathy had entered the bedroom of the father of her best friend and discovered that gentleman on his knees before her seated mother doing something the girl had never seen or thought of before but instantly understood. Lila considered that the moment when she lost her daughter, which always returned to her memory in the form of that stricken ten-year-old face, a face which a great enough amount of pleasure or success did not exist to erase from her mind.

Mark the computer person drove away in his sporty little whatever. Lila thought of Bernie, not guiltily, but urgently. She had his e-mail address. Rather than consider the evening with Mark, she wrote to Bernie.

> Dear Bernie,
> There is something I want to tell you now. In ending our marriage, I made a terrible decision. I don't mean a wrong decision. I mean a decision which I know caused a lot of suffering. Including my own. I tell you about my own suffering not to elicit sympathy from you but to let you know that my attachment to you was not and is not something I bear lightly. Perhaps by thinking I caused you and the kids so much pain I am exaggerating my own importance. Do you remember that time we went to see Othello? Do you remember how the play depressed us both for weeks afterward? And do you remember when Othello is about to kill Iago's wife—what was her name? Mrs. Iago I suppose, unfortunately for her—and she says 'Thou hast not half that pow'r to do me harm / as I have to be hurt. O gull, o dolt, / As ignorant as dirt.' My wish for you now is that you be Mrs. Iago to my Othello.

Lila's body ached. She was beyond fatigue. She phoned the internet and sent her e-mail, which made its way out into the ether, somewhere in which was also the entity still known by the name of Bernie. Lila climbed into bed. As far as how Bernie would read this e-mail in his coma, her reasoning was abstract; possibly the piece of equipment that monitored the electromagnetic activity of his brain was also an instrument that translated e-mail into the language of brain waves.

Lying in bed, she thought of the conversation with her daughter on the topic of religion. She envied Cathy her certainty. She was sure that as long as she herself remained an agnostic, her God would always give back to her what she gave to It, namely, ambivalence.

Without a thought for the young man whose fingernails had created the narrow raised red lines that criss-crossed the smooth skin of her upper back, Lila disembarked from waking life and joined her former husband in the undifferentiated territory of slumber.

17

Just after the 4 P.M. sunset of a Friday in late autumn, Chris Schwartz drove his father's unmagnificent gray Honda Civic down to Port Town. On the tape deck and out of the past, Paul Robeson sang "Danny Boy." The depth and resonance of Robeson's voice corresponded to Chris's sense of his own maturity when he got behind the wheel of his father's car. He knew how to drive better than the President of the damned American Automobile Association. It's just he was a little nearsighted and didn't like wearing glasses. Also he hadn't studied for his driver's test and had failed the written and nonwritten portions. So legally he wasn't supposed to be driving, but technically, and more important still, morally, no one deserved to be on the road more than Chris. Unless by *on the road* one meant *lying* on the road. Or unless one meant walking on the shoulder of the road, shivering in the early November air, for who should he see doing exactly the latter but Dr. Lisa Danmeyer. He spotted her at the same moment he came within visual range of Port Town General Hospital, as if she and the hospital were one inseparable entity. He swerved the car abruptly onto the shoulder several yards in front of the doctor. This jerky car maneuver that was uncharacteristic of Chris's excellent driving skills no doubt resulted from Chris's excitement upon seeing his father's doctor in a civilian context, plus his night vision sucked.

Chris rolled down the passenger side window as Danmeyer approached.

"You trying to put me in the hospital?" she said.

"Whoa. Danmeyer attempts a joke. That's some crazy shit. Hop in."

"I think not."

"You're shivering out there in your pathetic windbreaker." The lack of a winter coat was part of Neurology Fellow Danmeyer's regimen of money-saving and mental toughness.

"It's all right," she said, "I'm just a few blocks from the hospital."

"What's the matter, you think I have cooties?"

"I was inoculated for cooties at age seven."

"A second attempt at humor from Danmeyer." Chris felt his face heat up. He didn't know how he was able to come up with this much relaxed banter. Maybe it was because he hated this woman or because he was terrified that his father was going to die. "Come on, Danmeyer. Get in the car."

"Do you even have a license?"

"Would I be driving if I didn't have a license?"

Danmeyer scowled, put her hands on her hips, got in the car. Chris felt a dual surge of pleasure and power, for in medico-automotive terms, the driver is the doctor and the passenger is the patient.

"Why do I feel like I'm making a big mistake putting my life in your hands?"

"Like you said, we're almost at the hospital."

"Most accidents happen within five minutes of the hospital." She didn't know why she was behaving so unprofessionally—if indeed that was what she was doing—toward this relative of one of her patients. Perhaps because he'd gotten under her skin with his series of remarks about the imaginary podiatrist. For getting in the car and speaking playfully to the boy, she felt a pang of regret tinged with fear, as in the recurring dream in which she has cut open a patient's head only to find a group of squirmy green and brown lumps and tubes that are unrecognizable to her.

Chris parked the car in the hospital garage. Before getting out, Dr. Danmeyer said, "Chris, your mother did ask me to treat you like an adult." (Holy shit, she was going to make a pass at him. She was going to do him in his father's car!) "So I have to bring up a difficult topic. Does your father have a living will?"

"A what?"

"A living will is a set of instructions in which the patient—the person—has asked not to be kept alive by life-support systems in case of a terminal illness. In the case of your father this could be important if we continue to be unable to communicate with him."

"What are you saying? Are you saying my father isn't gonna wake up? Are you saying he's a vegetable now? Isn't that what you people call it, 'persistent vegetative state'? It's really charming the way you doctors talk about people who are people's fathers. Are you telling me my father's going to be a fucking vegetable from now on?"

"No. Please understand me. I'm still optimistic about your father's recovery. I'm just asking if your father has left instructions in case he should not regain consciousness."

"Oh fuck you, *Lisa*. I invite you into my father's car and this is what you say to me? If you want to talk to me about this, you should be sitting me down in an office inside the hospital with my sister present and probably also a lawyer, you cunt."

Chris was up out of the car now and so was Dr. Danmeyer, who said, "Don't you use that word with me. Don't you ever talk to me like that. I have given your father excellent care and you have not shown me one-tenth the respect I deserve. I don't care how difficult this is for you, you little twerp, you just keep your head when you're in my presence, you little nothing, you speck of dust, you presumptuous molecule."

Danmeyer walked away. Chris stood by the door of his father's car. He couldn't speak. Instead, he hurled an open vowel sound at her as loudly as he could. He screamed at her in the cavernous parking garage.

18

"I've done a terrible thing. I've made a series of mistakes of increasing magnitude, culminating in one very big mistake. More than a mistake. I've done harm." It was 3 A.M. Lisa Danmeyer had made her rounds, finished her paperwork, and was speaking with someone she considered to be an ally at the hospital, a sympathetic ear. "I yelled at a kid. I said something very unkind to him. Not just a kid. The son of a patient. A fragile boy whose father is quite sick, potentially terminal, though I don't think so. I'm only twenty-eight years old, did you know that about me? When I was in high school my own father used to call me Mr. Smarty Pants. That was his shall we say peculiar way of showing affection. It has probably messed me up in ways I'm not aware of. One might conceptualize parental insults as neurotransmitters of doubt. I frighten my father—my intelligence, my will, which I know people perceive as coldness. My father was a piano salesman, retired now. Mr. Smarty Pants. I'm competent, but tonight I demonstrated my immaturity and bad judgment as a professional. As a person. More than that. I'm insecure. *I'm* frightened, though the truth is I hardly have time to notice it and it's probably best that way, and anyhow who would I tell, besides you? But tonight, wow. Dr. McKelty, Ronald McKelty—he's been in here a few times, do you remember?—has never, I'm sure, spoken to the relative of a patient that way, or had the feelings I've been having lately. *He's* remarkable, Ron is, Dr. McKelty, my supervisor. He's so rigorous, a true scientist, but compassionate too. A good soul. He's gentle with his patients and their families. I don't know how he does it. The concentration required to be a good neurologist—you're responsible for the physical means by which these people are conscious, for the functioning of their bodies, for their lives—the concentration, the amount of knowledge you have to assimilate is backbreaking. And let's not even talk about how I'm the young female in the field of middle-aged men. I'm the girl neurologist. They detect any softness in me and they're all over me like piranhas on a wading cow. And I'm not just talking about my colleagues here. Patients and their families too. It's happened! Even Ron McKelty—no, he's gentle, he's great—but I can tell he respects me that much more because of my coldness. I'm his special one, his brilliant cold girl. Now I have to confess something to you. It's something I resist acknowledging in myself and it has to do with the coldness. I get interested in my cases in this particular way. Zeal might be the word for it. For the puzzle of them, the science of them. I become fascinated. I see a person's suffering and the suffering of that person's family as an opportunity. Now there's this case—you know about it—of serotonin syndrome. I've done a review of the literature and there's not much that's good. I'm going to write a paper, I'm going to add to the overall knowledge we have about this syndrome. I feel an enthusiasm about this that's totally at odds with compassion. And then I try to make up for it in fits and starts, and that's when the faux pas happens. I lurch into a conversation that ends up being way too personal. I thought I was being compassionate this evening with this boy, the son of this patient of mine. I thought I was being empathetic, but I was not. I was flirting with him. He saw me on the side of the road near the hospital and gave me a lift. I flirted with him, realized my error, and compensated disastrously. Let me reassure you, my medical technique in this case has been unreproachable. But I've nonetheless made a series of increasingly stupid mistakes in the area of doctor/client interface. And now, Mr. Schwartz—now, Bernard—now, at the very end of my shift, just before I go home, pour myself an eight-ounce beaker of undiluted rubbing alcohol, gulp it down, have a good cry, and tumble into what I hope will be pitch-black, nonideational sleep, I will commit one last professional mistake. Do you hear me, Bernard? Do you hear my voice? I am standing over you and I am your doctor. Your son and daughter need you. So Bernard, you listen to me now. I am your doctor and I am standing over you and I am telling you to wake up. I'm ordering you to wake up. I am commanding you to wake up. Wake up, Bernard, wake up, Bernard. Wake up!"

19.

As the second week of Bernie's coma came to an end, a change in
mood occurred among the group to whom the coma mattered most.
Sorrow is an emotion that demands of its practitioners vigilant
upkeep. Left unattended, sorrow is in danger of becoming annoyance. Thus Chris and Cathy Schwartz and Lila Munroe and even
Dr. Lisa Danmeyer, in isolated moments of carelessness, felt Bernie
was letting them down. They thought of him often and he did not,
as far as they knew, reciprocate. It was becoming inconvenient for
everyone to continue to wish for the best outcome, total recovery.
Each now had also begun to wish for the distant second-best outcome, death. They all dreaded the third-best outcome—more
coma—and even more the fourth-best outcome, an awakening with
severe impairment. Whatever happened, they all felt, without
meaning to, was up to Bernie, for one of the least examined opin-
ions shared by those closest to the coma was that it belonged to
Bernie. The coma was like a dog he had allowed to shit repeatedly
in the yard of the neighbors. The coma expressed a lack of commu-
nal feeling. The coma was a form of impoliteness.

20.

Chris Schwartz's life wasn't going so good. To make it worse there arrived, at the end of the second week of November, a nightmare educational event known as the Day of Dodgeball. The chief characteristic of the annual Day of Dodgeball was that it was not announced in advance. The rationale for the surprise element was history itself. The Day of Dodgeball was a vestige of the high school's yearly reenactment of the Battle of Bellwether, a not widely known incident of the American Revolutionary War in which an entire colonial battalion was killed in a surprise attack by the British Army over the course of two hours.

Early in the morning of the Day of Dodgeball, the moveable wall between the gymnasium and the cafeteria was retracted, and the wide doors between the cafeteria and the upper parking lot were thrust open. At the beginning of the first of the three forty-minute lunch shifts at the high school, all the students were herded into the large but bounded cafeteria/gymnasium/parking lot space. For the next two hours (the preservation of the two-hour time limit of the original battle being the one merciful element within the event's overall configuration of cruelty), the school's gym teachers, sports coaches, and other faculty with even halfway passable throwing arms were supplied with an unlimited number of semi-soft red inflatable rubber balls. Their objective: to hit every student currently matriculated at Bellwether High School with a ball thrown from not less than six feet's distance within the allotted two-hour time span. The objective of the students was, of course, to avoid being hit. Any student who remained "alive" for the duration of the "game" was awarded a $200 gift certificate, to be redeemed at any of a dozen participating Bellwether retailers.

Chris had often meant to research this little-known battle, a barely noticeable stain of ignominy on the historical fabric of his happy suburban town; he had also meant to find out what fascist had invented the Day of Dodgeball, but either no documentation of the battle and its sadistic remembrance existed, or Chris kept forgetting to look for them, or both. It was generally understood that in the loosest possible correspondence to historical events, the teachers were the Redcoats and the students were the Colonials. But in the contemporary Bellwetherian political overlay, allegiances of nation and ideology were not so straightforward. The referees of the event, for example, were faculty members who tended to rule in favor of their colleagues. And there were student "Colonials" who colluded with their "British" teachers by offering up fellow Colonials for sacrifice, a practice that was looked upon by the referees not as an act of treason against a free and democratic America, but as an act of valor and steadfastness and a shoring up of traditional authority. Only people like Chris, who did not wish to die in a war he did not believe in, were regarded as turncoats.

The game had begun. Each year Chris was shocked anew by its undisguised viciousness. Fear, bedlam, and carnage reigned in the gymnasium, the cafeteria, and the parking lot. All around Chris, students were hit and fell to the ground. He shouted an impromptu invitation to other students to protest the hypocrisy and violence of this festive celebration of the massacre of their proud and brave and decent forefathers, but few heard him, and those who did were too consumed with fear or bloodlust to care what he said.

Richard Stone appeared to Chris's right. With a seamless movement he stepped behind Chris and grabbed his arms, immobilizing him. The football coach, a massive and ugly man Chris could not recall having seen before, loomed much closer than the sanctioned six feet in front of Chris. He took aim at Chris's face with what looked like a much heavier and harder version of the regulation red rubber gym ball. At that moment, lithe and fleet-footed Frank Dial flew in toward the football coach from the left, feet-first, jujitsu-style. The pink sole of Frank's dark bare foot collided with the coach's ear. The coach went down bellowing, momentarily spasmed on the cafeteria floor, went silent and still. Frank picked up the ball the coach had been holding and carried it toward Richard Stone. Stone let go of Chris and backed away from Frank in horror. Frank was not in fact carrying the coach's ball, he was carrying the coach's head, the forehead of which he proceeded to smash repeatedly against the bridge of Stone's nose. Stone fell away from Chris's view, and now Chris did the right thing. He guided Frank Dial to the bathroom and washed the blood off Frank's hands for him, and washed his bloody feet as well. Beside Frank's feet Chris noticed the careworn notebook entitled *Everything in the World.* He picked it up, and though it was covered in blood and bathroom dirt, he offered it to Frank. Frank refused the sullied version of *Everything.* He said, "Let what has been thrown away stay thrown away. The best you can do is only your best, for you are a molecule."

Chris woke from his dream lonely and ashamed. The time was 7 A.M. Because he did not know what else to do, he described the dream as best he could in an e-mail to Frank Dial, which he concluded, "You saved my ass, even though I didn't know a molecule could have an ass. I'm very sorry for what I didn't do. Chris."

At 7:23 the reply came:

To the molecule it may concern:
My mother has asked me to invite you and Catherine Schwartz to Thanksgiving dinner at our house next Thursday. I am in full accord with both the spirit and the substance of this invitation. My mother has also conveyed to me that she has it on good authority that your father, Bernard Schwartz, is in a coma. Would you please confirm this extravagant and disturbing piece of news at your earliest convenience? Should my mother speak the truth, as I fear she does, I would like to suggest a private meeting between yourself and myself, to be held at the north end of the lower parking lot of Bellwether High School during the time normally given over to first-period French class and in lieu of said class. At that place and time I wish to discuss in detail this alleged coma of your father's, which strikes me as being in all ways more important than yet another reexamination of *The Little Prince,* by Antoine de St. Exupéry, a work of

literature undeserving of the immoderate attention it receives in secondary French classes throughout the land.

Meanwhile I offer this optimistic thought: the things in your life that suck right now—and the specialized *way* that the things in your life that suck right now suck—will not continue indefinitely.

Sincerely,

Francis Dial

PS: Regarding your dream: you are one fucked up motherfucker.

21

Sixteen days after he had fallen asleep, Bernard Schwartz woke up. This happened on a Sunday afternoon. Lisa Danmeyer came into his room to find him making a weak and haphazard attempt to remove the breathing tube from his throat. She called Cathy and Chris. Chris drove his sister haphazardly to the hospital. The doctor met them outside their father's room.

"Has he said anything yet?"

"Yes."

"What?"

"He asked where he was and what happened to him."

"Anything else?"

"He asked about you and Cathy."

Chris had hoped his father would emerge from the coma speaking in Symbolist poetry. He was disappointed that his reentry into the land of the conscious—if that was what you would call it—was so clichéd.

"I think I need to prepare you for how he looks and how he talks," Dr. Danmeyer said.

"No you don't," Chris said, and walked past her into the room. There was his diminished father, half-sitting up in bed. The breathing tube had been removed from his mouth, which hung open. Saliva collected along his lower lip. His eyes were watery and vacant. Cathy came in behind Chris and started to cry. She silently asked God to forgive her for the anger she'd been feeling toward her father. Chris was pissed off that his father didn't know how to come out of a coma with dignity.

"How's it going, Dad?"

Bernie's eyeballs moved in the direction of the question—that was the extent of his response.

"What do we do now?" Chris said to the doctor.

"You may try to communicate with him. Bear in mind that he may not respond, and that if he does, his speech will be very slow and not entirely accurate."

"What do you mean, not entirely accurate?"

"Well he's had a stroke. The mixture of the two drugs caused him to have an irregular heartbeat. The irregular heartbeat in addition to some very mild preexisting heart disease caused a small amount of tissue to accrue near his heart, and then to travel through his bloodstream to his brain. This little ball of tissue blocked blood-flow to an area in the left hemisphere of his brain that we think is quite small, though it's hard to tell at this stage."

Chris said, "Seems like no matter what stage things are at, your level of ignorance is pretty high."

"We'll know better in a few days, but right now the area of your father's brain that produces the names of simple objects or concepts or action words is functioning at a deficit."

"I," Bernie said. "Did," he said. "It," he said.

"What?" The three other people in the room looked at him. This was more like it, Chris was thinking. This was a good opening statement, suggesting as it did a sense of accomplishment.

"What did you do, Dad?"

"I– " (he made an unintelligible gesture with his left hand) "myself."

"You *what* yourself?"

"I– killed– myself."

"What?"

"I– cut– myself."

"Where? Where did you cut yourself?"

"I– stabbed– myself."

"What?"

"I– hurt– myself."

"Dad, you're scaring the shit out of me."

"The– candy.

"The– pearls.

"The– nodes.

"The– grain."

"The what?"

"The– thing.

"You– eat– it.

"You– eat– it– and–

"The– uh– sadness– uh–

"Vanishes."

"The antidepressants!" Chris said.

"I– cut– myself."

Chris said, "I think he's trying to say he hurt himself by taking the wrong antidepressants. What else, Dad?"

"Cigarette."

"What?"

Bernie made the gesture of smoking a cigarette. "Frank—

"Schwartz is–

"A film–

"Actor," he said, speaking at a rate of one word per five seconds. "A human–

"Cigarette–

"Burns down–

"His face." He said this urgently, impatiently, as if the people in the room were idiots for not understanding what he meant.

Chris said, "Don't worry, Danmeyer, he always talks like this."

"Is he dreaming?" Cathy asked the doctor.

"I don't think so. Not exactly."

"Say something else funny, Dad."

"Don't push him, Chris. Let him go at his own pace," Dr. Danmeyer said.

"He's my father and he'll go at whatever goddamn pace I tell him to go at. Dad, say something else funny. Who am I?"

"You're Chris.

"You're my– pet– cat– uncle.

"A cigarette."

Chris giggled. "Dad, you rock."

"Our father doesn't 'rock,' Chris," Cathy said. "I understand that you're frightened, but why must you cover it up with this immature glibness?"

"'Immature glibness,' wow. That's good. That's very nicely done. Subtle and sophisticated for a Catholic girl. Why don't you premaritally go fuck yourself."

"Hey!" Dr. Danmeyer shouted. "What is wrong with you two? Your father needs you."

"Who cares about *him*? What the hell has he ever done for me? He can go back to sleep for all I care, and wake up at my convenience, which is never!"

"That's— not— very— nice— Chris," Bernie said.

"Hey, Dad, I was just kidding, you know that, right? Not that there's much difference between you in a coma and you out of a coma." Chris became calm again, euphoric. From up out of the coma, his father was bantering with him, or so he believed.

"Get me— lung— fire— white— smoke— tube."

"Cigarette? I'll be right back." Chris ran down the hall to the nurse's station, saw a pack of cigarettes inside someone's open handbag, stole them, and ran back down the hall to his father's room. He tried to put a cigarette in his father's hand but his father couldn't hold it. He tried putting it directly into his mouth but it fell out. Bernie's eyes were vacant and watery again; his mouth hung open again. Two minutes went by in silence. All three watched Bernie. They saw something like alertness enter his eyes from somewhere inside his head.

"Take the cigarette, Dad." Chris placed the cigarette between his father's lips, which closed around it.

Lisa Danmeyer removed the cigarette and threw it on the floor. "What is the matter with you?" she said. "This is not a joke. Your father is still in grave danger."

Chris sat down in a chair by the door of the room and leaned forward and put his head in his hands.

"Doctor," Bernie said, in his stroky drawl. "Be— kind— to—

Chris. He is– suffering."

Without going anywhere, Bernie had traveled to a place that was mysterious even to Lisa Danmeyer. He spoke softly, calmly, reasonably. His children and his doctor could not help thinking that a traveler who had passed through the land of the coma was there granted access to the truth, and though he spoke in a strange and halting tongue now that he had returned, what he said nevertheless had to be considered with the utmost respect, and if it failed to sound like a message of wisdom, that may have been the fault of the listener and not the speaker.

"I'm tired," said Bernie.

"Rest, Mr. Schwartz," Lisa said. "Do you know where you are?"

"A café."

"This is a hospital."

"Hospital. Yes, of course. You are a– doctor," Bernie said. "I am a– patient. My– daughter is– happy. My wife is– faithful. My son is a– genius."

Well, be careful what you wish for, especially if your father is in a coma and you wish for him to be ironic when he wakes up from it. Chris's disrespect for Bernie was one thing; he'd be shirking his filial duty if he didn't disrespect his dad; but when Bernie disrespected Chris, that really stung. That was a breach of the social order. The ironic remark was especially brutal now, seeming to express that which lay beneath all the layers of politeness that the freshly non-comatose patient could not be expected to have mastery of.

Bernie closed his eyes and seemed to be asleep.

"Is he back in the coma now?" Cathy said apprehensively.

"No, he's just sleeping."

"Is he totally out of the coma?"

"Yes."

"Could he go back into it?"

"He could, but he probably won't."

"Is he the same as before?"

The doctor sensed she was being asked a question whose answer lay beyond the scope of medical science. She proceeded carefully:

"We don't yet know how much brain function has been affected by the stroke. After a stroke, some areas of the brain are only temporarily depleted, whereas others are damaged. We'll have to continue to do tests, and we'll also have to wait. Your father is speaking very well. He seems quite alert. Those are good signs."

"How long will he have to stay here?" Chris asked.

"Hard to say now."

"Could he come to Thanksgiving at my friend's house?"

"That's four days away. I think not."

"Don't be a pill, Danmeyer."

"Where your father's safety and well-being are concerned, I will be as much of a 'pill' as I have to be."

"What about his happiness?"

"That's not my area. I don't do happiness. I do safety and well-being."

The doctor's humor demoralized Chris, and she recognized she had gone too far once again.

Cathy admired the doctor. She liked the way she treated Chris, with a combination of medical efficiency and personal aggression. Cathy liked the way the doctor combined her own character with her professional demeanor. She wanted to ask her how she did it. She wanted to ask her something like, How do you conduct yourself as an adult in this world? What are your thoughts? What is the correct way to think about life? Cathy felt that if she only had a correct basic philosophy—two or three densely and perfectly articulated thoughts that constituted a unified theory of life—each of her life's individual situations and challenges would not seem so impossible to get through with dignity and decency.

22.

In the lives of Chris and Cathy Schwartz, hospital and school
exchanged roles. Hospital was now the place where they went to be
educated and socialized by illness and the resistance to illness;
school was the place where they visited their gravely ailing secondary education. It wasn't as if they'd been learning much in school
anyway. The hospital, on the other hand, offered them the opportunity to become wiser by way of pity and terror.

On the Tuesday night before Thanksgiving, Chris made his sixth
or seventh attempt to persuade Lisa Danmeyer to let his father leave
the hospital to attend the festival meal at the Dials'. She said no. He
insisted. She refused. Cathy could not stand the noise of this repeat-
ed argument and searched her mind for a new topic. She found one
she'd only half thought about, and blurted it out before she'd given
herself the chance to consider all its ramifications: "Dr. Danmeyer,
would you like to join us for Thanksgiving?" Everyone was stunned.
"I'm sure you already have plans. But I'm really serious about the
invitation. I hope that's not disrespectful. You saved our father's life,
and that would make you an honored guest at our table."

Chris decided to make use of the opportunity presented, for
once, by his sister: "And if you come—pardon the expression—you
can supervise the health of the patient."

"No, Dr. Danmeyer, that's not what I had in mind. I agree with
you that it would be best for our father's health if he remained here
for Thanksgiving. I just wanted to invite you. If you have other
plans we'd still love it if you'd stop by for dessert." Cathy couldn't
believe she'd used the word *love*.

"I really don't think that would be right," Lisa said, and wished
she didn't sound like a prig who'd been offended. "What I mean is

that it wouldn't be right for me to accept your invitation because I'd be letting down my own family." Letting down her own family meant letting down her father. Her whole life was virtually one big effort to please him, but the very formidability of her effort to please him was a source of discomfort to a father who wanted his daughter to have been a happy and well-respected music teacher.

Cathy didn't understand why Dr. Danmeyer didn't say, "You're right, I do have other plans already." She was writing down the address and phone number of the Dials, and saying, "This is just in case you decide to come by for an after-dinner liqueur," and then she had an uncomfortable moment in which she realized she was offering somebody else's liqueur to somebody when she didn't know if the person whose liqueur she was offering even had liqueur, not to mention that it wasn't her liqueur to offer; then she figured she could bring some liqueur, but then she realized she couldn't bring liqueur because she couldn't buy liqueur without breaking the law. "Or maybe just pumpkin pie," she said.

Lisa Danmeyer, who had grown angry at her father in the last half minute, said, "I am very touched by your offer, Cathy." With bitterness she added, "But you know how families are at Thanksgiving."

"I've made a fool of myself already," Cathy said, "so please take this piece of paper with the name and address." Cathy realized that she had just implied that the reason Dr. Danmeyer should take the paper would be to prevent Cathy from feeling like a fool, which was selfish and presumptuous. "I mean, don't take it because I've made a fool of myself, take it if you want to take it." Now Cathy thought Dr. Danmeyer was going to think she was rescinding the invitation. "Please take it," she said, almost aggressively.

Lisa took it, said "Thank you," and left the hospital room.

Throughout this entire transaction, Bernard Schwartz remained unconscious.

"That was suave," Chris said.

Cathy said, "Shut up, asshole."

23

Lisa Danmeyer sat in a hard straight-backed chair at the table in the kitchen area of her sparse apartment in Port Town. There was a chair in the apartment that was more comfortable and there was a couch that looked more comfortable but wasn't. When she sat in the comfortable chair she really was comforted, and when she sat on the couch she could also be comforted if she worked hard at imagining it was a different couch. But now wasn't the time for comfort, now was the time for phoning her father. She wished she had the sort of father whose voice on the phone would be a break in the almost unremitting routine of self-abnegation that her life had become. But, in the end, who really had that father? Possibly the Schwartz kids. For most of the time she had known him, Bernard Schwartz had been in a coma, and that alone made him more docile than most fathers, but the man who emerged from the coma—as well as the man who emerged in descriptions of him given by his children and his ex-wife—seemed to be the sort of man Lisa thought she would be comforted by.

"Hello," said the stern male voice. Why did this retired piano salesman whom everyone but Lisa thought of as jolly speak sternly only to her, even before he knew it was she who was calling him?

"Hi Daddy."

"Ah. When you coming?"

"On Thanksgiving, as we agreed."

"Yes, of course, but what time?"

"Let's see. My plane leaves New York at 8:05. I have a two-hour stopover in Chicago—"

"I don't need the whole itinerary, I just need the time you're arriving in El Cuerpo."

"Well my plane lands in San Francisco at 1:35 California time."

"I'm still waiting for the El Cuerpo arrival time."

"Well that depends on how fast you can drive," she said, hoping he'd realize she was being playful and not challenging.

"What are you talking about?"

"If you pick me up when my plane gets in we can probably be back in El Cuerpo by 3:00."

"What time does your plane arrive in El Cuerpo?"

"It doesn't. It arrives in San Francisco."

"What? What kind of a thing is that? You want me to drive all the way down to San Francisco to pick you up? How young do you think I am?"

"Oh. I didn't– I just assumed– "

Her father, despite being handy in the kitchen, wasn't going to cook a Thanksgiving dinner. Even if she offered to buy a turkey and cook it, he would insist on going to his favorite family-style restaurant (emphasis on *style*, because she couldn't recall seeing any families there, only old men like her father whose wives had died or divorced them and whose children had gotten out of El Cuerpo as soon as they were old enough to vote or think for themselves, whichever happened first) for a cheerless two-person meal of fresh-frozen turkey along with cranberry sauce of uniform smoothness and color served in the unaltered cylindrical shape in which it will have slid from its aluminum can.

Lisa stood up and walked over to the comfy chair and flopped down into it. She wished to be enfolded in the arms of the comfy chair. She wished to be swallowed up by it, to disappear into it, to vanish from her apartment and from her own consciousness, at least for the duration of the Thanksgiving holiday and possibly until sometime shortly after the New Year. "Daddy," she said. "I'm sorry. I already bought the ticket. I'll drive us back up to El Cuerpo."

"Aw hell, you're really gonna make me drive all the way down to San Francisco?"

"It's nice to hear how eager you are to see me."

"Aw sweetheart, don't do this to me. Don't inconvenience me

and then make me feel bad for being put out. It's Thanksgiving. I'll pay your cab fare all the way from the city, because I know you doctors are always hard up for cash."

"Daddy, when I'm done with my fellowship I'll hire you a chauffeur, and that way you won't have to exhaust yourself by driving ever again. In fact, I'll just charter a helicopter and land on the roof of your house."

"I hope I'll be dead by the time that happens."

"Oh my God how awful, why would you say such a thing?"

"What, what did I say? I made a joke. We all know I'm not so subtle. We all know the same jokes I've been making all my life that my friends and customers thought were funny because of what coarse people they are are not *really* funny."

Lisa paused for a long moment. She felt very tired. Sometime earlier this evening her throat had begun to hurt every time she swallowed saliva. "No, it's me, Dad. I didn't realize you were kidding. I think the long hours at work make me a little humorless."

"Well, I guess I play a little rough," her father said. "You're a good kid. I worry about you. Have you got a husband—I mean a boyfriend? I didn't mean to say husband, I meant boyfriend."

"I'll take a cab up to El Cuerpo Thursday afternoon. I'm tired. I gotta go to bed. I love you, Daddy."

"You're a good kid. You get your rest. I want you to be happy. I didn't mean to say husband."

"Good night, Daddy."

"Okay kid."

Moe Danmeyer put the phone back in its cradle on the kitchen wall and walked out onto the small cedar deck of the house he'd worked all his life for. He leaned forward and pressed his forearms against the railing, which he had stained a shade called "redwood." It seemed fake to him now. He should have chosen a darker, more sophisticated stain that his daughter would appreciate, like mahogany. The smell of the autumn air of northern California and the sensation of it against his arms were soothing to him. He liked being outside in a short-sleeved shirt well into the winter months.

He looked down at the yellow golf shirt covering his round belly, at his plaid golf pants, at his blue plastic house slippers, and wondered if he was the sort of man Lisa and her friends would laugh at if they were to see him on the street. Then he thought of his serious daughter, who didn't have time to laugh at anyone. His compassionate daughter. His daughter who was short one sense of humor. Too bad he couldn't even kid around with her. If she'd let him kid around with her then they'd be friends. She was the kind of daughter he could brag about. He did brag about her. Everyone he knew was sick of hearing Moe Danmeyer talk about how great his daughter was, but he kept telling them because he knew they liked being sick of it, because that was how people kidded around with each other. He could brag and even exaggerate a bit—add little things like how the head of neurology told Lisa she was the best neurologist he'd ever seen, which the head of neurology may well have done but Lisa would never tell him because she was too modest—and when he got to the end of his bragging he always wanted to add that his daughter, Lisa, the neurologist, was also his good friend, but that he couldn't do, because that was not even an exaggeration of something that was true. Lisa was not his good friend. Lisa was not his friend. His only child was only his child.

Moe Danmeyer went inside and poured himself a generous glass of single malt scotch and went back out to the porch and took a small sip of it. Three thousand miles away, his daughter poured herself a generous glass of the single malt scotch her father had bought her the previous spring, got into her disheveled bed, took two big gulps, and clicked on the TV with the remote. Over the next fifteen minutes, she sipped the rest of the scotch in her glass, felt her sore throat getting worse, watched the digitized dancers' bodies abruptly come toward her and recede from her to the beat of a series of nearly identical and impersonal songs she didn't recognize, and then she passed out.

24

Having experienced poor results in a prior attempt to alter his father's appearance, Chris Schwartz was tentative as he put the disguise on Bernie that the latter would be wearing when Chris snuck him out of the hospital for Thanksgiving dinner at the Dials'. There were aspects of dressing his father that Chris had to erase from his mind even as they were happening: slipping his white cotton briefs over his buttocks and privates was one; getting dark blue dress socks over his white, horny, yellow-toenailed feet was another. Chris also wasn't thrilled when, as he struggled to get his father's pants on, Bernie giggled and said, "Ooh, you're tickling me."

Though he had explained it to him carefully several times, Chris had no idea how much of his hospital escape plan Bernie understood. Bernie's relation to the world seemed to shift often and irregularly from total disorientation to hallucinatory distortion to total clarity. But then some of the things Bernie had been saying in what were generally agreed to be his hallucinatory distortion periods were so *true* in this weird kind of way that Chris began to think that maybe what most people thought of as total clarity was really hallucinatory distortion, and what most people thought of as hallucinatory distortion was really just raw perception minus years of education, and that all education was was the training of the senses to perceive a very limited bunch of stuff that wasn't even there.

The disguise Chris had developed for his father in order to get him out of the hospital was pretty much the same one Bernie had worn to the fateful Halloween party. In other words, he was making his father over as a creature whom no one would ever mistake him for: a normal dad.

After the mortifying struggle with the pants, Chris paused and regarded his shirtless father. In practical terms, it made no sense to put the pants on before the shirt, because in order to tuck the shirt in you had to undo the pants again. But in terms of manhood, that was simply the way it had to be done. Only women and children put shirts on before pants, and the older Chris got, the more he realized how precious little there was that prevented a man from becoming a woman, or a child. And that was a shame because to be a dad you had to be a man.

Now came the struggle with the shirt. "Hold your arms up over your head, Bernie."

"Why?"

"To get to the Dials' on time."

"What dials?"

"Not dials like dials. These are people whose name is Dial."

"Why are they called Dials?"

"That's their name."

"What's my name?"

"Oh come on, now you're just messing with my head."

Bernie laughed his creeped-out wooden mental retard laugh. Because of the damage to the left hemisphere of his brain, he could barely lift his right arm, so Chris lifted it and got a blue oxford broadcloth on him, and a tweed blazer, and a pair of tortoise-shell glasses with no lenses that he'd picked up at the pharmacy the day before. Bernie enjoyed the seriousness with which this young man, his son, put on his shoes, and especially the straight-faced way he retrieved the left shoe each time Bernie kicked it off his foot and across the room.

As they walked down the hall, Bernie was unsteady on his feet. His right leg and foot were not responding to his brain's attempts to control them.

"Have you been practicing walking?" Chris said.

"I don't want to answer that," Bernie said, at about one word per three seconds.

In the elevator down to the lobby, Chris stuck a box of cigarettes in the breast pocket of Bernie's jacket to complete the disguise, and also to allow Bernie to smoke if he wanted to. To be a man, you didn't have to be happy, Chris felt, but you did have to be free, even if freedom meant freedom to destroy yourself.

"I'm not going to be able to hold onto you to this extent in the lobby and possibly also not in the parking lot, depending who's out there," Chris said.

"Whatever," Bernie said.

Halfway across the lobby, unsupported by Chris, Bernie tried to light a cigarette and fell on the floor.

"Is he still drunk?" a man in a nurse's uniform said, mistaking Bernie for someone else. "Maybe we ought to keep him here longer."

"Oh, you've *gotta* let him out, Mister. It's Thanksgiving," Chris said in semi-advertent imitation of some nonspecific American classic feelgood cinematic holiday comedy. "I'll make sure he doesn't touch a drop."

The man nodded dubiously.

As Chris drove Bernie's car to the Dials' with one eye on the road and one eye on Bernie, Bernie smoked cigarette after cigarette, coughing out each lungful of smoke.

"What is your problem?" Chris said.

"I don't know," Bernie said.

Walking in the cool night air toward the Dials' house, which was illuminated by lamplight, Bernie said, "That's a very small house."

It was hard to know what Bernie meant by this comment. Maybe he meant that the house was much smaller than the hospital, which he may have come to perceive as the standard "house" by which all other houses were to be measured; or small compared to his own house, or compared to some inner ideal of "house" that formed the basis of all judgments made about actual houses; or small as the result of some neurological/visual damage wherein objects seen by him were closer than they appeared. Or perhaps Bernie deemed the Dials' house small by virtue of some previously repressed socioeconomic snootiness which the trauma had knocked loose inside his brain.

Bernie hunched over as he walked through the Dials' front door and into their living room, as if passing through a doorway built for children or midgets.

Francis Dial's mother, Renata Dial, in her bright red and purple flower print dress, moved toward the guests with a look of uncertainty on her face.

Cathy, who was sitting on the couch where Frank had sat when he ejected Chris from his home, stood up and cried out. "Chris! What is the matter with you? This is so dangerous. You could be killing him right now."

Bernie, speaking haltingly and slurring his words, said, "He's not killing me. He's bringing me to– Hanukkah– Easter– Thanksgiving at the dials. The dials are a kind of black people who have a small– physical– structure– window– house." Bernie looked at the people in the room to see if they understood what he was saying, because he sensed he wasn't making himself clear.

"Come and sit down, Mr. Schwartz," Renata Dial said, took the hat off his head and led him to a chair.

Cathy grabbed Chris's arm and pulled him away from their father and whispered to him, "You bring him back right now. Can't you see how fragile he is? This is scaring me."

Chris said, "Oh, you're no fun any more."

"Chris!"

"No. You think it'd be so good for his health to be sitting alone in that hospital on Thanksgiving?"

"You know our plan was to leave here at eight and visit him until ten. Besides, he doesn't even know it's Thanksgiving. He doesn't know what Thanksgiving is."

"He does too. Just because he can't talk right doesn't mean he doesn't know stuff. Lisa Danmeyer said his aphasia isn't a deficit of data storage, it's a deficit of data processing."

Cathy refrained from making a comment about Chris's barely concealed crush on the doctor because she could not bear to appear to be that most banal of creatures, a bitchy teenage girl, even though she felt that was probably just what she was. She and Chris looked over at Bernie, who was hunched in his chair, not only as if the ceiling were too low for him even while he was seated, but also as if the chair he was seated in was too small to accommodate his bulk properly.

"Mr. Schwartz," Renata Dial said with strained joviality, "How about a cracker with cheese on it?"

"Thank you, dial. May I say that your– red– yellow– green– brown– uh, thing that covers you, uh, skin, is, uh sensitive, uh, kind, uh, nice, uh, beautiful this night."

"Mr. Schwartz, my name is Renata Dial. I would like you to call me Mrs. Dial. I would also prefer if you did not keep talking about the color of my skin or your skin or anyone else's skin. This is a holiday. Let's just enjoy each other's company and forget our cares."

"Why can't we talk about skin color, Mom? It's not offensive, it's just the truth." Frank Dial had just strode into the room in his sky-blue tailored suit, black silk tie, black patent leather zip-up half-boots.

"Wow, you really look nice, Francis," Cathy said, and blushed.

Renata Dial said, "Frankie, I don't want to feel uncomfortable because of what people are saying who are guests in my house. I'm not going to argue with you about this. That's just the way it's going to be."

"Catherine, you are one good-looking white girl. I mean, girl." Frank kissed Cathy's cheek and said, "You smell really good."

"It's just soap," she muttered. She had not at all meant to look good or smell good or flirt. She was wearing a gray wool jumper and black tights and a black T-shirt and wanted to be neat and appropriate and unnoticed.

Frank said, "I'm sorry I'm late, everyone. I had to feed my fish their special Thanksgiving meal. Catherine, would you like to come to my room and look at my collection of tropical fish?"

"No. I mean, no thank you, Francis. I don't understand why anyone would keep wild animals in a small confined space for his own pleasure. Also my name isn't Catherine, it's just Cathy."

Frank didn't understand why his mother and this girl wanted to crush the happiness he'd felt when he entered the living room to celebrate Thanksgiving in his new, excellent suit. He wanted to say something to hurt Cathy, but because he admired and respected all the weird regimented systems he imagined she had invented to make her life the orderly-looking thing that it was, and because he maybe even had started to love her a little bit sometime within the last fifteen seconds, he wouldn't allow his mind to formulate an insult. "Well," he said. "Would you like some apple juice?"

"Yes, thank you, Francis." Cathy had not meant to speak harshly to him. She had had to invent that opinion about cruelty to fish in order not to have to visit Francis's room. She did not know what her feelings toward Francis were. Her skin was hot now in his presence. She could not allow Chris or her father or Mrs. Dial to see her doing anything with Francis that had even the appearance of impropriety, though she wasn't sure what impropriety she was guarding against the appearance of, or why.

On his way to the kitchen, Frank bowed mock-formally to his pal Schwartz, who returned the gesture. Frank stopped in front of Bernie Schwartz and said, "Bernie! How the gosh darn heck are *you*, my brother? You awake now, or what?" Frank raised his right arm up perpendicular to his body and intended to swing it in a downward arc toward a big slapping male handshake with Bernie, but Bernie, wildly misinterpreting the arm movement, stood awkwardly and dove at Frank's torso, giving him a tight and fierce hug. "Okay Bernie, okay." Frank hugged him. Bernie wouldn't let go. "You can sit down now." Bernie didn't budge. "Somebody get him off me."

Chris peeled his father off his friend. "Down, Daddy, down."

Bernie sat down, again as if he were Goldilocks in the chair of Baby Bear. "I don't want to break your little heart– glass– chair," he said to Renata Dial, who was trying to remember every second that this man was ill, not rude.

The coma had conferred upon Bernie a genius for turning the perceptual/cognitive hiccup that was happening within the boundary of his skin into the protocol fuck-up that was happening beyond it. For the rest of the evening, this Thanksgiving party would repeatedly witness the unhappy merger in Bernie of biological and social dysfunction. At dinner he spilled food on the table, the floor, himself. He handled dishes and cutlery as if they were doll dishes and doll cutlery. Despite the vigilance of everyone, he periodically managed to drink a sip of wine. Just after Renata Dial brought out the pumpkin pie, Bernie fell asleep in his chair. Cathy insisted that they bring him to the hospital. Renata, overcompensating for her anger at this horrible/not-horrible man and her anger at his son for bringing him to her house, offered to let Bernie lie down in Frank's room. Cathy really wanted to get Bernie back to the hospital, but she also took it upon herself to make up for the shameful manners of her father and brother by having the best manners humanly possible, and therefore accepted her hostess's generous offer so as not to offend her. Renata Dial, who had been hoping Chris and Cathy would have the decency and good sense to reject her offer and take their father back to the hospital where he belonged, instructed her son and his friend to carry Bernie to Frank's bedroom and tuck him into bed, which they did.

The doorbell rang. Renata Dial opened it and saw a young dark-haired, red-eyed white woman.

"Hello, my name is Lisa Danmeyer. Cathy Schwartz invited me here for dessert. Are you Mrs. Dial?"

"Yes dear, come in." Renata turned to Cathy and said, with a noticeable something-or-other in her voice, "Your friend Lisa is here. I suppose I would have prepared more food had I known about the extra guests you decided to invite."

Cathy blushed. Frank took his mother aside and said, "Mom, the Schwartzes, you know, they're kind of out of it on the best of occasions. But they're basically good people. I promise. I know it was my idea to have them over but please try to deal? I'll help you clean up."

"Oh, if this had been the easiest Thanksgiving we'd ever had, you would be helping me clean up. This Thanksgiving being what it is, let me give you an extremely clear picture of what the clean-up is going to be like tonight in this house: you will clean up."

"Yes, ma'am."

That morning, Lisa Danmeyer's flu symptoms had rendered her unable to get out of bed except to vomit, after which she'd gone back to sleep. When she awoke again, her flight to San Francisco had already departed. She called her father to tell him the news. He yelled at her and she cried. She hung up and was miserable. Her friends and colleagues had fled Port Town for the holiday. Lisa slept, vomited, tried to catch up on back issues of neurology journals, watched TV, stared out the window. At 8 P.M. she thought of the Schwartz family. Cathy and Chris were different from the relatives of any patient she'd had, insofar as none had invited her to dinner until now and none had insulted her so vigorously and consistently until now. Where most patients' families behaved toward her as if she were some great and inanimate force of nature like a huge Arctic glacier implacably breaking apart the modest pleasure ship of their healthy lives, Cathy and Chris acknowledged Lisa's humanness by being kind and mean to her, respectively. She was feeling less nauseated than in the morning, she knew that convivial human company had a positive effect on physical health, and she desperately wanted to get out of her stuffy little apartment. If Dr. Ronald McKelty were in her place, would he accept the invitation from Cathy Schwartz? No, because Dr. Ronald McKelty would not get the flu on Thanksgiving or have a dreadful argument with his father. She climbed out of bed, bathed, and called a cab.

Upon seeing Lisa Danmeyer, Chris leapt from the table. "Danmeyer! Dude!" he said, grabbed her hand in both of his and yanked it up and down in what was meant to be a comically exaggerated handshake. The cab ride had already jostled Lisa's labile stomach, and the handshake nauseated her further.

"You look as if you need to sit down," Renata Dial said. "Would you like some pumpkin pie?"

"Oh no, thank you, Mrs. Dial. It seems I've caught this flu that's going around. Physician heal thyself, or something."

"I'm so glad you could come," Cathy said to Lisa, blushing. To Renata she said, "I hope you don't mind that I invited our father's doctor. I really meant to tell you. Please forgive me."

Frank pulled a chair up to the table for Lisa.

Renata said, "What can I get you, sweetheart? A cup of tea?"

"Tea would be nice, thank you." Lisa didn't want tea. She wanted not to have left her apartment.

Chris said, "So Danmeyer, where's your podiatrist boyfriend this holiday season?"

Lisa, tongue loosened by fever and nausea, said, "Back off, you little *pisher*."

"Ooh Danmeyer." Chris turned to Frank. "Didn't I tell you she was huggable?"

Frank said, "Dr. Danmeyer, be assured that aggression is my good friend Chris's way of expressing his warm feelings for you."

"Yes, well, all my male patients want to marry me, and all my female patients want to be me." Lisa inadvertently looked at Cathy after she said this. Cathy looked down at the table and wished to erase Lisa from the mental list of women she thought she might be able to model herself on, but couldn't do it. Lisa knew she'd hurt Cathy and didn't understand why she'd done it.

Chris said, "Hey, Danmeyer turns out to be an arrogant bitch."

Cathy said, "Chris, you've gone too far."

Lisa said, "No, it's all right."

Renata Dial placed a cup of tea before Lisa. Lisa took a sip to be polite. Chris made a series of facial signals to Frank having to do with his fear that the doctor would discover the presence of his father, and Frank didn't understand them. Chris stood and said something about wanting Frank to show him his fish. Frank stood and the two boys left the room, but not before Chris gave Lisa a hearty slap on the shoulder.

The shoulder slap pushed Lisa past the point of oral continence. She asked Renata where the bathroom was. She went there quickly, closed the door, and vomited into the toilet, vaguely aware of broken glass and small brightly colored mobile objects on the floor, as well as something massive and out of place in her peripheral vision. When the vomiting loosened its grip on Lisa's body, she looked to her left and saw something that frightened her: Bernard Schwartz naked and unconscious in a bathtub filled with water and tropical fish. Chris and Frank entered the bathroom. Lisa vomited again. Frank surveyed the bathroom, rushed away, and rushed back with a little green net with which to scoop up his fish. Lisa Danmeyer knelt over the patient, checked his vital signs, and ordered Chris to call an ambulance. He did.

25

The Thanksgiving dinner had a demoralizing effect on all its participants. Chris Schwartz had made the central contribution to the second near-death of his father. Cathy Schwartz had stood by and watched her brother practically kill him off. Lisa Danmeyer had been placed in an ethically troubling position by the members of this family. Frank Dial lost several of his favorite fish. Renata Dial virtually admitted to herself that she would never have white people at her Thanksgiving table again, or at least not these white people. And when Bernard Schwartz woke up eighteen hours after he had been found passed out in the Dial bathtub, he was mute and still, and seemed to be functioning at the mental level of an unusually savvy four-year-old.

Frank Dial did not shun Chris Schwartz, but he was getting pretty sick of him. They rarely walked to school together any more. They didn't skip class to talk and lie in the woods. Frank transferred his allegiance to Cathy Schwartz. Cathy developed a justification for moderate intimacy with Frank Dial that was not in violation of the unofficial, unspoken, and unintelligible rule she believed non-pragmatic contact with him would violate. The justification was Christianity. As far as she could tell, the essence of Christian teaching was to perpetrate kindness. But that didn't mean Christian teaching forbade a person from *receiving* kindness. To complete the kindness equation, someone had to receive the kindness being perpetrated. Furthermore, getting it was good training for giving it: being the attentive object of Frank's good deeds provided Cathy the opportunity to figure out what worked and what didn't work, in terms of the execution of good deeds, and so the intimate contact with Frank Dial—the moderately intimate contact—was a sort of worldly Sunday school for Cathy Schwartz. Cathy knew she was both not kidding herself and kidding herself; she cared and she didn't care; she was a narrow-minded idiot and a broad-minded idiot. Oh, she just liked the notes he slipped inside her locker at school; she liked that one bouquet he brought to her house that one time, though of course she pretended she didn't; she liked his polite and carefully phrased inquiries about the health of her father and herself; she liked his occasional visits to the hospital, his stylish good humor. Even his concern for the well-being of her parricidal brother touched her and taught her not to hate Chris, or tried to teach her not to hate him.

"You do know that Brother Chris is basically good people, right?" Frank asked Cathy one day. "He didn't mean to do harm to your pops. My mother's been dragging me to—uh, I've been attending church all my life, so you must believe me when I say that the person you have the hardest time loving is the person God wants you to love the most." As Frank made this argument to Cathy, he semimonitored it for veracity. He himself was having a hard time loving Chris Schwartz lately, and while he could sort of convince himself that he was explaining to Cathy what he thought God wanted her to do partly to remind himself that God wanted him to do it too, he also had to admit that he was saying this half-full-of-malarkey thing just to impress a chick; no, more than impress her: help her move beyond anger that he knew caused her pain; but also definitely impress her; mostly impress her, plus maybe help her a little bit. The only thing Cathy didn't like was when Frank called her "Sister Catherine."

Chris drank and drove. Drinking more than a little bit of liquor made him sick, and as much as he thought he deserved to be sick at all times, he couldn't bring himself to be more than lightly drunk at any given time. At any given time, he was lightly drunk. He carried a flask of Wild Turkey with him everywhere and sipped from it as often as he could bear to. Slowly, carelessly, tipsily, and illegally driving his father's car, he rattled around Bellwether and neighboring towns, often with no destination. Sometimes he dropped by school for *that* kind of self-punishment. More often, he spent hours at the hospital communing with his retarded father.

On a Thursday evening in mid-December, in the presence of one of the orderlies who now always stood guard in the room when Chris visited, he halfheartedly sang "The itsy-bitsy spider went up the water spout," and tried to make his father do the thumb-to-fore-finger, my-hand-is-a-dumbass-spider gestures as a way of reconditioning his impaired spatial perception and motor coordination. "Down came the rain, and washed the spider out," father and son sang together. "Out came the sun, and dried up all the rain," they sang and, in a burst of awkward enthusiasm, Bernie knocked a bowl of compromised hospital succotash from the night stand to the floor with his messed-up right arm, which he had been using to imitate half the sun. Chris, who had been periodically running to the bathroom to take itsy-bitsy sips of whiskey throughout this evening's visit, apologized to the orderly who was in the room, and cleaned up the succotash. The orderly disliked and distrusted Chris Schwartz, and so did everybody else in the world except Bernie Schwartz, who loved Chris now more than ever, as if Chris had done him the biggest favor in the world by making him more of a retard, as if being a retard had liberated Bernie from the burden of intelligence he'd been carrying all his life.

Chris started the song again, having warned his father to go easy on the pantomime aspect. Chris hated the song even as he appreciated its perfect formulation of the cyclical nature of the futility of all existence.

Frank Dial entered the room.

"Where's Cathy?" Chris asked, wincing at the presence of his erstwhile best friend.

Frank said, "Do I have to visit only when Cathy visits?"

"I don't know. No."

Frank stood between the door of the hospital room and Bernie's bed. Chris stood on the other side of the bed, between it and the room's one window. Chris and Frank looked at Bernie. Bernie stared past Chris out the window and into the darkness. Chris had seen Bernie spend entire evenings staring into the darkness. Chris said, "What are you looking at?" Bernie continued to stare in silence. Chris tried to look into the darkness as well, and saw only the imperfect reflection of his own face, the pimples appearing as tiny dark spots, areas of perfect nonreflection, the not-Chris that was the essence of Chris. Frank looked at Chris and Bernie looking into the darkness. He thought this was some kind of Schwartz father-son communion, a silent form of vacant attentiveness not available to the unimpaired. "Do you have that flask on you?" he asked.

"What flask?"

"*The* flask."

"No, no flask," Chris said, and tried to make a furtive, pleading head gesture that indicated the presence of the orderly in the room.

"You still beating yourself up?" Frank said.

"What's it to you?"

"You heard the doctor: Bernie might have gotten worse anyway. Having that tube in him all that time probably would've given him the pneumonia whether you pulled that escape-from-Birkenau routine or not."

"So? Why are you even telling me this? What do you know about it?"

"Did you ever think your total misery might be selfish? What about Cathy? She's pretty upset too, but all you can do is wander around thinking about how bad you feel."

"Oh I'm not so worried about Cathy. When it comes to being nice to Cathy, I think you're doing the job of ten men. Maybe you should leave right now and go bring her some more flowers."

"Easy now, boy. What I bring Cathy is between me and Cathy."

"Oh, okay, boy. Whatever you say, *boy*."

"I have an idea," Frank said in a bright and happy tone. "Why don't I come over there and slap you?"

Bernie turned away from the darkness and looked at Chris and then Frank. "Hey, stop," he said. "Don't– fight. Fighting is– sad."

Frank said, "What should we do?"

"I will sing a– frill– dirge– song."

"You're going to sing for us, Bernie?" Chris said.

"Don't speak to me like I'm a– fink– shit– child."

Chris and Frank stared at Bernie, who closed his eyes tightly and opened them. Haltingly, he sang,

> One of these days
> And it won't be long
> You'll call my name
> And I'll be gone
> Fare thee well oh honey
> Fare thee well

part
three

26

Just before the long Christmas holiday, Lila Munroe flew back east to help Chris and Cathy place their father in a rehabilitation facility before the three of them took off for a California vacation. Chris and Cathy spent all their school holidays on the West Coast with their mother. Mother and brother and sister were glum on the plane ride. Not only were they embarking on another long awkward period of family togetherness, but they had just banded together to imprison Bernie. It was the worst thing they'd ever done.

They arrived at Lila's bucolic two-story wooden house in Heart Valley in the evening in the middle of a rainstorm. The house was damp and musty. The air inside it was hot and unmoving. For Chris, entering his mother's house was like entering his mother's reasons for divorcing his father. There was an order to the space and the objects in it whose logic Chris could not penetrate. The house remained dark and gloomy and incomprehensible. And each time his mother patiently, even affectionately explained the divorce to him, Chris felt more convinced than the previous time that her underlying answer was "It's none of your business." In the same way, as he walked from room to room of this house that his mother had insisted he live in for the next week and a half, he felt that each door—including the door to "his" room—was plastered with an invisible sign that read "Keep out."

Chris couldn't stand the stillness of the air. He opened a few windows. Rain sprinkled the sills, the floors, the edges of the rugs. Lila saw these things that belonged to her getting wet and she wanted to scream. Three seconds into his visit, the kid had managed to make messy inroads into her orderly little life. Not even so little. It was expanding all the time. She was building it while teaching herself how to build it. This was complicated and strenuous work that she loved. Every time her kids entered her life, they set about pulling it apart, and continued to pull it apart until it was no bigger than it had been when she was married. When she was married, her life could not exceed the dimensions of the marriage, which were roughly the same as those of a small closet. These visits amounted to sharing that one closet with two adolescents. And yet, she had to admit, the little airless closet had a coziness her life otherwise lacked, and which she missed when her children left.

Still: *That selfish bitch* was her nickname during her children's vacations, phrased just like that in the third person, though in reality only Lila called herself *that selfish bitch*, and never out loud; *not in reality*—that is, in the ongoing conversations all the people in Lila's head conducted without her permission—it was her children who had invented that name for her. Lila as seen by Lila's own mental Chris and Cathy was a Lila Lila couldn't stand: *that selfish bitch.* In the rest of her life—her life away from her children's dissatisfied gaze, real or imaginary— she was free to be *that fabulous bitch* or *that bitch who can do anything* or *that glorious woman* or even, as she unexpectedly became on the kitchen floor with the gardener when the kids were out of the house on the morning after their arrival, *you beautiful, intelligent, powerfully sexy woman.*

If desire may be defined as the maddening feeling you are left with even after you have obtained the thing you want, then the feeling Lila had toward the end of the remarkable morning she spent with the gardener was very possibly as close as she had ever come to desirelessness. He wasn't even *her* gardener, in the literal sense. At least he hadn't been before this morning. He'd been tooling around in his pickup truck knocking on people's doors trying to drum up business. He knocked, she answered, he said a few words to her about what he could do for her lawn and flower beds, and, Californianly, but uncharacteristically for Lila, she invited him in for herbal tea. Midway through the tea she was kissing him. And then the tea slowly went cold in the cups while that amazing event transpired on the kitchen floor. Lila would never fall in love with the gardener, but wow, was she ever fond of that marvelous man. He was the most relaxing person she had ever spent time with, would be one way of monumentally understating the case.

When Chris Schwartz walked in, Lila was laughing, and the gardener was laughing and slicing tomatoes on Lila's kitchen counter. In a freak alliance brought on by the emotional duress of vacationing, Chris and Cathy had gone out for breakfast together several hours earlier. They had taken a walk on the sand adjacent to the Pacific Ocean, or at least they'd stood sadly side by side facing the ocean and contemplated its crushing enormity. Chris had dropped Cathy off at the Heart Valley Public Library to read up on her saints' lives, and now here he was looking right at his mother and the guy he knew she'd just had sex with. How did he know? Their hair was wet, for one thing. Weirdly enough, it didn't bug him. He thought it was funny. There was his mother washing some arugula at the sink and laughing, and Chris laughed too, and the guy shook his hand and told him his name, which made the three of them laugh that much harder.

"People don't call you that, do they?" Chris said. "What do they call you?"

"Charlie."

"Is Charlie your middle name?"

"No."

Everybody laughed some more.

Chris pointed over his shoulder with his thumb toward the door and some nonspecific place in the world beyond the door. "I was just going to go for a walk in, you know, the woods."

"Which woods?" Charlie asked.

"You know, the woods that are over, like, there."

"I could show you some amazing woods after lunch," Charlie said. He was maybe fifteen years older than Chris and Chris wondered if he was the only one who thought that was weird.

"We're all three about to have lunch together, right?" Lila said, and laughed.

Chris said, "Okay."

They ate the tomato and arugula salad. In addition, Lila brought out a number of plastic containers of Aquarian-style salads and stews produced by local artisans and given names that called to mind the elegance and purity of the Far East as well as the goodness and simplicity of the developing African nations. While they ate, Charlie spoke of the dreariness of gardening in the rain, and of his preference for hard physical work under the sun, especially when the result was something as beautiful and pleasure-giving as a garden or well-landscaped lawn. He talked about surfing as well, and the brilliance of summer in California, whose reliable return each year was one of life's miracles.

While Charlie spoke, Chris looked over at his mom expecting to find an expression of amused disdain on her face. He found the amusement but not the disdain. In fact, several times, when she exhaled, she emitted this slightly disturbing kind of hum-sigh. This may have been the first time in his life that he'd witnessed his mother in a state of unmitigated contentment. He wasn't sure it was proper for adults to express their contentment in front of their own children.

27

The sun had come out and dried up all the rain. Chris and his mother's sex partner were walking through the woods. Chris said, "Tell me your real name again?"

"Sextus Mann."

Chris wanted to laugh again but he thought it would be impolite and maybe self-endangering now that his mother was not present.

Sextus "Charlie" Mann was pale and willowy and soft. He had blue eyes and thick long black hair and a native talent for making anyone feel as comfortable as possible, even that most uncomfortable possible teenage son of the woman he'd just made love to. Without saying so directly, Charlie conveyed to Chris that he, Charlie, had the utmost confidence in Chris's cleverness and overall suitability as a woods walking companion. Not that Charlie's confidence itself didn't make Chris nervous (Chris thought he might get molested).

The trail ascended. They were on the side of a small wooded mountain. The mountain smelled good. The trees on the mountain were pretty and made a gentle noise when the wind blew them. The dirt path they climbed on was clean and clear and there were little chips of wood on it that contributed to the good smell of the mountain. Some birds were chirping and some squirrels were running around—frolicking, Chris guessed—and little purple and yellow flowers were just sitting there near the ground looking unpresumptuously excellent.

When they got to the top of the little mountain, Charlie—aka Sextus, for Christ's sake—lay down on his back on a smooth, flat rock, and gestured for Chris to lie down near him. Chris hesitated. Charlie made a gesture indicating he would not molest Chris, which was of course indistinguishable from the gesture an adult man would make who really did intend to molest the teenage boy for whose reassurance he was making the gesture. Nonetheless, Chris decided to go for it; to go for lying on his back on the rock, that is.

For the first few minutes on his back, Chris thought of Frank Dial. He wanted to write to Frank about all that had happened to him on this trip so far. Mentally composing an e-mail to Frank Dial was Chris's habitual way of processing experience, of making encounters with reality more bearable. In these mental e-mail compositions, Chris failed to acknowledge the sad fact of Frank's being, as time went on, less and less the ideal audience for them. His physical position now reminded Chris of the moment when he and Frank had been lying on their backs in the woods near Bellwether High School and were then brutally confronted by football-playing Richard Stone, a moment that led to the current unhappy state of affairs between the two friends. He shook this thought loose from his brain and stared at the clouds above. He saw a cloud that reminded him of a throw rug, and another that looked like the timer on a VCR. He thought of sharing his observations with Charlie, but decided against it. Whatever his virtues may have been, Charlie would not have understood what Chris was saying. Charlie was happy, and that was all well and good, but there was a terrible sacrifice Charlie didn't even know he was making in order to be happy: he didn't embrace irony. Chris respected Charlie in a way, but he also thought that anyone who didn't embrace irony was a fool, because whether you embrace irony or not, sooner or later irony embraces you.

Chris allowed his thoughts to drift along with the clouds. After a period of time that was not measurable by him, he became aware that he'd been gazing idly at a cloud that resembled a middle-aged man lying in a bed. As he scrutinized the cloud, he did not know if his eyes were open or closed. The cloud resembled his father, naturally. He looked at the place in the cloud that looked like his father's face; specifically, the face of his father after the coma. He saw the droopy, sad eyes of Bernard Schwartz, and his simple stare. He saw the lips that were now always wetter than Chris wanted them to be. He saw the cool, pale, rubbery flesh, the tall, pale forehead, the dark hair which the staff of the rehabilitation facility didn't wash often enough and which was consequently stringy. This cumulus version of his father floating in the sky above him changed shape as he watched. It broke apart in the area of its mouth. A sound came out of the mouth. Chris listened.

"They are kind to me here," the cloud said. "But there is no one here I know well. Kindness is one thing and intimacy another. Intimacy is the house that shelters you from the weather, and kindness is comfortable furniture. You need the former to survive, you need the latter to feel good, and you need both to have a good life. The person who has good furniture but no place to put it is in constant danger of not surviving."

"Dad?" Chris said, and wondered if, when his father had said "They are being kind to me here," he had meant by *here* the rehabilitation facility, where Chris had last seen him, or heaven. Not that Chris had developed ideas about the existence or location of heaven. He was not among the faithful, and he was not an atheist or an agnostic so much as he was a nonstarter where religion was concerned. His tentative notion of heaven now was of some hazy aerial zone of the recently dead. He began to tremble.

"Your friend comes to visit me every day," the cloud said. "He is sharp-tongued. He makes remarks that are either jokes or not jokes. If they are jokes, they are insulting. If they are not jokes they are even more insulting."

"Please be patient with Frank Dial," Chris said to the cloud. He didn't know if he was saying it with his mouth, or with some other part of his body, or not with his body at all. "Frank is going through a hard time lately."

"I'm confused most of the time," the cloud said. "I don't know what I know. One moment the world is clear and the next moment people and rooms don't look the way they're supposed to. The air itself feels inside out. I wish I could look at something I recognize, but I am in a strange place surrounded by people I don't know."

This Cloud Dad wasn't talking like Chris's real dad, either before the coma or after the coma. And Chris, when he spoke to the

Cloud Dad, wasn't talking like himself. So Chris didn't know if he was imagining this whole thing or what. The face part of the cloud was now rapidly disintegrating. It was widening and lengthening and thinning out, as if Chris's father's face were being pulled apart, as if Chris's father were screaming. Chris shoved his knuckles into his own eyes and must have made a noise because Sextus Mann sat up next to him on the rock and said, "Are you okay, buddy?"

Chris said, "I need to call my dad."

"Do you want to use my cell phone?"

"Yeah."

Charlie removed his phone from his pocket and gave it to Chris. Chris dialed the number of the rehabilitation facility. "I need to speak to Bernard Schwartz please."

The woman on the other end of the line went away, returned, and said, "Mr. Schwartz is taking a nap. Can I give him a message?"

"No. Please wake him up."

"I can't do that, sir."

Perhaps the fact that the person on the other end of the line was a woman encouraged Chris to feel more impatient with her than he otherwise might have. "Oh I think you can do that and you will do that. This is his son and it's an emergency."

"What's the emergency?"

"The emergency is that I'm gonna come over there and stick my foot up your ass if you don't let me talk to my father."

The woman hung up. Chris remained seated on the rock with the phone to his ear. "Why?" he said.

"Why what?" Charlie said.

"Why do I do this over and over?"

"Do what?"

"Become somebody who I don't even know who it is, somebody who acts like an idiot, somebody who does the total wrong thing and accomplishes the exact opposite of what I want to accomplish."

"I don't know."

"Basically I have this idea of who I want to be and I never am that guy."

28

Cathy returned to her mother's house by foot from the Heart Valley Public Library on a winding road sheltered by tall trees. The road was dark, but irregularly shaped odds and ends of sunlight clung to the smooth black pavement, the few houses, the low-lying shrubs, and the pale skin of her arms. Cathy's visit was not and would not be satisfactory, but she'd be damned if it wouldn't be useful; now, on her walk, with the cool darkness of the road, the smell of eucalyptus, the unexpected fragments of sunlight, she was having an experience that seemed to her more than useful, more than beautiful, even: she tried to permit herself to call this all the grandeur of God.

Lila was lolling in her living room with a volume of *McKinney's Statutes*. She heard the noises of her daughter's arrival in the kitchen, and then that girl appeared before her, or perhaps materialized was a better way to put it. Cathy stepped into a narrow radius of late afternoon sunlight that illuminated the left half of her flushed face and lovely, womanly torso. Lila's senses, aroused that morning, were awake to the beauty of her daughter. Cathy looked down at Lila, and Lila took in her melancholy pride. She wanted her daughter to stand there for a while. She wanted to stare at her face and body and take in all the changes that were happening there. She was grateful for this moment in which she was able to apprehend her daughter fully—it didn't happen often—and she wanted to convey to Cathy that she loved her and wished for her happiness; no, happiness was a shallow way to put it; she wished for Cathy to fulfill her own finest promises to herself. What could Lila say that would signal to Cathy that everything was okay between them now?

"How are the saints?" was what she decided on, and with the help of Cathy's little scowl, recognized her mistake.

"Well I was reading about Saint Teresa of Avila."

"What did she— who— which— saint was she?"

"I'm grateful for your interest in my reading, Mother, but I wonder if you wouldn't mind if I didn't discuss Saint Teresa with you. I just need to think about her by myself for a while before I talk about her." Cathy would gladly have talked about Saint Teresa with someone who she felt could help her to understand.

She sensed some new kind of affection emanating from her mother. She was sorry she didn't reciprocate it. She knew if she'd absorbed the lesson of Saint Teresa's life, she'd have been able to open her heart to her mother. Instead, she waited out the encounter and hoped to get through it without making Lila feel bad.

"You look as if you've had a nice walk."

"Yes."

"Chris went out for a drive with the gardener."

"I see."

"Do you know the gardener?" Lila asked, though she knew that was impossible.

"No."

"Are you hungry?"

Cathy wondered how she could fix her own meal and make her mother feel that that was the best arrangement. Make her mother. She wanted to make her mother. She wanted to make her mother into the woman she wished her to be, but she could not imagine what sort of woman that was. Also, before she made the decision to have children, the mother should have already taken the responsibility to become the woman her daughter needed her to be.

"Do you mind if I make my own lunch?"

"No. There are lots of things for sandwiches."

Cathy went into the kitchen and hoped Lila would stay in the living room, but that was not to be.

"Grandpa Tim wants to see you," Lila said.

Cathy said, "Okay." She thought Tim was an absurd name for a grandfather and especially a Jewish grandfather. In fact, Grandpa Tim had begun his life only half Jewish, and had gone all the way only at the behest of his wife, Cathy's grandmother, now deceased. But he didn't act Jewish, even in that sweet, wry way that Cathy's father acted Jewish, which wasn't a religious way of acting but had its own cultural dignity with a whole long history of suffering and immigration behind it.

Lila said, "He sent this funny telegram."

"He sent a telegram?"

"Yes."

"He lives twenty miles away. He could have made a local phone call."

"He sent a telegram. He thought it would be fun, I guess. Do you want to hear it?"

They both knew the answer to that question and pretended its opposite was true. Cathy opened the refrigerator and looked inside, more to present her mother with her opaque back than to find something to eat.

"'Chris and Cathy,' it says. 'Welcome to CA. Looking forward to feeding you mountains of ice cream, buying you unnecessary luxury items, and engaging in other forms of grandfatherly malfeasance. Call me. Love, Tim.'" Lila realized about halfway through the performance of the telegram that it couldn't have been more offensive to Cathy's ascetic sensibility than if it had been designed to be so. She gazed wearily at the back of her daughter's stiff figure in front of the fridge.

"I'll call him tomorrow," Cathy said.

"Maybe you should call him tonight. He gets very busy."

"Really? What does he do?"

"I don't know. He makes lots of plans with his friends."

"His drinking buddies? They plan in advance to go to a bar and drink?"

"Cathy! Stop it! I can't take it any more."

Cathy felt a thrill in her belly and turned around.

"You're carrying this holy righteousness too far. I will not be judged by you in this way and I will not have my father judged by you. I will not tiptoe around you and try to say only things that will be acceptable to this narrow and naive and untested morality you are so goddamned aggressively thrusting on all of us. You're a child. You live in a comfortable house in a rich suburb. We have very carefully protected you and your brother from any of the violent or difficult events in the world for which people have had to develop the kind of stringent moral systems you think you know all about." Lila's daughter made herself remote from her. Standing still at the open door of the fridge and looking not at Lila's eyes but at her forehead or ear, Cathy receded into the fridge. She was at the back of the fridge, behind the rotted lettuce, almost invisible.

Lila tried to soften her speech. "I'm worried about you. No, not worried. Mothers aren't supposed to worry, right? Concerned. I misspoke a moment ago. I got angry and a little carried away. I apologize. I'm truly impressed by this strength I see in you, this rigor. But don't forget you're sixteen, Cathy. Don't forget to have fun. Don't forget pleasure."

The word *pleasure* brought her daughter back to her, in a bad way. With the word *pleasure*, all was revealed. Cathy got where her mother's weird friendliness in the living room had come from. It had come from *pleasure*—the same kind of *pleasure* Cathy had seen her enjoy when she was ten years old and walked into a dark room to see her best friend's father doing that thing to her mother. Pleasure indeed.

"I'm not hungry," Cathy said, and went to the room in her mother's house that she slept in at night, and closed the door.

29.

On the fourth night of the kids' visit to the coast, Chris, Cathy, and Lila drove down to South San Francisco to dine at the home of Tim Munroe. Tim Munroe was the only living grandparent of Chris and Cathy. Cathy didn't like him. Chris liked him but felt that despite all Tim's jolliness, the guy didn't really want to be his friend. Encounters with her father produced in Lila five or six different emotions that usually made her cry, which made her father wonder how this frail and volatile woman could have become a rich lawyer. Lila had been late getting home from work and had to stop on their trip down to South San Francisco to buy not just beer for her father but a bottle of scotch as well. It was nine o'clock by the time they arrived. The three of them were exhausted, but not Tim Munroe, who had awakened at eight from a two-hour nap, and had just finished drinking an invigorating concoction of four ounces strong dark-roasted coffee and one ounce bargain Cognac. Working with speed and force on a filterless cigarette, Tim stood on his unrenovated front porch and greeted his daughter and her kids. Each of them gave him a kiss, which meant penetrating with their faces the almost tactile bolus of smoke that encased his head.

"We're all really hungry, Daddy," Lila said. To hear her mother call this infantile man *Daddy* made Cathy feel sorry for the woman.

He looked at his watch. "Hungry, sure, it stands to reason. Where shall we eat?"

"You said you were going to cook for us."

"That's strange. I haven't cooked in thirty years."

"Yes you have. You sautéed me those shrimp when I moved here, when was that, five years ago."

"You know what I mean, I mean *generally* I haven't cooked in thirty years."

Nobody knew what he meant. Lila felt desperate. The breach of promise indicated he had no idea what kind of human suffering was at stake. Why did this fact continue to surprise her? She considered having the bottle of scotch for dinner, taking a cab to a luxury hotel in the city, passing out, and going in to work late the next morning.

He invited them inside to sit on "comfy chairs," at least until they worked out the conundrum of, as he put it, "where and how to eat dinner."

The chairs were old and ugly and threadbare; they had lost all fluff and gave no support. The house reeked of cigarette smoke.

"Who wants a beer or a scotch?"

"Scotch please," Lila said, and Chris echoed her.

"How old are you these days, kid?"

"Twelve."

"That's funny as hell." Tim left the room.

Chris knew his grandpa didn't think it was funny at all. He figured Tim would not find anything he said or did funny until Chris was about seventy, had a few heart attacks under his belt, and had taken a leg full of shrapnel in the Pacific theater of war.

Tim came back to the living room ten minutes later with four scotches—though Cathy hadn't asked for one—four cans of beer, and two books wrapped in old newspaper. "Here," he said, handing out the scotches and one book each to Chris and Cathy. Chris's was a yellowed and still somewhat dusty paperback edition of short stories by Jack London. Cathy's was a mystery by someone called Andrew Greeley that was not as discolored but stickier to the touch. "Your mother told me you were a Catholic now and Greeley was a priest who wrote bawdy mysteries, so I got you that. Chris, I don't know what-all you're into, but I figure you're a young man so I got you that." *I figure you're a young man* was an insult Tim had no idea he'd perpetrated, and *got* in this instance was a verb that elided the trip Tim made to the bookshelf in his garage just after he'd asked everyone if they wanted scotch.

Tim uttered a one-syllable toast that none of them could make out, upended a shot of scotch over his wide-open mouth, popped a beer, sipped it, lit a cigarette, smoked it.

Cathy said, "You're amazing."

"I know, I know," Tim said meditatively.

She stared at him for a minute with his slicked-back white hair and his gaunt, white-stubbled face. "Why do you do all that stuff, Grandpa Tim?"

"All what?"

It seemed to Cathy that right now he was doing about five decadent things, but she could only name two: "Smoke, drink."

"Easier than not doing 'em."

"But they're going to kill you and also they're disgusting. Maybe you don't know how bad it smells in here?"

"Ah kid." He blew some smoke and waved at it a couple of times with his free hand, which may have been a gesture of courtesy to Cathy. Everybody was silent for a while.

"Well Grandpa Tim, are you going to answer me?"

"Answer you about what?"

"Why you smoke and drink even though they're bad for you and gross?"

"Oh. Hm. Answer you. Sure, sweetheart. Think of it like this. Cigarettes are like a wife and mother to me. A drink is like a mother and a dinner." Tim brought his current cigarette close to his lips, paused to revisit the logical sequence of his answer to Cathy, and followed through with a deep confirming inhalation.

They ate in a south city pizza establishment with molded plastic furniture and fluorescent lights. Tim knew why everyone was gloomy. He liked Bernie and had thought of him from the first as a real sweetheart, one of those guys who used his own underconfidence to put other people at their ease. Tim would now honor Bernie with a little lighthearted pizza chat, but that was it. As soon as anyone got into comas or brain damage he'd change the subject, four or five times if he had to. He wasn't going to let anyone say anything serious about sick fathers.

"Bernie's as strong as an ox," he said, and knew that was the last thing Bernie was as strong as, so he blustered his way through and beyond the comparison with a vigorous, wordless 7-Up toast.

"Spend a little time with him," he said to the kids, "and then let him alone to do his healing. A man needs solitude and a man on the mend needs it twice as much."

"That's not true of Bernie, Daddy," Lila said. "He likes to have people around all the time. He needs people like crazy."

"Yeah, in our family it's not the man who needs solitude, it's the woman," said Chris, who had intended to make a humorous remark. Chris was once again tipsy though he wasn't really a drinker, though he might have been becoming one.

"I don't know," Tim said in response to something.

With her napkin, Cathy politely removed an anchovy from her mouth and put it in her pocket. She wondered what significance this dinner had in the overall story of her life. If being faithful meant that she was supposed to use even the most banal and annoying events like this dinner in the pizza parlor to serve God somehow, then she might as well have been an atheist.

There was a long silence during which they could have sworn Tim was quietly humming "She'll Be Comin' Round the Mountain."

"Hey Grandpa," Chris said. "An Irishman, an Italian, and a Polish guy are sitting in a bar drinking. After four drinks each, the bartender gives them one free. The Irishman says, 'In Dublin there's a bar even better than this one called O'Casey's. You buy two drinks and the bartender buys you one.' The Italian says, 'Oh yeah? Well in Rome we got a place called Dante's where you buy *one* drink and the bartender buys you one.' 'That's nothing,' says the Polish guy. 'In Warsaw we got a place called Szymborska's. You walk in, the bartender buys you a drink, then he buys you another drink, then he buys you a few more, then they take you out back and get you laid.' The Irishman and the Italian say, 'Really? Did that happen to you?' And the Polish guy goes, 'No, but it happened to my sister!'"

"Not bad, kid," Tim said without laughing. "There's an old lady living in Florida goes to visit her daughter in L.A. Lady walks in the front door, sees her daughter walking around the house naked, says, 'What're you doing? Didn't I raise you right?' Daughter says, 'Mom, this is the new fashion in L.A., it's called the nondress.' Couple weeks later, the lady's back in Florida, her husband comes down to breakfast, and there she is standing in the kitchen stark naked. Husband says, 'What is this?' Lady says, 'It's the new fashion, it's called a nondress.' Husband says, 'Yeah? Well yours needs ironing.'"

Chris laughed and slapped the table and wanted to hug his grandfather but knew that would ruin everything that was still left to be ruined.

Lila and Cathy were like a pair of teenage girls, angry and embarrassed and mute and desperate for the dinner to end.

Tim's red-nosed friend Sporty Swenzler walked into the pizza place and said, "Am I late?"

"Just on time, just on time," Tim said, and to his family: "Well it's been nice seeing all of you. I'll pay for this and then Sporty and I have some serious business to attend to."

Sporty Swenzler laughed at this worn-out euphemism more than Tim had laughed at anything all evening. The younger generations of Schwartzes and Munroes were defeated, crushed. Lila said, "You brought us to this pizza place because this is where you agreed to meet up with your drinking pal?"

"I wouldn't put it that way."

"How would you put it?"

30.

Chris Schwartz shook hands with Francis Dial at 6 A.M. on a Friday in Bellwether, Connecticut. The handshake was solemn, the air was cold, the sun was not yet up. The boys stood on that place that was neither Chris's house nor Chris's street—Chris's driveway. At 6 A.M. everything seems possible, and that was a burden on the boys.

"What's happening with our screensaver apothegm venture?" Chris said.

"I don't know."

"You were supposed to be sending out query letters while I was away."

"Oh, I visit your father every day and send out screen-saver apothegm venture query letters while you're frolicking in California."

"I wasn't frolicking, I was brooding."

"Like I care."

That actually hurt Chris. "You're telling me you didn't send out letters."

"I sent out twenty."

"And?"

"Nothing."

"What do you mean, 'nothing'?"

"Seventeen rejections, and the other three companies are probably stealing the idea."

"You followed up with phone calls?"

"Yes."

"And?"

"Nothing."

"What do you mean, 'nothing'?"

"I mean fuck off."

"Did you include a broad enough sample of the individual apothegms? The individual apothegms were so witty."

"It didn't work. Get it? It didn't work."

"So now what?"

"Now we keep sending each other apothegms, if we feel like it."

"Why?"

"For our own enjoyment."

"What a stupid reason."

"Fine, don't then."

"What should our next business venture be?"

"Nothing."

"What do you mean, 'nothing'?"

"I mean let's give up and fail."

"Oh thank God," Chris said, and they got in his car.

He drove in the gloom. First it was too cold in the car, then he turned the heat up, then it got too hot, then he turned it down, then it got too cold, and so on.

"This isn't how you get there," Frank said.

"Is too."

"No, you should have taken a left on Plymouth Avenue."

"Listen, all the streets on this continent are interconnected, so if we keep driving randomly, we'll eventually get there, given enough time."

Frank punched the passenger-side window of the car several times almost hard enough to smash it. The boys, on their way to visit Bernard Schwartz at the Roosevelt Rehabilitation Facility, competed for who was in the crappier mood.

Despite the effort the management of the Roosevelt Rehabilitation Facility had made to ensure that its patrons would not feel shut in, quarantined, hospitalized, warehoused, imprisoned, or abandoned, a lot of them did, and some of them were. Not the three acres of uniformly green front lawn, nor the colonial-style brick mansion, nor the elegant but homey American antique stuffed chairs and Persian carpets could conceal that quality of atmosphere that was half smell and half mood, and signaled that this was one of the dwelling places of the living damned.

Chris found Bernie in the exercise room crawling on a nearly motionless treadmill. "This has both physiological and psychological benefits for your father," a lady said. Chris refused to acknowledge the lady. He pointedly did not notice any of her singular features, talk to her, look at her, listen to her, or imagine having sex with her.

Bernard Schwartz continued to crawl toward the front end of the treadmill without arriving there. Chris stood amazed, watching his father perform a metaphor of Chris's life.

"Why," Chris asked Frank, "are they making my father humiliate himself like this?"

"I can see why you'd think that's what they're doing," said the lady whom Chris wasn't noticing. "But we are retraining his brain's connection to the muscles of his arms and legs. We're also allowing him to revisit the early stages of human development so that when he becomes a functioning adult again he'll have a sense of wholeness when he reviews his own progress."

Chris looked at the surface of the young woman as if inspecting a pair of shoes he was about to discard. The woman shut off the machine and helped Bernie into a chair. Chris looked around the exercise room at the other feebs and idiots being guided by condescending mentors through methodical, pointless tasks on or entangled in padded chrome torture machines.

"How you doing, Bernie? It's me, your son, Chris, back from California."

"I'm okay," Bernie said in his halting, stroky drawl. "Sometimes I feel sad and I don't know why. Chris what's a– a– frugal– what's a– blowjob?"

"What?!"

"What's a– blowjob?"

"I heard two of the– people with– with– ladies talking about it in the– lengthy area– long thin area. One of them said it was fun. The other said it was disgusting."

"Oh it's fun," Chris said. "It's when one person closes their eyes and the other person blows gently on their eyelids. It feels nice. Do you want to try it?"

"No, it sounds disgusting."

Frank Dial laughed uncomfortably and Chris punched him in the arm and Frank punched him back twice as hard. One or two tears sprang from each of Chris's eyes and a light sob issued from his mouth before he was able to get ahold of himself.

31

February arrived. Some people celebrated this fact, others bemoaned it. Chris was among the latter, always the latter. Time moved forward, erratically perhaps, but never so erratically that it moved backward, or to the side: just that one outrageous direction, as if Time were a dutiful idiot sent on an infinitely long errand. Space, on the other hand, could move backward and to the side. Not that space was any great shakes. Space was pretty stupid too. Space was limited. In Time, at least, two or more things could co-exist in a given space, whereas in Space, only one thing could exist in a given space. The worst was when you put Time and Space together. They diminished each other. They added up to less than the sum of their parts. Thought, however, could do things Time and Space couldn't. Thought could go backward and forward in time, and legend had it you could hold up to seven thoughts at once in the single space of your head. But Thought was weak compared to Time and Space, and entirely dependent on them. One little puff of nitrous oxide to the brain and Thought was obliterated, whereas Time and Space had always existed and would always exist, world without end.

Chris visited Roosevelt Rehab every day. He figured these visits were a more efficient way to get over being young than showing up for senior year of high school would be. Chris's father's room wasn't like a hospital room, nor was it like a hotel room, and it certainly wasn't like a bedroom in a house. It was somewhere in the group home/flophouse range of living quarters. Sometimes Chris found his father in there with the lady he had done his best to ignore, but now begrudgingly had to acknowledge as a sexy but annoying speech pathologist, someone who made Bernie name simple household objects and describe line drawings. Sometimes Chris found him in there conversing with a woman whose aphasia was so severe she could say only "Down the hatch." Sometimes Chris found Bernie staring at the wall, sometimes sitting in the soft, worn vinyl chair half-dozing with fluttery eyelids. On the particular day in mid-February in question, Chris found Bernie sitting in his pajamas in a wheelchair at "his" desk, trying to draw a circle on a piece of paper with a black pen. The end of Bernie's tongue stuck out the side of his mouth as if Bernie himself were a drawing of a child making a sincere effort to accomplish some pathetically easy task.

"Why you in a wheelchair?" Chris asked panickily.

"Because it's fun," Bernie said.

Bernie's circle was a lopsided spiral. That couldn't be a good sign. Chris played tic tac toe with him for a while, then dots.

"These are kids' games," Bernie said petulantly. "I want to play a grown-up game. I'm a grown-up."

"So act like one."

"I'm trying."

"When do you think you'll succeed, out of genuine curiosity?"

"Jennifer told me I shouldn't worry about it."

"Who's Jennifer?"

"The talking– the– talking– "

"The talking dog?"

Bernie glowered at Chris.

"The speech pathologist?"

"Yes."

"She looks like a bitch on wheels."

"What's a– bitch?"

"A female dog."

"You are mean to– people who are– women."

It was gloomy in the room. There was a small high window that faced north, letting in the dull glow of a cloudy winter afternoon. The hard low carpet was of a pale color that had no name. The walls were beige and the moldings were an artificially natural dark wood color which, along with the high ceilings, gave Roosevelt its genteel feel, or at least gentile feel. The Schwartz boys sat in gloomy silence. Bernard thought of notable clouds he'd seen in his lifetime, and tried to remember the name of the president of his country. Chris thought of the speech pathologist, Jennifer, with pique and vague groinal stirrings. Jennifer had told Chris to do anything he could to aid in his father's linguistic recovery. Chris neatly tore two long strips of paper and handed one to Bernie. "This is called the exquisite corpse game. It's for your aphasia and my amusement. How this works is I name a part of speech, like noun or verb or adjective, then we each write one of whatever part of speech I just named at the top of our strips of paper. Like let's say I say 'verb.' Then you'd have to write 'give' or 'sleep' or 'die' on your paper. After you've written the word, you fold the top of your paper just enough so it covers the word you've written, and you pass your paper to me, and I pass my paper to you. Then I call out another part of speech—say, 'adverb'—we each write an adverb, fold our papers to cover the adverb, switch papers again, et cetera, until we've collaboratively written two sentences, if I haven't screwed up the sequence of the parts of speech."

Bernie neither understood Chris's instructions nor could he identify the different parts of speech. So they ended up playing a modified version of the game in which they took turns saying nouns to each other.

Chris said "Snow."

Bernie said "Ice."

Chris said "Cheese."

Bernie said "Pizza."

Chris said "Face."

Bernie said "Blowjob."

Chris said "Whoa."

Bernie said, "You lied to me about that word."

"What? How do you know?"

"Jennifer told me."

Chris rejected the existence of that remark and carried on with the game. Bernie was doing well in this format. They practiced naming farther, naming faster:

"Germ."

"Speck."

"Mote."

"Dot."

"Glob."

"Ball."

"Chair."

"Man."

"Car."

"House."

"Alp."

"Sea."

"World."

As the afternoon ground implacably forward, they muttered, called, and shouted the names of physical objects at one another, not because it was fun but because it was the closest approximation to that makeshift breastwork against the desperation of solitude, a meaningful connection of souls.

Over time, or against time, the game evolved. By early evening, they were building whole phrases out of nouns.

"Facility."

"Rehabilitation Facility."

"Roosevelt Rehabilitation Facility."

"Roosevelt Rehabilitation Facility Fundraiser."

"Roosevelt Rehabilitation Facility Fundraiser Dinner."

"Roosevelt Rehabilitation Facility Fundraiser Dinner Menu."

"Roosevelt Rehabilitation Facility Fundraiser Dinner Menu Committee."

"Roosevelt Rehabilitation Facility Fundraiser Dinner Menu Committee Chairman."

Jennifer, the speech pathologist who had an extralinguistic pathology of her own to contend with, entered the room and remarked, "I see you're making the most of his aphasia. Good."

"Don't talk to my father about blowjobs," Chris said.

"Well, it's interesting you should say that, but I haven't. That's not something I would ever talk about with a patient."

Jennifer put some pictures on the desk and asked Bernie to point to the picture that best illustrated the sentence she uttered. "The girl is reading a book," she said. "Good. The dogs are not chasing cats. Good. The man greeted by his wife was smoking a pipe. Good. The boy kissed the nurse. Nicely done. The boy was kissed by the nurse. Okay, try that one again. The boy was kissed by the nurse."

Not only did Chris now fail to ignore all attributes of the speech pathologist, Jennifer, but he noted with despair how her presence provoked the involuntary pairing of adjectives and nouns in the place inside his body where words had their origin: "Full lips," he said silently to himself against his own will and better judgment. "Golden hair. High cheekbones. Red lips. Sparkling eyes. Passionate temperament. Lovely anger. Round breasts. Pointy nipples. Strong hands. Good God."

Jennifer saw him staring at her. "Don't lie to me, bitch," he said more or less apropos of nothing.

"Listen, jerk," she said. "There's no earthly reason I should take crap from you. I came in here to do an extra session with your father. Why don't you do something a little extra for him instead of ogling me and insulting me. He could use a walk in the back yard. You go wait for him at the bottom of the back stairs near the exit. I'll get him dressed and send him down."

Chris stood there and said nothing.

"Go!" Chris stood up and walked toward the door. "Oh and by the way," Jennifer said, "I'm not a bitch. I'm really nice."

As Chris was leaving and Jennifer was beginning to remove his father's pajamas, did she wink at Chris?

Jennifer dressed Bernie in his street clothes, told him she'd be right back with his winter coat, and left the room. Chris was waiting in the dark empty hallway. Jennifer approached him. "Hey there," she said.

"Where's my father?"

"Upstairs."

Jennifer continued to approach Chris, who was scared. She walked right into him. Their bodies collided. She kept walking as if she would go through him. So as not to fall down, he backed up, until his back met a wall. Their faces were an inch apart. "Hi," she said.

"What are you doing?"

"I'm going to kiss you." She did. First closemouthed, then, when he realized what was happening, openmouthed. She unbuttoned and unzipped his pants. Chris wondered if he was dreaming. She yanked his pants and his underpants, quite unromantically, Chris thought, down to his knees. She knelt before him, looked up, and said, "I don't know why I like you. You haven't been nice to me."

"I'll try really hard to be nicer," Chris said.

"You don't have to. I don't mind."

What happened next didn't feel to Chris as if it happened *next*. Things got kind of unchronological. Time, for once, went all spirally, backward and forward, long and short and long again. Behind Chris's eyelids, egg yolks burst and coated his brain with their soft bright liquid. Jennifer stood and pulled his pants up for him.

"That was so nonverbal," Chris said.

"It was adorable." Jennifer mussed his hair, said, "Come again soon, y'all," and mounted the stairs.

This was Chris's penis's first immersion in any part of anyone's body since prior to his birth. Chris was moved that this young woman had understood his hostility as an expression of desire, his crude insults as a form of flirtation. He tried to make the timeless feeling of the blowjob last and in doing so, didn't.

Jennifer reentered Bernie's room with his coat and put it on him. She was wearing her own coat, and was thinking ahead to the thirty-mile drive to her empty house and the long evening of agitation she knew awaited her.

"Okay now, Bernie," she said. "Go all the way to the bottom of the stairs. Your son is waiting for you there."

"How will I know when I've reached the bottom of the stairs?"

"When there aren't any more stairs."

32

On Saturday, Cathy Schwartz hung around the house suffering. What caused her to suffer was ostensibly the biography of the Jew Edith Stein aka the Catholic Saint Teresa Benedicta of the Cross. Not just her birth and death, but everything Edith Stein did and everything that happened to her meant something. Each moment in the existence of Stein could be read as a commentary on holy scripture. Cathy's existence, on the other hand, was random, meaningless, indecipherable. As a child, Edith Stein had secret, silent sufferings that eventually led her to faith in God. Cathy had secret, silent sufferings that led her to more secret, silent sufferings. Edith Stein was a woman with a destiny. Cathy was a girl with a bicycle. For a long while, Edith Stein's intellect held her back from holiness. Intellect was not Cathy's special cross to bear. She hoped her special cross would be revealed to her because she was feeling defeated by all this non-cross-shaped pain.

An imaginary picture of her male friend, Francis Dial, appeared before her eyes, while in nonimaginary reality, Frank was walking toward her house. His skin—both in her mental picture of him and on his flesh—was lovely; his skin and his hair and his teeth; his thin hands, his long fingers. She pictured him against a white background: first his whole body clothed in that blue suit he'd worn on Thanksgiving, then his torso and arms and head, then just his head, then the area of his face that went no higher than his eyelashes and no lower than his wet bottom lip. Along with the Francis Dial for whom the sole audience was Cathy went a sort of musky scent. Cathy's skin became hot, plus a few other bodily changes she chose not to think about. Edith Stein's soul had become a fool for God, but that was not what Cathy's soul or any other part of her was becoming a fool for. She stood up and went outside. The subfreezing air that whipped her face and the skin of her bare arms, the icy flagstone that pressed up into the bottoms of her feet: such gorgeous suffering she could hardly stand for more than half a minute. She went inside.

The weekend in question was a transitional period in the life of Frank Dial. Just as the annotated catalogue of Everything was a hubristic project for whose destruction he no longer blamed anyone but himself, so the catalogue of Everything He Hated was a project he would have to save for a time in his life when there would be fewer distractions from the bitterness and suspicion necessary to it, i.e., old age and retirement. In the mean time, he had made a tentative start on a project whose scope and tone he felt were more appropriate to this time in his life: descriptions of naturally occurring phenomena. In so doing, he hoped to find within himself a greater love of nature and humanity, especially the latter, which, on the whole, disappointed him. The first phenomenon he had chosen to describe was one of nature's unequivocal triumphs, the body of Catherine Schwartz, beginning with her hands. "The palm of Catherine Schwartz's hand," Frank had written,

> is soft, pale red, often wet, and faintly mushy. If one looks carefully at the pale redness, one finds it is composed of tiny little irregularly shaped areas of darker red, and other tiny little irregularly shaped areas of lighter red, and still other tiny little irregularly shaped areas of pure white, as is warranted by her Caucasianicity. As to the softness and so-called "mushiness" of the palm of Catherine Schwartz's hand, it might not inaccurately be compared to that of a thick slice of Muenster cheese that has existed in a room-temperature environment for twenty to twenty-five minutes. Now imagine that someone—it matters not who—has washed his or her hands and not yet dried them, and proceeds accidentally to touch the Muenster cheese. The cheese now also approximates the aforementioned wetness of the palm of the hand in question. The wrinkles or "lines" in the palm are few and insignificant. The palm is not without contour and topography, but to say the palm is "lined" would be to mislead the reader of this description. Lined paper is "lined."

Catherine's palm is, as previously specified, contoured. The palm of Catherine gives off a variety of scents. The palm is a place on the body of Catherine where her nervousness is made manifest, and therefore sometimes gives off a metallic scent, as of ozone or American coinage. At other times, the palm of Catherine smells of pencil shavings; at others, salmon. One can imagine licking this palm. Because of the palm's previously detailed similarity to Muenster cheese, a certain disgust would obtain in licking it. This disgust would, however, not only be accompanied by a palpable thrill racing throughout the body of the person who has licked the hand of Catherine, it would be inextricable from and almost synonymous with that thrill.

When Frank had reached that moment in the description, he left off writing it, read it, hated it. He wondered if Catherine would kiss him when he went to her house that afternoon, or if he would kiss her. He wondered if he and Catherine would kiss before he died.

He rang the doorbell of Catherine's tidy Colonial-style home. She answered it. Before he spoke or thought, he handed her an envelope. On the envelope he had written "Catherine" in his almost typographic hand, though she had told him more than once that her name was Cathy. Inside the envelope was the description of her hand. He'd printed it out in a digital simulation of the Palatino font, but the Palatino had seemed too bland, neither fast nor virile enough for the occasion. He'd printed it again in Bodoni, in response to which he'd said to himself, "Oh please, Frank, what are you trying to prove?" He ended up going with Gill Sans Medium. Now he was standing in the bitter cold just outside Catherine's house, watching her stand inside her house and read his description of her hand in Gill Sans Medium. He was horrified that he'd chosen Gill Sans Medium, as if the description of her hand were a sidebar in a quasi-pornographic men's magazine. Cathy read the description and Frank despaired over his font choice. He wanted to fall into a crack in the earth. When she was done reading, she laughed. One side of her mouth went up, the other went down. What did that mean? She turned away from him, walked to the far end of the entrance foyer, turned back, walked toward him. She stared at him. She turned away again and went into one of the rooms off the entrance foyer—Frank had no idea what the room was for, nor what went on in there. He couldn't see her.

Cathy sat in a hard-backed chair in this room that had been her father's home office before he became a drooling imbecile. She did not know what to do or say. She did not know which to be more offended by, Frank's wish to lick her hand or his sense that licking her hand would be disgusting. But really she was something that being offended was much easier than. She checked her posture in the hard-backed chair. It was okay but not great. She tried to think of a prayer but she couldn't remember any. This is the one she improvised: "Oh God God God God God God. Help me help me help me help me. Please please please please please please please."

Massive amounts of cold air entered the house through the open front door. Cathy sat stiff-bodied and shivering in her father's hard-backed chair, and Frank stood rigid with frost and anger on the flagstone that was directly in front of the impenetrable doorway to the house of Catherine. He felt like a nigger. The N feeling—which was with him all too often in this town his mother had forced him to move to for the sake of his secondary education—had not arisen with Catherine until this very moment. Didn't she know how cold it was outside? He stood on the very flagstone on which Cathy had stood earlier that day trying to cool off. He punched the side of her house with his gloved hand. "Catherine!"

In her father's office, Cathy heard Frank calling that funny, formalized version of her name. She wished he wouldn't. She wished he understood that he ought to come inside her house and go into her kitchen and make them both some calming tea, which she would then refuse to drink.

"Catherine!"

She wished he would disappear from the earth. She was moved that he called her Catherine instead of Cathy, as if responding to the essential formality that existed in her heart.

"Catherine!"

What was the matter with him? Was he a black maniac? She was a white racist prig with mushy hands.

"Catherine!"

She had better go out and lock the door or he would come in and rape her with his black rage.

"Catherine!"

She loved Francis Dial, an interesting person. Why this state of affairs had to be so painful she did not know. She went to him. He was gone. She closed the front door, put on her shoes and coat, left the house, and rode off down the street on her purple bicycle. Where was she going? Away.

Frank Dial, like a demon, crouched behind a bush on the edge of Catherine's property as she rode past him on her purple bike, wished her ill.

33

Cathy pedaled in the February wind. She did not have a destination in mind. Because most of her resources of perception and cognition were directed toward the place inside her that was the temporary residence of her chaotic feelings and thoughts, she missed salient clues to her external whereabouts, such as street signs and familiar landmarks. Without knowing it, she crossed the border from Bellwether into Port Town, which is to say she rode beyond the edge of civilization as she understood it. In fifteen minutes, she was riding her purple three-speed high school girl's bicycle along a silent and desolate industrial street less than a hundred yards from the edge of America. The air was cold and the wind was strong. She decided to ride to a familiar stop of the number 97 bus, which would take her to the town of Stevenson, where the Roosevelt Rehabilitation Facility was located. But now she did not know where she was, nor how to get to the safety of her father's high-ceilinged room. As she rode, the wind whipped menacing scraps of paper or plastic into her leg or the spokes of the wheels of her bicycle. She saw a pair of husky, angry-looking men who belonged to one of Connecticut's disenfranchised minority groups standing by a metal-shuttered cargo door of a closed place of business wearing checkered working-class flannel jackets, smoking cigarettes, waiting for God knew what type of transaction to "go down." She rode in the direction that she thought was away from the coast and toward the commercial center of Port Town. She had no idea how big Port Town was, nor how much of it consisted of streets and old low buildings seared and bleared with toil.

Cathy had ceased to think of Francis Dial and now directed her senses toward the discovery of someplace inhabited by friendly, helpful people who could tell her how to get to the number 97 bus. She saw a metal cross above a glass door. Above the metal cross, in metal lettering, a sign: HARBOR OF LIFE. Cathy rode toward the cross and the sign. Outside the door, she couldn't find a thing to lock her bike to, so she brought it inside the building with her.

"That's a nice bicycle," a boy said. He was small and blond, roughly nine years old in Cathy's estimation.

"Thank you. I need some information. Is there a grown-up around?"

She and the boy were standing in a smudged white corridor. To her right there was a crude white wooden counter with a phone on it and some old black office chairs behind it. "They're in a meeting," the boy said.

"How long do you think they'll be in the meeting?"

"I don't know. They're having an intense talk."

Cathy looked at the boy. He was wearing a colorful striped T-shirt that looked like a hand-me-down, and rigid new blue jeans with about a foot of extra length at the bottom, which had been folded halfway up his shins. Cathy unzipped her dark blue quilted down jacket.

"They're having an intense talk?" she asked.

"Lady, do you know what this place is?"

"I know it's a Christian place."

"It's a battered women's shelter."

"What are you doing here?"

"My mom is a battered woman."

Cathy flinched at the boy's answer. "Oh. I'm sorry."

"It's okay. She's getting help now. She's turning her life around. She's in a meeting with other battered women. They're having an intense talk. Could I please ride your bicycle?"

"Where are you going to ride it?"

"Up and down the hallway. I'll be very careful with it. I'll be quiet, too."

Cathy gave him the bicycle. "What's the address here?"

"I don't know." The boy rode away down the hall. Cathy went

behind the counter to look for a phonebook.

"Who are you?" a woman asked her angrily.

"I'm looking for a phonebook."

"And if I ask you what you're looking for will you tell me who you are?"

"What?"

"Who said you could come in here and look around?"

"I'm sorry. I'm lost." The woman was skinny and wearing a beige trench coat. She had reddish-blond straight greasy hair and the kind of rough-textured skin and gaunt face that Cathy associated with economic difficulty. Cathy had had a difficult life too, but she'd always been more than adequately fed and housed and she never used drugs or cigarettes and was young and educated and had access to high-end medical care.

The boy rode toward them on Cathy's bicycle. "Mommy!"

"You get off that bicycle now!"

"Yes Mommy." The boy had the conciliatory tone of someone who knew how to take care of his mother by obeying her. He gave the bicycle to Cathy.

"Where'd you get that bike?" the woman said.

"From the girl."

"Why'd you let him ride it?" she said to Cathy.

"He admired it and he asked me politely."

The woman seemed to accept that with a modest amount of skepticism. "Why are you here?"

"I'm lost."

"Where do you want to go?"

"The 97 bus."

"Oh, you're a Stevenson girl." The woman didn't look directly at Cathy, but consistently a little to the side of her.

"Bellwether," Cathy said.

"Big difference."

"Where are you from?"

"Port Town, where'd you think I was from?"

Cathy felt she shouldn't have said "Where are you from?" She should have said something honest and open like "I don't have to apologize for being from Bellwether," or, better yet, nothing.

The woman gave Cathy directions to the nearest stop of the 97 bus. Cathy thanked her and extended her hand and said, "I'm Cathy Schwartz."

"You Jewish?"

"Yes, but I'm thinking of converting to Catholicism."

"That's all we need," the woman said.

Cathy continued to hold her hand out. "Connie Hyde," the woman said, and grabbed the tips of Cathy's fingers for an instant, then took several steps back away from Cathy.

"Thank you for your help."

The woman did not respond.

"What's your son's name?" The woman stared at Cathy's shoulder. Cathy regretted asking. The boy waved to her and Cathy didn't wave back for fear of offending the boy's mother, Connie Hyde. Connie Hyde took her son by the shoulder and yanked him to her and gathered him against her legs and held him there, not as if he were likely to try to escape, but as if he were likely to melt, or to float away like a helium balloon. Cathy steered her purple Bellwether girl's bicycle out the glass door, mounted it, and rode away from the Harbor of Life.

34.

Celibate neurology fellow Lisa Danmeyer was on her way down the second floor hallway of the Roosevelt Rehabilitation Facility to visit her healing patient Bernard Schwartz. Bernard was communing with his only son, Chris. Chris had just finished reading his father the poem "Leda and the Swan," by William Butler Yeats.

"Who is Leda?" Bernie asked.

"Leda is a Greek woman who is sort of like a swan."

"And who is Zeus?"

"Zeus is the same guy Cathy calls God."

"Who is Agamemnon?"

"Agamemnon is a war hero like General Norman Schwarzkopf, only he gets eaten by his wife, Clytemnestra, no *jew de mots* intended."

"What is a *jew de mots*?"

"A person of Hebraic extraction with certain hangups."

"What is 'indifferent beak'?"

"*Indifferent* is the opposite of *different*. It means *the same as*. *Beak* is a bird's mouth. So Yeats was saying Zeus was basically the same as all the other guys in Leda's life—rape 'em and leave 'em, type of guy."

"What is rape?"

"Rape is when two people are having sex and only one of them wants to."

"I think I raped your mother."

"I could have done without hearing that today."

"Hello Bernard. Hello Chris." That was Lisa Danmeyer at the door.

"Look Bernie, La Danmeyer has come to give a little diva love."

Bernie was bewildered by 90 to 95 percent of the things his son said. Part of one of the language centers of his brain had been destroyed, but, Darwinianly, the area of his brain which enabled awareness of familial love remained intact: Bernard knew Chris loved him. In order to be worthy of that love, he tried to understand what Chris said.

"Hello Dr. Danmeyer," Bernie said.

"How's your recovery going?"

"My re– My re– I feel good."

Chris said, "His recovery is going shittily, thanks to your excellent initial work on him, La D."

Chris reminded Lisa of her father, for whom she was also often the straight man. On impulse, she kissed his cheek, on which a light, thin crust of drying acne was ever present. Chris thought it was possible that all semifriendly, semihostile female healthcaregivers wanted to give him blowjobs. Thus he floated the suggestion "Blow me."

"Chris," Bernie said. "I don't think it's nice of you to say that to Dr. Danmeyer. I'm your father and I want you to apologize."

Chris was about to say something mean to his father, but was prevented from doing so by speech pathologist Jennifer Gramsci, a person who was being lightly toyed with by mental illness, had indeed blown Chris, was now standing in the doorway of Bernie's room, and had witnessed the kiss. "I agree with your father, Chris," Jennifer said. "That wasn't nice at all. I, too, want you to apologize to Dr. Danmeyer. Hello Dr. Danmeyer."

"Hello Jennifer."

"I'm sorry," Chris said. "To everyone. For everything."

Jennifer grasped Chris by the crook of his arm in such a way as to cause him pain without anyone's knowing except him. "Chris, I'd like to talk to you about your father's progress in my office please."

He left the room with her.

Bernie was sitting on a soft padded chair in his pajamas. Lisa saw the volume of poems by William Butler Yeats open on the desk. She sat down in the desk chair and said, "Was your son reading you a poem?"

"Yes," Bernie said. "It was a poem about rape. Would you read me a poem?"

Lisa chose "The Second Coming." Coincidentally, down the hall in Jennifer's office, Chris was about to receive the second blow job of his life.

"'Turning and turning in a widening gyre
The falcon cannot hear the falconer;
Things fall apart; the center cannot hold;
Mere anarchy is loosed upon the world,
The blood-dimmed tide is loosed, and everywhere,'" Lisa said, while Jennifer harshly unzipped Chris's pants.

"You want someone to blow you?" she asked him.

Lisa said, "'The ceremony of innocence is drowned;
The best lack all conviction, while the worst
Are full of passionate intensity.'"

"Wait, wait," Chris said. "I don't want you to do this if you're mad at me."

"I'm not mad at you."

"'Surely some revelation is at hand,'" Lisa said.

"'Surely the Second Coming is at hand.
The Second Coming! Hardly are those words out
When a vast image out of *Spiritus Mundi*
Troubles my sight.'"

Chris, who had been standing, slid down to the floor of Jennifer's office. Jennifer worked feverishly, as if possessed.

"'Somewhere in sands of the desert
A shape with lion body and the head of a man,
A gaze blank and pitiless as the sun,
Is moving its slow thighs, while all about it
Reel shadows of the indignant desert birds.'"

In Chris's mind, all consideration was obliterated.

"'The darkness drops again; but now I know
That twenty centuries of stony sleep
Were vexed to nightmare by a rocking cradle.'"

Chris's body jerked and shuddered.

"'And what rough beast, its hour come round at last

Slouches towards Bethlehem to be born,'" Lisa said, and shuddered.

"I like you, you're so nice to me, even when you're mad at me," Chris said, as if he had become, for a moment, his own innocent father.

"That was a nice poem," Bernie said.

35

Chris strolled into his father's room. Lisa Danmeyer was laughing. The effect of the rhythm of the two miserable poems by William Butler Yeats on Bernie's autonomic nervous system was beneficial. He looked clear-eyed and sophisticated in his dark blue flannel pajamas. He looked like the grown-up he was and was not. Chris didn't know what was going on, here or elsewhere. Cathy arrived. She was worried about her purple bike. It was possible that she hadn't remembered to chain it to the street sign near the bus stop on the Port Town border.

Chris and Cathy stood in the doorway and looked at Lisa Danmeyer, who sat in the desk chair smiling. They looked at their father looking relaxed in his dark elegant pajamas. Their father's hair was kempt. The livid half circles beneath his eyes were slenderer than when they'd dropped him off at Roosevelt. His face was more uniform in color than it had been in the last half dozen years. They imagined they were in the den at home. They expected their father to say, "Now children, come gather round. Your mother and I . . ." The mother in question would have been Lisa Danmeyer. Cathy and Chris both wished that the four people in the room right now were everyone in their immediate family. Bernard wished to be a good father to his children. Lisa wished for a full recovery for her patient Bernard, and something more that she could not name. Wouldn't it be amazingly nice if all their wishes came true? Wouldn't it be amazingly nice if, for once, everything were amazingly nice?

Chris's penis ached; Cathy's conscience assaulted her; Lisa felt hungry and tired; as happened on and off throughout the day, colors, shapes, sounds, and smells became unintelligible to Bernie; all four started talking at once, and became silent again. The phone rang.

Bernie, on instinct, picked it up.

"Bernie?"

"Who's this?"

"It's Lila."

"Lila?"

"Your wife. Your former wife."

"Oh yes. I think I raped you."

"My father died."

"Remind me of his name."

"Tim Munroe."

"Yes, Tim Munroe, your father."

"Yes."

"Are you– sad now?"

"I think so Bernie. I think I'm sad now, yes."

"Oh. I'm sad now too."

"Why are you sad?"

"Because you are sad."

"Bernie," Lila said, expressing a well-trod exasperation. "You don't have to be sad just because I'm sad. You can be however you want."

"No, I don't think I can be however I want."

Chris said, "Bernie, what's happening? What's wrong with Mom?"

"Her father, Tim Munroe, died."

Cathy crossed herself. Chris took the phone from his father.

"Mom, what happened?"

"Grandpa Tim died."

"How'd he die, from drinking?"

"Heart attack."

"Are you okay?"

"What kind of a question is that? Of course I'm not okay. Why do people always ask if you're okay precisely when you are least likely to be okay?"

"Yeah Mom, I guess you're right. I suck."

"Oh listen Chris, don't listen to me right now, I'm crazy. I guess I need you and Cathy to come out here again."

"What for?"

"The funeral and shiva."

"What's shiva?"

"Oh that's right, I forgot, I've got a Catholic and a— what are you, anyway?"

"Ignoramus."

"That's right, an ignoramus, sweetie. Shiva is mourning. I cover the mirrors and the windows of my house. I stay at home and sit on a low stool. People come over and console me. I don't cook for them, they bring food. It's a sort of miserable social occasion that it would be nice if you and your sister could be here for."

"I've got school, and Dad."

"Chris!"

"What?"

"Your grandfather just died."

"He didn't even like me."

"That's irrelevant. This is what you do when you're a human being and your grandfather dies."

"I can't even deal with this conversation right now. You wouldn't believe how many weird things are happening to me all at once."

Lila was silent.

"Mom, are you there?"

"My daddy is dead."

"Oh. Oh I didn't think of it that way. I'll come. Um. Here's Cathy for a minute."

Cathy took the phone. Chris walked out into the hall, cried a little, called himself a list of obscene two-syllable names.

Cathy said, "What happened, Mom?"

"Grandpa Tim died."

"Are you okay?"

"Yes."

"How did he die, cirrhosis of the liver?"

"Heart attack."

"Did a clergyman come to see him?"

"Before or after he died?"

"Before."

"No."

"How about after?"

"No."

"When is the funeral?"

"March first."

"We'll leave tomorrow. I'll call the airline and pray for his soul."

"Couldn't hurt."

Chris came back into the room. Cathy got off the phone. Chris told Lisa his mother's father had died. She asked how old he had been. No one knew.

"Father, do you remember Grandpa Tim?" Cathy asked.

"No."

"Tim Munroe, the father of Lila Munroe."

"Oh yes, Lila Munroe's father. I didn't like him."

Chris said, "Isn't it cool how being stupid makes him honest?"

"No, it's awful."

"Why didn't you like him?" Chris said.

"Because he didn't like me."

"How do you know?"

"Because I raped his daughter."

"Chris, what have you been saying to him?"

"Dad," Chris said. "Would you drop the stupid act already?"

Bernie glowered at Chris.

Lisa said, "Well, I'm so sorry about your grandfather. I'm afraid I have to go. Bernard, it was good to see you. I'm glad you're feeling better."

Bernie said, "I'm not feeling better. I'm feeling terrible. Everybody in this room is angry. Why?"

Lisa left. What she hadn't said was that she, too, would be in northern California in a few days, to visit her father. She thought these people were a crazy, backbiting, vindictive little family, and she was charmed by them.

"Well Father, we have to go to California for Grandpa Tim's funeral."

"No."

"We'll be back, Dad."

"The last time you went away I ended up in this terrible place, alone. Please don't leave me here."

Cathy said, "We can't take you with us."

Chris said, "Maybe we can."

Cathy said, "Shut up!" And to her father, "So long. We'll be back in less than a week." She hugged him.

"How long is a week?"

"Seven days."

"I'll never remember that."

"We'll call you every day."

"How will you call me?"

"By telephone."

"How will I know you're calling me?"

"The phone will ring."

"How will I know it's ringing?"

"It will make a noise like a bell."

"I don't know if I'll remember all this."

"You will." Cathy hugged her father again.

Chris hugged him and tried to kiss his cheek, but he turned his face away. "I'll communicate with you too, Dad. Remember last time when I was in California and you were that cloud and we talked to each other?"

"Yes."

Cathy, to her surprise, loved her brother when he said that. She and Chris left the room and opened the door to the stairwell and descended the stairs.

Bernard Schwartz cried out, "I'm scared! Please don't leave me! Please!"

36

The funeral was a joke. Some oratorical jackass presided over the death of Tim Munroe. Even to irreligious Chris, this rabbi was an asswipe, eschatologically speaking. He was beyond Reformed, he was Overhauled. He showed up at the funeral in Bay Area Rabbi Casual: low-riding granola-suede sandals, gossamer drawstring pants, navy crewneck tennis shirt, and matching polo yarmulke with "Go 'Niners!" embroidered around the perimeter. In a speech that was one part Talmud to five parts daily horoscope, this rabbi confessed that he'd met the deceased only once, when he was a windsurfing instructor, and offered the following summation of the dead man's existence: "He was the second-best seventy-six-year-old windsurfer I've ever seen. He only fell off the board twice." Words to live by. Something to take home for consolation during the dark hours of the soul.

And so Chris found himself back in California, the dreariest state in the union. As the landmass of California was in constant peril of breaking off, of crumbling away from the continent and languishing far from the coast that it itself once was, so Chris Schwartz was in danger of disconnecting from the continent of causality and floating out into a sea of pure anxiety: anxiety without an object in sight, anxiety as far as the eye could see in every direction, an ocean of unprovoked, unmitigated, unrelenting anxiety: angst angst everywhere and nothing to be feared. As for the house of Lila Munroe in particular, that was merely the extension of Chris's depression beyond the borders of his own body. The shuttered windows, the covered mirrors, the dimmed lighting and darkened floorboards, the gravely amiable post-funeral sociability: these were the concrete manifestations of the awfulness of adolescence and its inevitable consequence, death.

Chris cowered in his room of his mother's house for most of the reception and emerged late at night to begin the long shiva trudge. When he opened the door, Cathy was passing by—or possibly hovering—in the hallway.

Chris said, "Are you mad at me for hiding out during the reception?"

"No."

"Did you go to it?"

"Yes, but I didn't talk to anyone."

"Nice funeral, huh?"

"Oh Chris, it was so bad. I didn't know Grandpa Tim very well, and I maybe didn't like him. But still I think we should have tried to hand him over to God with as much dignity as possible."

"Me too, that's totally what I was thinking."

"It was?"

"Yeah."

"I didn't know you thought things that were anything like that. I didn't think you believed in God."

"I don't. But sometimes I wish I did. Sometimes I act like I do even though I don't, just in case."

"Really?"

"Yeah."

"That's what *I* do, only all the time."

"You? You're like Miss Perfect Piety."

"Well, thank you, I guess, but the truth is I'm not sure. I wish I were sure. I try to behave like I'm sure, so that maybe I'll become sure from the outside in."

"Huh."

They looked at each other, looked away, looked back at each other.

"Poor Grandpa Tim," Cathy said. A sob issued from her, then leveled off into moderate, regulated crying. Chris cried too. They stood in the upstairs hallway of their mother's house watching each other cry, their hands hanging down at their sides. Though they could not bear to touch each other, it was as if the same tears were springing from their separate pairs of eyes.

From down in the living room, where she sat with the guest who just wouldn't leave, Lila heard her children crying. She excused herself and climbed the stairs. Hoping for a happy threesome of criers, she let go a moan and a dozen tears. This had the opposite of the desired effect. The kids' eyes dried up. That made Lila cry more. Her children couldn't cry with her as they could with each other on this one special occasion, but they did each take one of her hands. This wasn't as intimate as two children crying, but it wasn't fake. It was real. But it was awkward. It was real awkward divorced family comforting.

37

"D'ya crack that will open yet?" That was Jerry "Sporty" Swenzler, the sole remaining nonfamily mourner, drunk in the living room of Lila Munroe late on the night of the funeral.

"Yeah Jerry, I cracked it."

"Ah, Lila, toots, call me Sporty."

"Yeah Sporty, I cracked it."

"Anything in there for me?" Sporty was the same fellow geezer Tim Munroe had arranged to meet several months earlier in the pizza parlor after the abbreviated dinner with his daughter and grandchildren. As if to keep his drinking buddy alive in his drinking buddy's daughter, Sporty was now speaking to Lila as he would have spoken to Tim Munroe—with a crusty irreverence to fine sentiment that was itself a form of fine sentiment to one initiated in its subtleties, which Lila was not.

"Million dollars," Lila said. She was drunk too, and was glad to have him there because he was roughly the same sort of annoying asshole her father had been. He laughed loudly and often, in a manner incommensurate not only with the situation at hand, but with the human condition in general.

"Million?" Sporty asked.

"Yep. But 75 percent goes to taxes, five percent goes to funeral expenses, and the other 20 percent I'm taking because I'm a lawyer and that's what lawyers do. In fact, the legal profession is founded on the principle of taking money away from people like you."

Sporty Swenzler was hurt by that. Tim's kid always insulted him, he thought. She came at him with a brand of humor he couldn't make sense of, a generational irony that was the central reason he'd remained drunk and confused ever since the Cuban Missile Crisis.

The children entered the living room. Cathy never drank, and Chris seldom drank unless he was about to get behind the wheel of a car, and then only enough to make it interesting. They were uncomfortable and disgusted as befits two sober youngsters in the presence of two drunk adults on the night of their grandfather's funeral.

"Well it's time to break out the good stuff, wouldn't you say?" Lila said.

"What 'good stuff' would that be, Mom?" Chris said.

"Yeah, what good stuff?" Sporty Swenzler said.

"Well, the medium stuff. Chivas Regal." Lila pulled a bottle out from under the couch. "I've got a case of it. Cost me half my inheritance." Everyone winced at her inheritance joke. "Swenzler. You Jewish?"

"Scottish."

"Tim, my daddy, had a Jewish mother and an Irish Catholic father. In honor of his mixed heritage we will now be sitting Chivas." She loved her joke and laughed at it and toasted it. No one else got it. Cathy, in fact, said "Mom!" and left the room.

Chris, who had no consistent position on sacrilege, broke his drink-only-before-driving rule to join his mother in a scotch, though in his heart he thought scotch tasted like throw-up.

Everything that had happened in the last twenty seconds went right over Sporty Swenzler's head except for the fact of the bottle of Chivas in the room. "Let's do it, Mama let's fall in love," he said to the bottle in a faux Armstrong growl.

Lila made a toast to Tim Munroe in heaven, or wherever Jews went after they died, she couldn't remember. Chris asked Sporty what he remembered of Franklin Delano Roosevelt. Sporty said, "He knew the Japs were gonna bomb Pearl Harbor. He had the Jap code! He let it happen so he could get the American public behind the war. Then he shipped us all off to Europe and the Pacific theater to die. FDR was a Commie-lover and a murderer, that's what I remember of him."

Chris found this response absurd, and dropped the subject.

Sporty continued the diatribe in his own head, where he blamed Roosevelt for the death of Tim Munroe. He knew no one in the room would understand because they were Jews. He drank his final glass of scotch, took a zombielike walk to the bathroom, made his nightly offering of vomit to Bacchus, came back to the couch, and passed out. Cathy returned to the living room and stared down at Sporty in disgust. Lila announced that as a result of deft estate management, Tim had managed to leave Chris and Cathy $75,000 each, after taxes. The kids went to bed. Lila covered Sporty with a blanket and kissed him on the forehead. She turned off all the lights in the house, rent the sleeve of her garment, sat on the living room floor, and looked at the dark until morning.

38

Sporty Swenzler woke up in a bad mood and demanded to see the will. Lila showed it to him, he couldn't read it because of his headache, she put him in his beat-up car and sent him away feeling lousy. Lila continued to sit Chivas in her living room, minus the traditional mourning activities of sleeping and eating.

Chris and Cathy staggered around California in the special daze known only to people who've received a lot of money and done nothing to deserve it.

In the afternoon, Sextus "Charlie" Mann, the gardener of love, came up from his hometown of Las Pulgas to offer Lila his brand of consolation, but when she greeted him at the door, said, "We're sitting Chivas," and staggered back to the living room, he thought better of it. Charlie was neither prim nor persnickety, but he perceived sex to be infused with a light holiness that precluded sloppy doings with a drunk woman.

Lisa Danmeyer drove down from El Cuerpo in the rain with her father. Moe Danmeyer had never met these people, but out of respect for the dead he brought a meatloaf, and for the kids, a lemon chiffon pie. At the time of the Danmeyers' arrival, Cathy was out staggering around Heart Valley in inclement weather without the proper protective attire, opening her soul to the sorrow of the rain. Chris was in his mother's home office composing an e-mail to speech pathologist and all-around oral wizard Jennifer Gramsci. Lila was dozing on the toilet. When no one answered their knock at the kitchen door, Moe, who'd visited more grieving homes in the last half dozen years than all the others combined, insisted to his reluctant daughter that they enter the house. He put his food on the kitchen counter and walked into the living room. Sextus Mann sat upright on the low couch where Sporty Swenzler had fainted the previous night. Sextus had been doing some solitary tantric breathing and had only semiheard the knock at the kitchen door. "Moe Danmeyer," Moe Danmeyer said, and stuck his big piano-salesman's hand in the direction of the seated ponytailed groovester. Sextus Man said "Sextus Mann" and, California-polite, extended his hand while remaining seated on the low couch. "Okay, sure," Moe said. He'd lived in California long enough to pretend to give the kid the benefit of the doubt, which was as close as he felt like coming to giving him it, now that he was retired from sales.

Lisa Danmeyer said her name to Sextus Mann and opted for the prefeminist head-nod and half-wave, something nice and passively rude to fall back on when you'd sized up the situation and decided you couldn't be bothered.

"My daughter here is a doctor. She's the neurologist of the exhusband."

Sextus Mann said, "I'm a friend of the family."

"Uh-huh. Anybody around?"

"Lila's in the bathroom."

Moe assessed the living room. "Upright'd look nice along that wall," he said to Lisa, as if she were a junior sales partner.

"Brain surgery'd look good in the backyard," she said.

"What? What's that supposed to mean?"

"It was a joke."

"Oh yeah. I'm a piano salesman and you're a brain surgeon. Now I get it."

"Sorry."

"No, it was funny."

Lila returned from the bathroom, saw the two visitors, didn't know who they were. "We're sitting Chivas," she said.

Moe said, "Really? I can't stand Chivas."

Lila laughed and embraced Moe Danmeyer. "You're wonderful," she said. "Who are you?"

"Moe Danmeyer. I brought you a meatloaf." Still being held gently by Lila Munroe, he looked at his daughter. "The mother's a warm person," he said.

"It's remarkable what a depressant will do for some people," Lisa muttered.

"Oh, I recognize you, you're the doctor," Lila said to Lisa, and embraced her. "I love female competence."

She looked back at Moe Danmeyer. He smiled at her. He was six feet two inches tall and weighed 250 pounds. "I love stature," Lila said, and embraced Moe again.

Sextus Mann took it all in from the low couch. Mellowly, he wondered what point of entry there might be for him in the configuration of people looming above him in the living room, which had been, after all, on occasion, a place of splendor for him.

"Why don't we fix you up with some meatloaf," Moe said to Lila. To his daughter he said, "This lady is charming and warm. I think she could use some meatloaf." To Lila he said, "I'll see what else you have in the kitchen, make a nice meal for you."

Moe went to the kitchen. He liked to take over when he felt people needed him to, which was often. He liked to be moving around in a kitchen doing useful things with admirable speed. He'd pull together a meal that would help Lila sober up and prevent her from getting sick.

The little fuckwad Chris Schwartz, as he liked to call himself, in his mother's home office on the second floor, composed a letter to Jennifer Gramsci. "Dear Jennifer," it went, at first. Then it went "Jennifer:" Then "Hi Jennifer." Then "Hi." "How are you?" it began, until it began "I miss you," but only for the most embarrassing of instants. "Hi Jennifer," it went. "This is Chris Schwartz writing to you from my mother's e-mail address." Mention of his mother in this context he then thought better of. "Jennifer, you amazing woman. Chris Schwartz reporting from California the day after my grandfather's funeral. Because of his death, I am now the proud owner of $75,000. I will take you to Aruba when I get back to Connecticut." For the e-mail's closing salutation, Chris tried "Love," "Luv," "Lust," "Yours," "Yours truly," "Affectionately,"

"Fondly," "Cordially," "Sincerely," "Sincerely yours," "Best," "Best wishes," "With best wishes," "Kisses," "Kisses and hugs," "xo." If the x in xo stood for "kiss" and the o stood for "hug," which letter of the alphabet, Chris wondered, stood for "cunnilingus"? Briefly, he pondered a possible next business venture with friend and fellow capitalist Francis Dial: to assign a form of intimate carnal contact to each of the remaining twenty-four letters of the alphabet; to patent, copyright, and/or register as a trademark each letter so assigned; to sell the letters—individually or in packages of twenty-six—to the worldwide market of letter-writing Roman alphabet users. In a moment of intoxication with his own genius, Chris signed his e-mail to Jennifer "With an odd exuberance," sent it, died.

An extended moment of extreme spaciness followed, not just for Chris, but for everyone. Over a period of time which by definition must be indefinite, no one knew what they were thinking or doing.

Chris heard a knock on the door of his mother's home office.

"Who is it?"

"It's your father."

"Hi Dad."

"Jennifer Gramsci does not love you."

"Okay."

"She will hurt you."

"Okay."

"Love—at least this kind of love—will bring you pain for many years and many cycles of years. There is nothing for you to do about this but love."

"Okay."

"You cannot do otherwise."

"Dad?"

"Yes."

"Nothing."

Next thing Chris knew, he was in the living room gazing into the eyes of Danmeyer herself. "Oh Danmeyer," he said, as if speaking to one of several ex-wives.

"Chris," she said, and shook his hand. It is nice to share grief with someone with whom one has previously shared anger.

Moe Danmeyer emerged from the kitchen, face flushed, bearing a giant tray of food. He set it down on the coffee table in front of the low couch where Lila was sitting. Somewhere in here, Sextus Mann had floated up and out of the scene. No one missed him on a day like today. If Lila had been actively and happily married, and if it had been her husband and not her father who'd died, then someone like Sextus Mann would have been useful in the present situation. But she hadn't, and it hadn't, and he wasn't, and off Mann had floated to be alone on the beach.

"Who's this?" Moe said of Chris.

"The redoubtable Chris Schwartz," Lisa said.

"Moe Danmeyer. You like meatloaf?"

"It doesn't suck," Chris said.

Moe fed everyone. He made sure Lila Munroe got a decent portion of food in her stomach. He subtly moved the bottle of Chivas beyond her reach.

As luck would have it, another thing Moe Danmeyer liked to do was take skinny kids under his wing, as he had once done with his sweet skinny daughter. The group of mourners all seated and enjoying their meals, Moe said to Chris, "So kid, tell me, what are you into?"

"Capitalism."

"Nice answer."

"Thank you, sir."

"Gimme a for instance."

Chris wasn't yet ready to disclose his concept for the packaging and sale of the alphabet, so he vamped: "Well I don't think I've found my market niche yet."

"You don't find the niche, you create the niche, my friend."

"Right, exactly," Chris said. "Like I have this business partner, Frank Dial? And one day a few years ago we were just hanging out, tossing the ideas around in a comfortably capitalistic setting on the grass."

"You were smoking grass?"

"On this occasion, no."

"Because I'm not against grass, in its proper place and time."

"Who is? My point being that we came up with the walking sushi idea. You know what I'm talking about? It's sushi, and it walks."

"The best ideas have an elegant simplicity."

"Yes, because we tried to add stuff to it, like it's sushi that walks and is also a refrigerator magnet, but that was no good."

"How could it be a magnet and walk?"

"It couldn't, and not only that: it shouldn't. So we've got our walking sushi idea. Now here's the rub: we happened to know that someone else had already come up with the idea. We knew this *going into the design stage*. We knew that someone else had already created the walking sushi and put it out there in the world in stores where they sell this type of thing, which is novelty and stationery stores. Long story short: we went into the design stage anyway. We were well into the design stage when it occurred to us to police ourselves for lameness, and you know what? We had to make a bust."

Moe Danmeyer shook his head in sympathy.

Cathy Schwartz staggered across the sand by the ocean in a white long-sleeved T-shirt, gray wool jumper, no socks, and black slip-on flats that rubbed away the skin on the backs of her ankles. Her clothes were wet. This was early March at the edge of the Pacific Ocean. Her muscles quivered involuntarily and she didn't care, she insisted she didn't care to anyone who was present, which she feared was only herself. She looked at the ocean. It was a mess. The waves were dark gray and white and taller than her body. Tens of thousands of drops of water rushed down from the clouds to join the chaos. Each wave of the ocean was composed of promiscuous molecules of water that gathered together passively in great hillocks of liquid that moved across the surface of the earth with purposeless force. Cathy disdained the ocean. She disdained the sand. She disdained the air. She lashed herself to her own disdain and piloted her little soul through the world. How pathetic. Her body shook in spasms of increasing breadth. She locked her jaw tight. She stumbled in the sand and fell down. She curled up in a tight ball to prevent herself from shivering. She clung to herself wishing she knew how to unlock her jaw, how to relax her body and surrender her soul to God. She recalled a line from the biography of Edith Stein, aka Teresa Benedicta of the Cross: "The self is the individual's way of structuring experience . . . the primary source of delusion and a potentially dangerous threat." She looked again at the drops of water. Each drop was without a self; no drop structured its own experience, but let the ocean make of it what it would. If she was to live other than the tiny life she had managed thus far, she needed the sort of drastic lesson the ocean could teach. She stood up and walked toward it. The shock of the cold water racing over her feet and ankles and calves was almost unbearably exciting to her. She advanced toward the promising cliffs of water just ahead. The water rammed her thighs and hips. She held her arms up above her head in greeting to the glorious ocean. The edge of a wave slammed the top of her head. She did not fall down. Though her knees wobbled, she remained standing with her arms stretched above her. Not the edge but the full body of another wave threw her down on the ground, crushed her body into the large, harsh grains of sand beneath her, dragged her away from shore. She remained inside the water for a long time in a groggy ecstasy. Her mouth and nose found the gray air for a moment, she breathed, and then she was in the water again. She hadn't meant to kill herself but she understood that that was what was happening. She became so angry with her own stupid fake religiosity. What she was hopeful for now, at the bottom of the Pacific Ocean, was a special soul connection to someone else alive in the world, the way Chris sometimes had to their father. Maybe her father would reach out to her mystically from within the shroud of his idiocy. Maybe her mother, drunk, could extend herself beyond the borders of her own stingy skin and stingy thoughts. Maybe Chris or even the courtly and acerbic Francis Dial . . . By making the sincere effort not to breathe, she tried to be worthy of contact from any human being, but it was so painful and difficult not to breathe. With a final surge of disappointment in herself and her life, Cathy Schwartz inhaled her first teaspoon of salt water.

*

There had been a moment early into the group consumption of meatloaf and salad, back at the provisional family manse, when Moe Danmeyer casually moved the bottle of scotch beyond the reach of Lila Munroe. So concerned was Moe for the sobriety and well-being of Lila Munroe that he wasn't paying attention to Chris Schwartz's increasingly deep and frequent forays into the bottle, nor to the ascent in number and volume of the loose, aggressive quips, asides, and non sequiturs that Chris had been contributing to the supper-time conversation over the last twenty-five minutes. Thus Moe could say to Chris, "So how exactly is your father doing back east?"

"My father?" Chris said. "Back east?" he said. "Moe?" he said. "May I *call* you Moe? Oh no, don't answer, I know what you'll say. You'll say, 'You can call me anything you want, but don't call me late for dinner.' Well, Late-for-Dinner, you ask about my father, so I'll tell you. When it comes to my father, I am merely finishing what your daughter, 'Doctor Lisa Danmeyer,' so incompetently began. La Danmeyer botched the rewiring of my father's head. She attached the red wire to the blue switch and the blue wire to the red switch. So what I'm doing, I'm working with the materials I was given. I'm doing a, like, a radical experiment in miseducation, if you will, Late-for-Dinner. See, I'm teaching my father all the wrong stuff. I'm starting with the basics. I'm teaching him that nouns are adjectives, adjectives are adverbs, adverbs are verbs, and verbs are nouns. We practice sentences such as, 'The sleepily crimson meatloafs the flee,' or 'The you run briskly the yellow,' or 'Renata refrigerator philosophy clockwork rictus verily some.' And spelling! I've got him using a system of spelling that's too elaborate for me to describe without taking off my shoes, but I'll just say that it involves all wrong letters, including many letters from the Cyrillic and Arabic alphabets that I don't even know what they mean, but my father does, now, though he won't be able to use them to communicate with anyone else. And then there's arithmetic. Two plus two equals four has got to be the biggest roadblock civilization has ever put in front of the creative and independent-minded individual. I'm just a kid, Mr.

Late-for-Dinner, I'm a kid trying to find my place in this crazy mixed up world, and I can't. One thing I do know: my place in the world isn't in the home. But I can't leave the home. Wanna know why? I didn't think so, but I'll tell you anyway: because two plus two equals four is blocking the doorway with its hands on its hips. I take a run at the doorway and smash my head against two plus two equals four. But once I break my head against two plus two equals four, a nice little thing happens: I see a group of pale ballerinas dancing. They are dainty and shimmery and light ballerinas and they are dancing in a little pattern that is the pattern of two plus two equals five. And then it all comes clear: the way I've been taught arithmetic and spelling and grammar and science and history and religion is just a load of horseshit handed to me by the decaying white male European Western military-industrial establishment. And that's why, even though it's too late for me, I can still save my father. I don't want him to grow up to be like he was the last time he grew up. I don't want him to grow up to be like you, Mr. Late-for-Dinner. A piano salesman. How perfect. My people—the Jews—struggle for generations to get a little money, a house, some leisure time, and what do you do? You sell them some huge piece of weird-looking, obsolete furniture that doesn't make them better, it just makes them *think* they're better, it just makes them *look* to their *neighbors* like they're better so the neighbors will buy one. And now that you've retired from bilking Jewish people in exchange for this worthless piece-of-crap emblem of middle-class life, you're this panicked *gorilla* who's threatened by his own daughter, a daughter who actually used her own middle-class childhood as a taking-off point for a life of genuine achievement, and you can't even stand it, it horrifies you to see this half-person, this *woman* achieve more than you. So how do you deal with it? You pretend to be a take-charge guy, when really what you are is just a bully. 'Chris, please emasculate yourself by telling me about your inconsequential hobbies.' 'Lila, sit down, don't drink, don't mourn, and shut up.' 'Lisa, my daughter, recede into the goddamn wallpaper so I don't have to think about how much better a person you are than me while I rush off to the kitchen and turn myself into a fucking meatloaf-making *fairy.*'"

Lisa Danmeyer stood up and slapped Chris Schwartz in the face as hard as she could. Chris fell backward onto his mother's lap on the couch. Lila held her son's head against her own cheek with her left hand and caressed his face and made soothing noises. The phone rang.

Sextus Mann had been bobbing along the beach by the ocean in bright foul weather gear. He had been experiencing a rare moment of unhappiness. To bring other people in contact with their own misery may have been the special genius of the Schwartz family. In Sextus Mann the misery was certainly not all that deep. Misery was not what was deepest about Sextus Mann. He was enjoying a good vigorous cry. Crying consoled and satisfied him. He liked an all-involving physical activity or sensation: a sprint, a sneeze, a cough, a laugh, a sob, a fuck, a fit; a puke would do in a pinch. Oh, he liked to be sad on the beach on a rainy day! He stopped walking and turned toward the melancholy gray horizon. At the bottom of his field of vision, he saw a flicker: something odd in the ocean. What was it? Oversized flotsam, twenty to thirty yards from shore. Driftwood? A human hand. He got out of his rain gear and swam toward the body in question with clean, elongated strokes. He felt the strain of his muscles moving against the awesome power of the surf. He hoped the person was still alive. He grasped the hand of the person. It was a woman. Her body was limp. He wedged his left arm under hers, and with his right arm he grabbed the rough water and pulled it past him again and again until he reached the shore. He carried this limp woman fireman's style to a gazebo by the beach's parking lot and laid her on her back on the cement floor. He blew hot breath into her mouth and pumped her sternum with the palms of his hands. He did this repeatedly for nearly a minute. Cathy Schwartz threw up and opened her eyes. Sextus Mann thanked her for being alive. Cathy threw up again. He put her in the cab of his truck, drove her to the hospital, checked her wallet for identification, and telephoned Lila Munroe with the news.

39

Lila Munroe stood with her children in that carefully random
mélange of tiny-wheeled luggage, TV noise, swirled e-z-wash car-
peting, sleep deprivation, and fake air—an airport waiting lounge.
There they were, the three of them, standing awkwardly over an
extended period of time, and Lila wished she knew how to maintain
prolonged but casual body contact with her children. She knew
Cathy was mentally traumatized and physically hurting, and she
wished she could give her something for it in the form of ongoing
motherly touching. Lila was good for a genuine soft hug, a cheek
kiss, a quick hand squeeze, and then—back off—*back the fuck up*,
to put it the language of urban American T-shirts. Many moms—
she'd seen this done in parking lots next to the big silver bus head-
ed for sleepaway camp, in airports even—could unobtrusively leave
a hand somewhere on their kids' bodies. Two moms chatted, once
upon a time, on the concrete steps of a Connecticut elementary
school, Lila being one of them, and throughout the conversation,
the one who was not Lila idly palmed her girl's head. No fanfare,
just palming, one among the reflexive activities in motherhood's
bodywork, like peristalsis. The head-palm came back to Lila now in
the wake of her father's death, and caused her to reflect that she had
been and probably always would be close to her father after all; not
close insofar as she had cleaved to him or shared interests or intimate moments or spoken to him often—he wouldn't have wanted
that, nor would she; not close by proximity but by resemblance: she
stayed close by imitating his distance from her with an equal and
identical distance from him and, extending out into the world
beyond the father-daughter dyad, from all of humanity.

"So, any thoughts about what you kids are going to do with your money?"

"Not really," Chris said.

"I could help you, you know."

"I thought the whole point of $75,000 is that it's the minimum amount you need so that you don't need help any more."

"Oh no, Chris. Quite the opposite. The more money you have, the more help you need. Look at millionaires. They've got people running around helping them in every aspect of their lives—servants, executive assistants, shipping clerks. Wealth is a precarious state of affairs that is always in danger of falling apart and must be held together by the hands of many. Wealth creates a huge helping economy. Really, Chris, what are you going to do with the money?"

"Not telling. Don't want to jinx it," Chris said.

"Oh don't tell me you're going to spend it on screensaver apothegms or walking sushi."

"Nope. Something humanitarian. You'll see."

"Cathy, how about you?"

"I'm going to give it all to a battered women's shelter run by the Catholic church in Port Town," she said, without meaning to sound defiant.

"Oh honey," Lila said.

"What's *that* supposed to mean?" Cathy said.

"It means I understand that you feel battered. I'm just saying think about it first."

"That's what you think? You think the only reason I'm giving money to an organization that's doing good in the world is that I identify with the people it's helping? You think the only way you can empathize with another human being is if you've been through what they're going through? My gosh, Mom, that's so amazingly limited."

"You moralistic little prig," Lila said. "You just don't quit with the holier-than-thou attitude, do you? Go ahead, give away all your money. You'll enter adulthood and you'll find that being an adult with no money is a hell of a lot rougher than the Pacific Ocean."

"Yeah, woo," Chris said. "Good one, Mom, you really got her with that one. Way to vanquish your own daughter in an argument." As was often the case, Chris didn't know whether he was kidding or what.

Lila was sad. Truth be known, she got her father's white trash house in South City and no money, and her feelings were hurt. And now they were doubly hurt because her daughter was going to do something with her money that was so different from what Lila would have done with hers.

"Last call," the flight attendant said. Chris hugged his mom, and Cathy hugged her too. Lila and Cathy said "I'm sorry" at the same time, and then the children's bodies disappeared beyond the threshold of the collapsible hallway that led to the flying machine.

Lila pressed her face and the front of her torso against the huge picture window next to the gate as the airplane slowly backed away. She raised her arms over her head and pressed the palms of her hands against the window like a small child watching her mother and father sail off to paradise on their honeymoon.

part four

40

Seventy-five thousandaire Chris Schwartz rolled up to the Roosevelt Rehabilitation Facility in his father's midsize gray hatchback, which he'd been driving around for four and a half months with no license and a bucketful of impunity. As he pulled into a parking space, unbeknownst to him, the love of his half-life, Jennifer Gramsci, was kissing a man in a $700 suit whom she hadn't met before. The man was holding onto a clipboard for dear life. Jennifer was making her mouth all soft and delicious and pressing her breasts up against him and rubbing them around in an unprincipled fashion. After she finished kissing him she wanted to knee him in the balls, but decided not to. Instead, she jabbed him in the ribs with a stack of tongue depressors that she didn't know why she was holding. He walked down the hall with his clipboard, off to inspect the kitchen or visit a cardiology patient or have a job interview or file a lawsuit, it hardly mattered.

Chris found Jennifer in her office. "Did you get my e-mail?" he said.

"Yes."

"How come you didn't write back?"

"Didn't feel like it."

"So listen, I'm checking my father out of the facility today. I'm going to give him homecare with that money I inherited. I was thinking I could hire you to give him speech therapy twice a week."

"No, you couldn't. This is a full-time job for me. I don't work freelance."

"Then I guess we can just see each other socially."

"No, we can't."

"Why not?"

"Because you're a child and I'm an adult. I'm a woman with a responsible job and you're a high school student with an attitude that is incommensurate with the puny nothing self that you are."

"But you made me feel good."

"I made you feel. You didn't make *me* feel. Whatever feelings I had I brought to the situation. You were neutral and passive. You almost weren't even there."

"What about that e-mail I sent you?"

"You gonna send me romantic e-mail? You should have thought of that when you were acting all snooty to me when you first got here."

"What?"

"Get out."

Chris stood there inside the open door of Jennifer's office. She gave him an economical "get out" head gesture. He left. She shut the door of her office, picked up a couple of pens from her desk and threw them one by one across the room as hard as she could. She gathered up all her curly brown hair and piled it on top of her head and let it fall. She grabbed small bunches of it and pulled them up over her head and teased them because she wanted to look like the Bride of Frankenstein. She kicked her desk. She kicked her desk again. She looked in the small, cheap mirror on the door of her office and saw an enormous smooth-skinned red ant, which then resolved into the inverted image of her own face.

41

O Sunday afternoon in Connecticut! Chris Schwartz drove the car backward down Roosevelt Lane with his trusty sidekick, Dad, on the passenger seat. He flashed his right turn signal and took a left off Roosevelt Lane onto Hoover Place. Backed down Hoover Place. Sweet joy of heartache. He went fast and stepped on the brake, went fast and stepped on the brake. Chris Schwartz was employing the Chris Schwartz backward driving style in tandem with the Chris Schwartz start-and-stop driving style in further tandem with the Chris Schwartz elliptical driving style. This last entailed swerving erratically from curb to curb and beyond. He liked the feeling of a wheel or two or three of the midsize gray hatchback rolling over the grassy shoulder. He liked to hear the giggle of his father. O sweet mystery of life! O sirens and flashing lights! O to be pursued by an officer of the law on a warm Sunday afternoon in March just after your heart has been reamed with a pointy fucking rustproof mace.

Chris brought the vehicle to rest in the center of the street and savored that special betwixt-and-between time, that time out of time after the cop has stopped you and before the cop has come to the door of your car to speak to you about the dearest principles of community life. The particular cop in Chris's life at this moment spoke from his own vehicle with the aid of a powerful amplification system: "Hey idiot, pull over to the side of the street." Chris did not respond. Bernard widened his eyes and put his hand over his mouth and bobbed his head low in a gleeful we're-in-trouble gesture. Nobody had the faintest idea what was going on within the rehabilitation center of Bernard Schwartz's mind at a moment like this.

The cop: "Pull over your goddamned car."

Chris: silence and stillness.

Bernard: davening.

The cop: anger, energy, action.

The cop strode toward the car, stood looming over Chris. "What the hell is a matter with you? I said pull your car out of the middle of the goddamned street."

Chris said, "I can't do it. I've been through too much."

"You're telling me you can't do it?"

"I can't do it."

"Get out of the car."

Chris got out. Bernie sat still.

"You too, asshole."

Bernie became sad, but didn't get out of the car.

"Out!" said the cop.

Bernie stayed, shivered, glanced up at the cop.

"He can't get out," Chris said, standing next to the cop, a tall, broad, handsome man with brown hair and blue eyes. "You see, he's slow, due to adult-onset retardation induced by metabolical coma with cardio-cerebral complications."

"What?"

"This is part of what I was telling you when I was telling you I'd been through too much, a minute ago. You see officer, this is my father."

"Get onto the curb and stay there."

"You mean like walk onto the curb?"

"Yes!"

The officer, whose name was Kenneth, climbed into the driver's seat and pulled the car to the curb himself. He reached in front of Bernie, removed the registration from the glove compartment, found it three months expired. He got out of the car and asked for Chris Schwartz's license. Chris had to confess to Kenneth quite honestly that he did not have a license, and explained that the mitigating circumstances of the thorny situation they all found themselves in at that moment were (a) Chris's father was a retard, (b) Chris had checked him out of retard rehab earlier that day after returning from (c) his grandfather's funeral in California where (d) his sister had tried to drown herself in the Pacific Ocean, and that it was therefore not only imperative but also unavoidable that Chris back his father's unregistered car down Hoover Place without a license on that particular afternoon, which Chris felt Kenneth would have to admit was a fine, sunny Sunday afternoon in March, and furthermore Chris found it all—perhaps even the sunshine itself—regrettable in the extreme. Which was how Chris and Bernie ended up in jail, and how Cathy ended up bailing them out, and how the three of them ended up riding home in the back of a squad car long after sundown, each child holding a hand of their silent, mysterious father.

42

Chris had no plan for the home rehabilitation of Bernard. He had done no research and little thinking. He would perpetrate the thing by gut. It was going to be a long, tangly, homebound, improvised father-son pas de deux with ambient dirge for normal family life.

On morning one of the rest of the life of Bernard Schwartz and Chris Schwartz, after a nutritious breakfast, Chris began the task he was going to refer to as "The Education of Bernard Schwartz," for which Chris was willing to sacrifice the final few months of his own secondary education.

Bernard was capable of forming letters and words with a pen or pencil at a rate of one letter per five seconds. However, from the outset, it was Chris's decision to discourage his father from taking notes on his semiformal/semi-informal lectures, not only because it would take forever, but because Chris was disturbed by the sight of the tip of his father's dark pink tongue, which emerged from between his lips like a snail's head from its shell when Bernie applied himself to—in all fairness to Bernie—the enormously difficult task of representing the world in words. Chris counseled his father to allow his son's educational talks to wash over his head in the same way he had allowed the warm, hard water from the spigot to do earlier that morning when Chris had supervised him in his first post-coma home bathing experience.

"Okay to begin with there's, like, the whole world," Chris said to his father. They were sitting in the room that had used to be Bernie's home office—the same room in which Cathy had recently hidden from Francis Dial on that cold winter afternoon, shortly before she'd almost died in the Pacific Ocean. "For his own convenience, man has divided the world into categories, and subdivided each category into subcategories."

"Who?"

"What?"

"You said there's a man who did this."

"Oh, yes. *Man* is an example of a category. If I talk about *man* as opposed to *a* man or *the* man, I'm not referring to anyone in particular, but to a select group of powerful and intelligent people who, throughout the ages, have come up with most stuff."

"Are you *man*?"

"No, I'm not even *a* man."

"Am I man?"

"Yes Dad, now that you mention it, you are, in a profound sense, *man*."

That seemed to make Bernie happy, though again it cannot be stressed enough how little was known about what was really going on inside the prison house of his skull.

"Today," Chris said, "I'm just going to give you all the broad categories for things and answer any questions you may have because even for people who aren't brain damaged it's very taxing to hear the truth in its naked form. In coming days, I will go into greater and greater detail about each category. Okay so are you ready? The basic categories of everything are: Time, Space, Living Things, Nonliving Things, Real Things, Fake Things, Concrete Things, Abstract Things, The Relations Between Things, The Movement of Things, The Quality of Things, The Quantity of Things, The Power of Things, Heat and Coldness, Sports, Jobs and Occupations, Crafts, Religion, Food, History, Science, Psychology, Health and Sickness, Aeronautics, Periodicals, Advice, Color and Colorlessness, Noises, Meteorology and Climatology, Sex, Death."

Chris felt like crying, he wasn't sure why. His father stared at him. "Any questions so far?"

"What's a category?"

"Are you kidding me?"

"No."

"All those things I just said are categories."

"But what *is* one?" Bernie said in the slow, halting, cretinous voice that made Chris cringe. "In the rehab center the lady would hold up a pen and say *pen*."

"You can't do that with a category. A category is like a mental place where you put all things that have things in common. Like *tree* is a category, and all trees go in the category of *tree*."

"How can tree be a category? I thought tree was a tree."

"Well, each individual tree *is* a tree, but the word *tree* refers to any object in the world which is a woody plant with a trunk and branches."

"But if *tree* is all trees, does that mean every time I say *tree* I'm talking about every tree everywhere?"

"No. If you want to talk about a specific tree, you say 'That tree over there,' and you point." Chris pointed out the window at a tree in the yard, and instead of looking at the tree, Bernie looked at Chris's pointing finger. "Another way to do it would be to give the tree a specific name."

"Like what?"

"Shirley."

"Can we do that now?"

"Do what?"

"Name a tree."

"How do you mean?"

"Let's go outside and point to a tree and give it a name."

"Okay."

Chris helped Bernie into the lightweight red Wu Tan windbreaker he'd bought him on the occasion of his release from the hospital. Chris grabbed his own colorless down parka and they went out into the yard. "Pick a tree and name it," Chris said.

Bernie pointed to a forty-foot-tall grayish-brown tree with rough bark and no leaves, ten feet in front of the house and ten feet to the right of the front door. "This one is Bob," he said. "Now you try one."

Chris pointed to a similar tree in a symmetrical position to the left of the front door. "I call that one Lou."

Bernie pointed to a small, pale, elegant tree at the bottom of the driveway. "That one is Su."

Of a majestic tree across the road Chris said, "That one is Al."

"That's Don."

"That's Phil."

"That's Mike."

"That's Jacqueline."

"I'd like to call this one Cathy."

Chris said, "Don't."

"Why?"

"It'll get confusing."

"Why?"

"You have a daughter named Cathy. When you say *Cathy*, how will anyone know if you mean the person or the tree?"

"*I'll* know."

"Yeah but the thing about words is they're mostly for when one person talks to another person."

"Okay, I'll call this one Phyllis."

In all his life, Chris had managed not to learn which tree was which; he had been a tree illiterate. Holding hands, he and his father wandered down the driveway and out onto their street, and they named all the trees they saw. When they were done naming the trees, they named the animals great and small. Then they named the blades of grass. Then the houses and other man-made structures, and then the clouds. They named the sky, and the light that was leaving the sky. They named the far-off sounds of car horns, and the sound of one another's voices, and the sound of the wind against the bare branches of the trees. When the sky was dark, they named the darkness. After they had named the darkness, they returned home, ate dinner, and went to bed.

"Good night, Dad," said Chris.

"Good night, Chris," said Dad.

43

Cathy Schwartz loved her purple three-speed girl's bicycle. She loved the purpleness and the girliness of it. She loved the freedom of movement it afforded her, the feeling of the wind against her face, the sensation of mild strain in the muscles of her legs as she propelled herself forward across the surface of the earth. She cherished the miracle of the wheel. She gave herself to the pleasures of the bike. She knew she would have to give up riding soon: the satisfaction she derived from it was too involving, and distracted her from her life's work. She didn't know what her life's work was—that was how distracting the satisfaction was. She would give it up soon, but not yet. She would give it up when the weather got warm and Bellwether turned sweet and smelled of spring. Yes, spring would be the most satisfactory season in which to give up the great pleasure of riding her purple girl's bicycle. She could barely wait until the fullness of spring and the fine hardship of renouncing the bike. She would of course be careful not to enjoy the renunciation too much.

Cathy registered and did not register the reality of almost having died in California. She felt devastated and she felt fine. She was getting used to feeling devastated and fine at once. She was beginning to recognize devastated and fine as the tonic and dominant of her life. Well *fine* might be overstating it: not fine but normal: normal for Cathy, that is: okay but not great: so-so: bearable: bearable with a nagging sense that something major was wrong: devastated and fine. The near-death experience—which, by the way, did not entail an out-of-body experience or a moving-toward-the-light experience—was factored into the timing of giving up the bike. She was cutting herself a little slack for once in her life. So, for now, she continued to do the bike and the stuff that went along with the bike. She liked to invent and perpetrate with meticulous attention whatever rituals she felt were needed to sustain or enhance any bike journey she took. Luckily for her, she had a terrible sense of direction, and thus on any journey to another town, or to a part of her own town with which she was not familiar, Cathy made a map. A map was a kind of divine thing, being a view of earth from heaven. A road map in particular was a celebration of that great achievement of humankind, transportation infrastructure. Cathy liked to replicate small parts of the world in pictures. She was a fine draftsman who knew the importance of faithfulness to reality, but did not underestimate the value of a fanciful flourish. On her map she drew hills and trees, ponds, mansions and shacks, windmills, office buildings that mirrored the sky. She used a ruler and a compass and a protractor and a slide rule and seven colored pencils. Her map was an accurate and beautiful confection on 11 x 17 paper. If Cathy had a flaw as a traveler it was that, in the age-old battle between map and territory for dominion over the mind of man, Cathy's mind tended to side with the map. And that was perhaps why, on her first intentional bike trip to Harbor of Life—the battered women's shelter in Port Town—gazing lovingly at her map while riding, she crashed into a stop sign and bruised and bloodied her forehead.

The day before her trip, she had called Harbor of Life, spoken to an administrator whose name she'd failed to write down or remember, and told this woman of her wish to donate a substantial sum. Today when she arrived, she assumed it was because of her status as prospective donor that she was ushered straightaway into a room where a group therapy session was about to begin.

Twelve folding metal chairs were arranged in a circle in this plain room of scuffed white walls and cheap gray carpet. Eight of the chairs were occupied by women in states that seemed to vary from agitation to calm. But not desperation, not that Cathy could tell. She had expected to see desperation stamped on their faces, but it wasn't. No bruises or scars, no pock marks signaling emotional anguish. Round and pleasant faces, mostly. Then two more women came in, and one of them had the kind of face Cathy'd been expecting them all to have, and that woman was Connie Hyde, the one Cathy had met on her previous, accidental visit to Harbor of Life, the one whose son had ridden Cathy's bike up and down the hallway. Connie's face hid nothing. Everything bad that had ever happened to Connie was written on her face. It was tight, it was pockmarked, it was scarred, it was acned and sallow and dark around the bloodshot eyes.

The woman who came in with Connie Hyde was heavy and middle-aged, with short gray hair. She sat down and said, "We've got some new faces here. Let's go around the circle and introduce ourselves."

Introducing oneself in this context turned out to mean saying one's name as quickly and inaudibly as possible. The one person who did not introduce herself in this way—who, in fact, seemed to take umbrage at this mode of self-introduction as a form of self-effacement—was Connie Hyde, who practically shouted, "Well my name is Connie Hyde!" as if daring anyone to contradict her.

When it was Cathy's turn to introduce herself, she noticed that all the women turned special looks of sympathy on her. "Cathy Schwartz. I don't want to be given any special treatment," she said, realizing immediately that her plea for no special treatment might be perceived as a plea for special treatment.

"Okay," said the big, tough, kind woman, whose gray hair, loose black shirt, black pants and black sneakers seemed to be the uniform of the leader of the group therapy session for battered women. "I'm Sister Theresa," she said. Cathy was moved by this statement. Teresa was the Jewish martyr Edith Stein's church name, or whatever they called it; and the way that Sister Theresa said her name implied that she, the bearer of that name, was a living stronghold of mercy and compassion, a place to come to in grief and defeat. Cathy did not realize tears were dripping from her eyes. "Call me Terry," Sister Theresa said. Cathy was less moved by that remark.

"Connie," Terry said. "Last week you said you were starting to feel safe enough here to tell us a little bit of your story. How do you feel today?"

Connie stared at Cathy.

"Maybe start out with just a few words, anything you want. Maybe something you've done that you feel good about."

"I don't feel good about anything. My life is one mistake after another. Last week you said that every time someone in here speaks, they're performing an act of generosity for the whole group, they're helping everyone in the group. Well that's a lot of pressure. I didn't come here to help anyone. Why's that girl crying?"

Everyone looked at Cathy again. Cathy decided to risk sounding like a fool in order to demonstrate her own generosity to the group beyond the impersonal gesture of donating money, which she assumed everyone already knew about. "I'm crying because Sister Theresa seems strong and good to me."

"Yeah right," said Connie Hyde. "You're crying because you've got a big shiner on your head."

"Oh no, I got this riding my bike over here. I accidentally ran into a stop sign."

"Now I remember you," Connie said. "You're the girl who came in here a few weeks ago with that bicycle, saying you were lost. And now you're back, saying you hit a stop sign. Well I'll tell you something. You weren't lost and you didn't hit a stop sign. You're not even a good liar. This is a battered women's shelter. You're here because someone's been beating you up. I don't want to be in a group with a liar. Check your lies at the door. Check your lies at the door!"

"Connie, back off," Sister Theresa said, with a mix of authority and compassion that Cathy found almost disorienting.

Connie looked stunned. She stood up as if she were about to run out of the room, and sat down again. She looked around the room, but not at anyone in particular. Her grayish-yellow unsupple skin seemed to tighten over the hard muscles and bones of her face. She said, "I'm sorry, everyone. I'm sorry, *Cathy*. I'm new at this. I tend to get out of control. I don't– how do you call that? I forgot what I'm trying to say. I'm trying to say something Sister told us last week but I can't remember. My mind is so– damn! I'm trying to say to all of you that if you see me fuck up like this you have to tell me. You have to just tell me, like Sister Terry just did, because I lose my—that's what I like about Sister is she'll just say it, but without being judgmental. I definitely need it said to me even if it is judgmental. My father used to say it to me. He'd say it to me and also smack me. 'You've been bad,' he'd say. 'I don't see how you could be my daughter,' he'd say. That was his big thing. I wasn't his daughter. I think he really thought I wasn't his daughter, even though I looked just like him and had his same bad temper and I still have it.

"My first husband used to tell me when I was bad too, only he'd use the words, 'You fucked up, Connie! You fucked up, Connie!' And a lot of times he'd tell me I fucked up when I didn't fuck up, though it took me about three years to figure *that* out. Mine is the typical story, as they say. First my father beat me, then my husband beat me, then my other husband who is the father of my son beat me. I'm like a little walking tragedy, boo-hoo, but I'm only making fun of myself and not you, what's-your-name over there who got hit in the face with a stop sign. I don't know. I have a bad temper. I say things to my husband that provoke him, I do. Okay now you're all staring at me like you think I'm pathetic. Well there's your act of generosity, Sister, I just made everyone feel a little better because they all know they're better than the pathetic loser who just made an idiot out of herself by talking and talking and saying absolutely nothing. Now *you* say something, stop sign girl."

"I'm about to donate $75,000 to this shelter," Cathy said.

44

Before she dumped him, speech pathologist Jennifer Gramsci had imparted a number of pieces of information to Chris about speech rehabilitation. She had stressed the importance of functionality and communicative competence. The clinician should join the patient in simulating various real-life situations which required that the patient be able to recognize different ways of structuring speech—like a story or an explanation or a description—as well as different ways of structuring social interaction—like a wedding or a baseball game or a picnic or a spousal argument. The spousal argument was Chris's favorite simulation. Chris felt that if he could get his dad in shape for having a spousal argument, he could get him in shape for having a spouse. Chris had given up hope of having neurology fellow Lisa Danmeyer as a stepmother, partly because he was cultivating the hope of having her as a wife. He had moved on to hoping to have a stepmother who was also a mental retard. Not that the middle-aged women he'd encountered at the Roosevelt Rehabilitation Facility hadn't been pretty demoralizing to be around. There was that one lady who had the kind of speech disorder where the only thing she could say was "Down the hatch." To her credit, she had done a lot with "Down the hatch." She could make it mean "Hello" or "Goodbye" or "It's snowing," or "Give me the remote." But most amazing was when she said "Down the hatch" when she was about to take a drink.

Nonetheless, Chris felt "Down the hatch" did not one half of a spousal argument make, and was spending the afternoon trying to get his father to yell at him about charging too many luxury items to the credit card when Cathy, dizzy, entered the kitchen. Frank Dial was also in the room at the time, looking out the window, paying no attention to anyone, thinking about things no one else in the room knew about or would be able to understand.

"Cathy, what happened to you?" Bernie said, and got to his feet. Bernie still said and did everything as if under twenty feet of water, or twenty feet of blood.

"Whoa," Chris said.

Here Frank Dial missed an opportunity. He had known that Cathy was in the room even before Chris and Bernie did, not because he'd seen her reflection in the window he was looking out of—which he had—but because he'd felt her presence like a rash on his skin. In a fit of humiliated anger, he had chosen to ignore her until someone else noticed her, at which point he'd planned to turn around with withering economy of movement and say, "Oh Catherine, how good to see you again." But when Bernie unexpectedly said "What happened to you?" Frank was thrown. He couldn't tell from Cathy's reflection in the window he was looking out of—looking *into* was more like it—what Bernie was reacting to. He fought his impulse to turn around and see what was wrong. He found himself in the untenable position of looking out the window when evidently some thing had happened to Catherine Schwartz. Five, eight, twelve seconds were gone and more were getting away from him. All kinds of events to which Frank's back was turned were taking place in the kitchen. The kitchen was abustle with family activity and he, nonfamily idiot, was looking out the window.

The kitchen went quiet. Chris and Bernie were gone. "Frank," Cathy said. His eyes were squeezed shut now and he gauged by the sound of her voice that she was standing four feet behind him, possibly three and a half or three. He tried to turn around but he couldn't.

"I loved the description of my hand that you wrote," she said.

Oh, how this girl understood just what to say! He turned and rushed toward her and took her hand and kissed it. They stared at each other. Frank's eyes widened in loving horror as he took in Cathy's head wound. As if of its own accord, the space between their bodies shrank down to nothing and they hugged.

Chris walked in with a glass of extracold water from the bathroom sink and said "Holy shit." Frank and Cathy shifted from hugging to light hand-holding.

Bernie came in behind him with the first aid kit and said, "Don't say that word. That's not nice. Why did you say it?"

"I don't know. I'm sorry. Everyone in this kitchen please forgive me."

"I forgive you, my brother," Frank said.

"I forgive you, my brother," Cathy said.

Chris was displeased that Cathy had chosen this moment to develop a sense of humor.

Bernie said, "Oh, hello, it's the young– the young– Negro Francis Dial, embracing my daughter."

Frank said, "I think we have an interesting situation here wherein it is proved that racism is a direct result of brain damage."

"Why? What did my father say that was racist?" Cathy said, and released Frank's hand.

Once again, Cathy and Frank were not touching. Frank grimly predicted that the state in which he had lived his whole life not counting the last fifteen seconds was the one in which he would live the whole rest of his life, namely, the state of not-touching-Catherine.

"All I was saying," he said, "is it's weird to walk into a room and comment on the race of one of the people in the room. I was kind of making a little joke."

Cathy said, "It just wasn't that funny because it was a joke about my father's misfortune."

"Well, to be fair to me, it was also a joke about being identified as a 'Negro' when there was absolutely no point to it and when its effect was to make me feel uncomfortable."

"Who wants to be fair to you?" Chris said, adding his own inappropriate joke to the tangle of misunderstanding and bad feeling.

"I guess not you and not your sister and not your father," Frank said, and walked out, ending his brief reunion with Cathy as he had begun it—by ignoring her.

"See what you did?" Cathy said to Chris, who left too.

Over the next half hour, sitting at the kitchen table, Cathy patiently allowed her father to clean and bandage the small wound on her forehead.

45

Late one Thursday morning, Cathy Schwartz was hanging around Harbor of Life, the shelter for battered women. She had come over on her beloved purple bike hoping to scare up some paperwork relating to her generous donation, but she couldn't scare up any because there wasn't any, unless the check itself could be regarded as paperwork, and in any case she'd already signed the check and handed it over to Sister Terry, the big all-social-working, all-administrating nun who was as kind a nun as Cathy had ever met, and as remote and competent as a giant, soft office building. Cathy thought that no one on God's earth could have found a kinder way than Sister Terry to tell her that she was not allowed to attend any more group sessions at Harbor of Life because she was not, strictly speaking, battered, in the sense defined in the Harbor of Life mission statement. Sister Terry's rejection was so considerate of Cathy's feelings and so protective of the women whom Cathy hoped her donation would help that Cathy felt she had spent her money wisely.

And yet Cathy was not satisfied, Cathy was not happy, Cathy was not fulfilled. She had discovered she could not succor her father too often or too closely without making her brother jealous. She saw that in his haphazard, ungainly, and at times idiotic way, Chris was doing a fine job with the rehabilitation of their father. Well okay he wasn't doing a fine job, he was doing a job, and maybe if she weren't sixteen she'd have been able to figure out some way to offer Bernie the kind of adult rehabilitation he needed and deserved, but she was sixteen, and mustering all the wisdom and forbearance of her sixteen years, she decided not to interfere in Chris's Dad-rehab rhythm. Cathy sacrificed the comfort she would have derived from comforting him in honor of that mysterious connection between boy and man that she did her best to try not to be jealous of, since it wasn't really something that anyone was doing to spite her, and wasn't even something that anyone was *doing*; it just was.

Making little effort to help her father was a sacrifice that left Cathy at loose ends. Not that she minded a sacrifice. She just wanted one that wasn't so passive. She wanted to make a *big* sacrifice that required palpable exertion, clear and visible activity, a sacrifice entailing pain that could be apprehended by any of her five senses, rather than one that left her body intact and rattling around the greater Bellwether County area on her sad purple girl's bike. So here was Cathy all prepared to give herself, and nobody wanted it.

She harnessed her bike attentively to a parking sign in front of Harbor of Life. What love she had to give to humans, rebuffed, found its diminished object in objects, like the little bicycle that was her helpmeet and companion.

"You're locking that bike up pretty good." That was Connie Hyde's blond son talking. He stood in the glass and metal doorway of Harbor of Life, an inveterate loiterer at age nine.

"I don't want it to get stolen."

"Who would steal it?"

Cathy wondered if he was insulting her bicycle, and decided that because he was nine, he was not. "Lots of people want bicycles and can't afford them," she said.

"Nobody'd want that one," he said. "Purple's an ugly color."

"You didn't seem to mind it when you were riding it last month."

"That was inside. I'd never ride it outside."

"Nobody's asking you to," Cathy said.

"My Dad lives around here."

"I don't think he'd want to steal my bike."

"He already has a bike."

"Do you get to see him much?"

The boy looked at her as if she'd said something foolish, a sort of Connie Hyde look minus the almost total hopelessness and years of personal tragedy. "I see him every day."

"Oh. You live with him?"

"Of course. He's my Dad."

"It's just I thought you lived with Connie Hyde." Cathy meant to say *your mom* but it came out *Connie Hyde*.

"Of course I live with Connie Hyde. She's my Mom."

"Your mom and dad live together?"

"Yes. We're a family."

"I thought if a woman went to a– oh. Yes, of course, you're right. I don't know. My mom and dad don't live together."

"My mom and dad didn't live together but that was only for a month. Now they live together again and my dad hardly ever hits my mom any more."

"That's . . . good," Cathy said.

Connie Hyde appeared in the doorway. Cathy braced herself for the assault she had come to expect, not as a consequence of speaking indiscreetly to the son of Connie Hyde, but as a consequence of being Cathy. But assault was not where Connie was coming from today. She was in a softer, more forgiving place. She even looked soft, such that Cathy thought she had discovered a new and much-needed technique of applying makeup, because sometimes it's the little superficial things in life that give rise to deep and dramatic changes in a person's whole basic approach to reality.

"Oh, hey, you're that funny girl, the one who ran into the stop sign," Connie said, hugging her boy from behind. "Charlie, you been trying to buy this girl a drink? Charlie loves the girls."

"Charlie and I were having a refreshingly honest conversation," Cathy said, as if she couldn't do without a little punishment today. A bolt of angular lightning shot through Connie Hyde's face, passed down into the ground, and was gone.

"Well honesty is good," Connie said with rote composure. "Charlie, don't I always tell you honesty is good?"

"No."

"Well from the gospels you know Jesus thought honesty was good—though I couldn't actually quote anything where he said that—so from now on, Charlie, I'm going to be telling you it more often. This is my favorite time of year." Connie looked around at the dingy buildings of lower Port Town as if the time of year were written on them.

"Springtime?" Cathy asked.

"Lent," Connie said. "We're going to lunchtime Mass at Saint Andrew's. Do you want to go?"

"Um," Cathy said. They started walking and Cathy walked with them. She had heard of Lent but she didn't quite get what it was. She had heard the expression "giving it up for Lent," and that was something she could relate to. She had been to Mass before but she didn't remember it. She didn't know much about the calendar of Catholicism, or its rituals or doctrine or history or liturgy. She sensed she was therefore missing the main point of Catholicism, but she also had to come at it in her own way. She had to love God before she knew who He was because that was what faith was. If she had learned anything from the example of the life of Jewish martyr and Catholic saint Edith Stein, it was that too much knowledge impedes faith. In faith, she felt she had finally found an endeavor which made maximum use of her stupidity and ignorance. She was adamant about not becoming a know-it-all. The exalted shall be humbled and vice versa.

First Connie, then Charlie, then Cathy walked into the Church of Saint Andrew, a building that looked like nothing special on the outside, but was tall and dark and stony and cavernous and, well, exalted-looking on the inside. Connie said, "This used to be an office building. Then the church got a big donation from someone even richer than you and they gutted it, took out the floors and everything, and renovated it using church-type touches."

Just to the left inside the door, there was a little container of water that was a hollowed-out quarter-sphere of masonry attached to the wall, with a small masonry crucifix above it. Connie dipped her fingers in the water and spread it over her face and neck in a cross shape. She told Charlie to do the same and he did. "Should I do it?" Cathy said.

"What are you asking me for?"

"Because I don't know how to do this."

"You're not Catholic?"

"I told you I'm Jewish."

"Oh shit I forgot. I can't believe I just brought you here." Connie seemed about to say something else and stopped. "No, actually, I guess it's good I brought you here. Skip the holy water. Come sit down with me and Charlie. Basically when everyone stands up, you stand up, and when everyone sits down, you sit down. Then there's this part where people in the audience go up front and the priest gives them grape juice and a cookie," she said, winking at Charlie. "You better not take the cookie or the grape juice. They're laced with something that you don't even want to know what it is."

Cathy knew Connie was saying something kind of dirty vis à vis Catholicism but she didn't know what or why. "Should you be saying that?" she asked.

"The Jewish person asks the Catholic person if she should be saying that," Connie said, and stopped herself again, because it was Lent. "Actually, that's a good question. Should I be saying that. Maybe not."

"What's Lent?" Cathy asked.

"It's where you atone for your sins and you give up something you like."

"What are you giving up?"

"I'm giving up letting people who I think are foolish get on my nerves and I'm also giving up expressing the irritability of them getting on my nerves."

"People getting on your nerves is something you like?"

"Well, Sister Terry said I'm really good at noticing when people are fools. She said even though I'm probably right most of the time, maybe being right most of the time isn't such a good thing because it's kind of like pride, which is bad. Except Sister Terry doesn't use words like good and bad because of her social work training, even though everybody knows when Sister Terry thinks something is good or bad, which makes Sister Terry kind of a liar, but in a nice way."

"Well you're being nice to me," Cathy said.

"That's to keep myself from slapping you. Hey I'm just kidding."

"Mommy never slaps me except when I'm bad," Charlie said. Cathy wondered if perhaps Charlie was a little dim-witted for his age.

They walked up the aisle of the church and found an empty pew halfway to the altar. Connie Hyde got down on one knee next to the pew, made a quick hand gesture in her face area, and scooted in. Charlie did the same.

Cathy said, "Should I do that? What does that mean?"

Connie said, "You ask a lot of questions that a person would say were dumb if that person didn't give up saying things were dumb for Lent."

Cathy looked up at the faux vaulted ceiling and wondered what it all meant. Connie looked over at Cathy, who was tilting her head back and exposing her throat. Connie hoped this girl didn't ever expose her throat like that outside of church. She imagined a knife blade or actually the serrated blade of a band saw coming at that exposed throat somewhere out on the docks. She imagined the saw blade slicing into that smooth white throat. She tried to make herself stop imagining it, but she kept imagining it. Connie would never expose her throat like that, not even in church. If she were going to look up at the ceiling, she'd do it with just her eyes, not her whole head. She thought being nice was something you could not do if you wanted to survive. Niceness was for saps like this Jewish girl who would probably get killed at a young age as a return favor for being nice. Connie knew this was a bad thought. No, not a bad thought, a thought that wasn't *commensurate*. Wasn't *commensurate with Christian teaching*. And more than that, she knew that whether it was commensurate wasn't even the real point. The real point was something else she couldn't name.

Cathy noticed two three-story-tall purple ribbons hanging down from the ceiling of the church. The priest came out of somewhere at the back of the church—or maybe that was the front of the church— dressed in a long-sleeve floor-length white formal gown and wearing one extra-long purple scarf draped over the back of his neck and hanging down the whole front of his body, as if the priest himself were a kind of human church dressed up to match the décor of the architechtural one. He raised up his arms such that they formed a shallow arc or bowl into which God might pour sweet wine or holy water. He said some things, and a man in a suit came up and read from the Book of Isaiah. "Treachery" was one word he kept reading and Cathy felt she ought to remember that word though she didn't know why. The priest came back to the podium and read from the Gospel According to Matthew. Cathy listened and watched from someplace inside herself, a place of dizzy alertness, a small core behind her ribs to reach which all stimuli and all thought had to travel through durable layers of flesh, muscle, and bone. By the time sentences in the English language reached her all the way in there, they sounded like some other language—Latin, maybe. She stood up and sat down, stood up and sat down, following the crowd. The priest asked everyone to pray together and encouraged people to speak up about what they needed from God. "Physical healing for Dan," one woman said. "Help for people addicted to drugs or alcohol," said a man. "Special attention," one man, then another, and then a woman said. Cathy wondered what special attention was, and what would happen in terms of things Cathy could see or hear or touch or know, if God were to give her special attention. She would never ask God for special attention, but she was moved to see people who were *really* suffering ask him for it. She hoped Connie Hyde would ask for something but she didn't. Other people far away from Cathy were murmuring indistinctly the names of things they needed from God. In lunchtime Masses all over Port Town and throughout Bellwether County; in churches anywhere in America, anywhere in the world where it was time for Mass, people were murmuring indistinctly the names of things they wanted God to do to them; thousands, millions of people speaking all at once to God in voices smeared by echoey church acoustics into one great plaintive unintelligible voice of suffering. This single, terrible voice sounded in the small core of nerve awareness within Cathy's ribs. Cathy wanted all the people talking to get what they wanted, and knew that most if not all would get nothing but more of same. What a bunch of wretches people were, how pathetic they must all have seemed to

God. Connie saw Cathy crying, grabbed her hand, found it to be wet and soft like some unborn sea mammal, and let it go. The priest said, "Our Father who art in heaven, hallowed be thy name."

Due to light-headedness, Cathy had to sit down during the sacrament. She couldn't believe what was happening up there: people having carnal union with God—sex with God, judging by the looks of post-ecstatic serenity and exhaustion on their faces as they left the altar and returned to their seats. Cathy was weirded out, but in a really interesting way.

When Mass was over, she gave a sparrowlike kiss to Connie and one to Charlie and excused herself. She felt beautiful, almost religious; she felt open and did not want to close up again just yet. She needed to make a connection with her bicycle, which she loved. She ran the several blocks to her bicycle, unharnessed and climbed astride it. She rode furiously down to the docks to be near the enormity of the water. She was not afraid of the water. Jesus was a sailor, some bible passage or pop song once told her, and she felt the moisture of Long Island Sound on her face as she pedaled her purple bike along its shore.

She rode across the edge of lower Port Town. The mass had imbued her with a feeling she often thought God was guarding as a secret from humanity—joy—and now she wasn't sure whether to hoard it or spend it. It was not Christian or Catholic to hoard it, but she didn't want to lose it. What she looked at in town she looked at fearfully, lest she should see some awful miserable creature who, by virtue of his greater misery, would constitute a void of good feeling into which good feeling would naturally have to enter, thereby fleeing Cathy's body.

She made it out of Port Town. Now it was mostly tree-lined streets she had to endure before arriving home.

46

For reasons that were secret, Francis Dial was the only soul at the Schwartzes when Cathy pedaled up the driveway bearing the intact flower of her religious awakening. Not only was Frank at the Schwartzes, he was standing in the front doorway of the Schwartzes, gazing out at what could be seen of the world from the Schwartz home's singular vantage, framed not just by the doorway but by the entire house, an equal amount of pale house flowing out to the left and to the right of Frank, who appeared to be the small dark head and thorax of a magnificent creature with two-story-high luminescent wings.

Now Cathy longed to throw her bike down on the lawn and run to him but she did not, because her salvation was surely predicated on the loving care of her bike. She made three attempts to get the kickstand down while gazing at the sunlight on the skin of Francis Dial's beautiful face. She was open and joyful and afraid she would become her usual closed-off self before she could reach Frank and make a connection with him. She fiddled with the lock, fumbled with the lock. Fuck the lock. CAREFUL WITH THE LOCK. Locked. Cathy approached Frank at a fast skip. Leaning in the doorway, he had no idea what was happening nor what was about to happen. Skipping wildly at fifteen miles per hour toward Frank, neither did Cathy. Her lips crashed into his lips. She pulled away, tried to examine what she was doing, couldn't, plugged her mouth into his mouth. She was doing something that was like weeping but wasn't weeping. Frank was doing something like laughing but wasn't laughing. She pushed him through the bright façade of the house into its dark penetralia. Somehow they were on a rug on the floor in the room that used to be her father's office and in which she had once hidden ignominiously from Frank after he'd given her a print-out of his description of her hand.

"Where are Chris and my father?"

"Gone fishing."

"Fishing?"

Frank kissed Cathy on the floor. One of them began the mutual struggle to get out of clothes; not clear who was doing what any more. The part of Cathy that commented—usually ungenerously—on what Cathy was doing had all but disappeared. What little of it remained wanted to know—when she grabbed the sinews of his upper arm, when she bit into the flesh of his bony shoulder and drew a drop of blood and he winced and she felt the wincing as a jolt in her own chest—how these could not be the very things God intended her to do and feel after He had entered the body of Connie Hyde and led her into his church. And then nobody knew who was making what sound any more, nor whose flesh had turned whose into some kind of food like a juicy tropical fruit or succulent cake. If there was still a Cathy who was separate from Frank down there on the floor in Bellwether, Connecticut, this was not some little timid church Cathy hiding inside her own ribs observing all from there. She was at every turbulent nerve end of herself, and beyond: she was in the body of Francis Dial, too, feeling the pleasure she gave him. Oh what a lovely man, what a gorgeous feeling, what a terrible man, he was pressing down on her and trapping her and hurting her, she would never be free of him. Where were they anyway? She looked around. They were behind or next to the couch somehow, half on the rug, half on the hard floor, a stubby leg of the couch in the small of her back. Then she lost track of where she was again, shocked that she couldn't tell where she ended and he began. She had to escape this hideous feeling. She opened her eyes again and saw a red deer running by the window of her house. This coincided with a physical sensation that was so unbearably good that she had to shout to make it stop. Then it stopped. Then she noticed how Frank was slamming her against the side of the couch. Then he stopped doing that. She wanted to cry but no tears would come.

Her back was pressed against the side of the couch. Her front was still joined to that of Francis Dial. The back of her head was pressed against the molding of the wall, and the side of her head was resting on the one-foot-wide portion of the wooden floor between the rug and the wall. She looked down at the black and tan slashes of the grain of the floorboards. She examined the tiny wrinkles in one of Frank's fingers that happened to stray into her field of vision. She felt lonely. She didn't move or speak and neither did Frank. They remained immobile and silent on the floor of her father's former office for a long time. She felt stupid for having confused sex and God. She was a tiny bit frustrated with both. Not because either had failed to arouse in her a passion more intense than she had ever expected to feel in her life, but because when she tried to understand what that passion meant, or tried through an act of willful remembering to recover the exact feeling of its presence in her body, she could not.

"I love you," Frank said. Cathy thought this a preposterous remark.

47.

Nighttime, late spring, Bellwether, Connecticut, U.S.A. The air was mellow and soft above the Schwartzes' hard black drive. Chris and Bernard craned their necks to look at the sky, which was filthy with stars.

"What are the names of the stars?" Bernie asked.

"I know one is called Serious."

"Which one?"

"I don't know."

"Let's make up names for the stars the way we did with— plants— bushes— shrubs— trees."

"I'm too tired right now."

"Do you have any cigarettes?"

"God, you're so non-self-reliant. You asked me that fifteen minutes ago."

"I did?"

"Sometimes I get the feeling you're not as brain damaged as you let on."

In the glow of the moon and of the electric light above the back door of his house, Chris looked at his father's head. A few strands of its wiry gray hair were wagging in the soft spring breeze. The horizontal and vertical grooves in the skin of his forehead, and the grooves that started at the edges of his nostrils and made of his mouth a parenthetical statement looked deeper than before. His chin and wet eyes contained melancholy. It was complicated to be the son of a man.

"Let me go inside and see if I can rustle up a stray cigarette from somewhere." Chris walked in the back door, heard human noise in the kitchen, and went to investigate. He stopped in the doorway and saw Frank and his sister seated at the kitchen table with hot drinks, leaning toward one another. Under ordinary conditions, he would have burst in with a sarcastic remark. But something that might have been maturity took over. He walked away shaking his head. What he had seen gave him a feeling he didn't have the energy for, so he put the feeling someplace inside himself where thought would not disturb it, though not someplace where it would not disturb thought, for there was no such place.

In his room, he found a pack of mentholated 100s he'd bought a year ago with the intention of taking them to parties and somehow using them to pick up women, or, failing that, girls. How long ago that seemed! How few parties he'd been invited to since that time, or before it!

He brought the pack down to his father on the driveway and handed him a cigarette. Bernie held the ultralong in the palm of his right hand, which was still not making every fine move Bernie's brain tried to tell it to make, nor would it ever. He made a fist such that half an inch of the tobacco end stuck out beyond his folded pinkie finger and another half an inch of mentholated filter end stuck out near the bottom knuckle of his thumb. "Light me," he said, holding his fist in the air near his son's face.

"Are you kidding?"

"What?"

"Where did you get this idea that you smoke cigarettes?"

"I don't understand the question."

"Where'd you get the idea that you are a person who smokes?"

"Are you asking me where ideas come from?"

"Do you *know* where they come from?"

"Cathy says ideas come from God."

"Cathy's fucked."

"Chris."

"Sorry, Dad."

"Dr. Danmeyer says ideas are electrical impulses tran– tra– moving through the human body."

"I can't believe how hard it is to have a basic conversation with you."

"Sorry, Chris."

Moonlight and lamplight and filial projection all converged on the face of Bernard Schwartz to make Chris feel his father's sadness, yearning, possibly terror. Chris was worn down by Bernie's sweet and pathetic helplessness, and by the inexhaustibility of his own wish to help this man who'd always loved him but rarely helped him.

"Okay," Chris said, "let's take this nice and slow. Best way to learn how to smoke a proper cigarette is to imitate the masters of the art. Unclench your fist."

Bernie opened his hand and the cigarette fell on the ground. Chris picked it up and put it between his teeth. "All right now I notice you're still having some hand coordination problems so let's start with the Clint Eastwood smoking style which involves minimal hand use. Chris squinted and grinned on the driveway. He pulled his lips back away from his teeth. "This is the Clint Eastwood face."

"You know who you look like?"

"Who?"

"Marlene Dietrich."

"Who's that?"

"German film actress with a deep throaty voice and great– uh, great– uh, sexual power."

"That makes a lot of sense. Now that you've said that, I want to say Clint Eastwood westerns are no more than the German mythology and ethos grafted onto the plains of the North American continent."

"How do you know this?"

"I don't, but I find that if I throw a couple of different kinds of jargon together, most people believe me."

"They do?"

"No. They think I'm full of bullshit, but at least *that's* fun."

"It is?"

"No."

They stood in the quiet night air, staring at the black pavement of their driveway. Neither son nor father had a thought in his head, as if they were two mystics. They heard the cry of the tires of a car a mile to the north,, then a loud bang.

"More comas for Danmeyer," Chris said.

He looked at his father's face again, he stared into the face of his father.

"I want to see you try that Clint Eastwood/Marlene Dietrich technique please, Father," Chris said. "Now stick that butt in your puss and grin, kid."

"What's a puss?"

"It's an old-fashioned slang word for face."

"I thought it was a slang word for vagina."

"That's *pussy*. Open up your choppers, big boy."

"Are you asking me to open my helicopter?"

"Teeth, man, teeth."

"English slang vocabulary is very confusing."

"Open up for daddy."

"Are you saying something dirty to me now?"

"Not that I know of, which isn't saying much."

"Why do you speak to me this way?"

"Let me just tell you something important about human behavior. Most of the time, people aren't doing or saying things for a reason, so this type of question won't get you very far in life. Let me put the cigarette in your mouth, would you? You're distracting me from my lesson plan here." Bernie opened his mouth and Chris put the cigarette in. "Now grin like a cowboy outlaw desperado German nightclub singer." Bernie flared his nostrils and worked his face into a grotesque rictus. With his two-day beard and droopy eyes, he looked like an impotent, down-on-his-luck gargoyle. "Stop it, stop it, that's not working," Chris said. "Let's try the Dean-o, the Dean Martin. This one should work for you. It calls for total facial relaxation." Chris modeled facial relaxation for his father. He gave his head a little shake and let his lips flap a bit and vocalized. Bernie did the same as best he could. "No teeth are involved in this one. It's all lip. Let the cigarette just hang off the side like this." Chris stuck the butt in his own puss and said, "Now when you talk you just use your natural lip moisture to keep the thing hanging in place, keeping your whole face as relaxed as possible all the while." The cigarette bobbed as he spoke. "Open up and try."

"I want to put the cigarette in my own mouth," Bernie said. "I don't like when you put it in."

Chris gave the cigarette to Bernie, who put it in his mouth. "Let's see the Dean-o," Chris said.

"I just want to smoke the cigarette." Chris shoved a pack of matches into his father's hand. Bernie shoved it back. "Light me." Chris lit him, and was about to stalk into the house and slam the door when Cathy and Frank walked out onto the driveway holding hands.

"Lovely night," Frank said.

Joyously, Bernie inhaled the smoke from his cigarette. Similarly, Cathy inhaled air. When it came to human relations, Chris was no savant, but he knew Cathy and Frank had had sex, and it was freaking him out. Cathy looked warily at the three men around her. Frank felt happy. Bernie loved his cigarette. They remained speechless and heard the sound of sirens approaching the car accident a mile north of them. Frank worried about his mother, who often worked ten hours a day at her secretarial job; Cathy wondered what happened to the soul after death; Chris hoped the accident involved someone he knew; Bernie was lost in his cigarette; Cathy and Frank studied one another's faces; each tried to guess what the other was thinking; Frank hoped Cathy was loving him as much as he was loving her; Cathy wished for the strength to love him as much as she knew he loved her; Chris looked at his best friend and his sister and harbored feelings of envy, outrage, disgust; Bernie thought of his ex-wife, Lila Munroe, felt it would be nice to be married to her again, sensed he would never be married to anyone again, took a consoling puff on his cigarette. Chris excused himself and went inside. He climbed the stairs and went to the window of his room that overlooked the driveway. Now that he had left, it seemed to him that the three others looked more relaxed. They were standing closer and talking. Chris spread discomfort wherever he went.

How could that jerk Frank have fucked his sister? How could that Catholic simp have fucked his best friend? What abominable joining of flesh and body fluids had taken place in the very house where Chris's own body now was? How dare she, who was both his younger sister and his younger Sister, have sexual intercourse before he did?

Chris lay down on his bed and wondered when he was going to change. He gazed up at the flat, finite sky of his ceiling. Somewhere in here he was supposed to start becoming an adult. How was that going to happen? Wasn't trauma supposed to speed the process along? Wasn't a divorce plus a dad permanently damaged by a stroke supposed to make a person either noticeably wiser or noticeably stupider with grief? Nothing was happening. Or rather, a great many things were happening while Chris remained at a standstill. He wondered what sort of grave personal inconvenience it would take to make him wiser.

48

Summer arrived. Lila Munroe wasn't really a litigator. She wasn't anything. She was on a little jaunt up to El Cuerpo, California, hometown of Morris Danmeyer. A little something was going on between Danmeyer and herself that she would be putting an end to this afternoon because she didn't like driving. Also he was an overbearing philistine ass. Mostly it was the driving though, not just her own, but his too. Time spent on the road from Heart Valley to El Cuerpo or vice versa was lost time. It didn't matter who was in the car and who was in the house waiting for the car to arrive. No thought or work or recreation could be accomplished during the trip, whether it be Lila's own trip or that of Moe Danmeyer, retired piano salesman, cook, raconteur, fuzzy bear, controlling bastard. Whenever he drove down to her house in Heart Valley, Lila drove herself to distraction inside her house, raging around doing nothing. That's right, she was a wealthy and powerful forty-five-year-old lawyer who coped with romantic love much the way an insecure twelve-year-old with too many braces and not enough breasts would do, only where the twelve-year-old loved love but was terrified of it, Lila hated love and the prospect of love. So much the worse that she and not Moe Danmeyer was driving today. Her trip to El Cuerpo was one long narrowly averted car accident. This was it, this was quits and kaput for the Munroe-Danmeyer affair.

Best sex she'd had in years. All right, best sex she'd had in years except for the sport sex she'd had with Sextus Mann. But here was another category: best postcoital attentiveness; or, to be more accurate, best postcoital attentiveness to the fact that she didn't like postcoital attentiveness: best postcoital I'm-over-here-on-my-side-of-the-bed-not-crowding-you-but-not-abandoning-you-either attentiveness.

So if this was the end, why was she driving up there? She was driving up there because Danmeyer was a reasonably decent person for someone who was an uneducated brute, and he'd managed to inspire in Lila if not actual honorableness then a wish to employ its agreed-upon forms. Given the frequent closeness of, at the very least, their bodies over the last several months, a phone breakup seemed impersonal even to Lila. So she was driving all the hell the way up there to have a five-minute conversation, only to drive all the hell the way back. She had no illusion that the drive back would be any easier, nor that the entire Saturday was not ruined, voided, canceled, a waste, a non-day, the equivalent of if she were to end up dying a day sooner than she was currently slated to do.

She walked up the half dozen redwood-stained stairs of Moe Danmeyer's deck. He had perversely had his front door removed so that everybody who entered his house had to come around the back and cross the deck first. She didn't even know what it meant to have a door removed. Wasn't a door already a removal of something? Maybe he'd been pulling her leg when he told her that. For some-one who was a fat loudmouthed hairy scotch-guzzling tub-thumper, he had a subtle sense of humor that she didn't always get. El Cuerpo was hot and Lila hoped she wouldn't have a stroke.

Moe greeted her in black-and-white plaid golf pants, a black terrycloth beach shirt, and the navy plastic sandals he'd favored since retirement. It was always summer at the Danmeyer residence. He opened his sliding glass door and stood blocking the way into his living room. "You've come to break up with me," he said.

"No, I haven't," she said. Unbelievable that he'd already outma-neuvered her: an incredibly stupid man using the stupidest tactics known to the civilized world.

"Please," he said. "I'm 14,000 years old. I've been broken up with more than a billion times. My own wife broke up with me five minutes before she died. Her idea of a funny joke."

"You can't mention your dead wife. That's not fair. I've got an ex-husband who was in a coma," Lila said irrelevantly.

"She had a brain tumor, which was funny because our daughter had just started training to become a neurologist."

She hated these situations that suggested men were smarter than women, "these situations" being any time Lila was heterosexually involved with a man.

"We both knew she was going to die any minute because I was about to euthanase her or whatever the word is, and she says, 'I'm breaking up with you.' I say, 'What?' She says, 'This is it. You're about to murder me and I consider that grounds for a breakup.' Then I say, 'But we agreed to do this.' She says, 'I was getting sick of you anyway.' My wife's about to die and she's got me playing Martin to her Lewis. I'm all set to crank up the morphine and my wife's coming at me one last time with something I don't understand. My daughter has this same sense of humor, only worse."

Faltering, Lila said, "And you're telling me this so I'll feel sorry for you. You would rather have me stay with you out of pity than not at all."

"Who's talking about pity? I'm trying to tell you about the track record of ladies who break up with me. They usually don't live to enjoy it."

"Now you're threatening me?"

"I'm supplying you with the facts. That some self-interest may be involved I would not deny in a court of law."

"You're threatening me."

"I'm saying if you came to break up with me, why'd you wear that sexy tank top and those cutoff shorts that if they were cut any higher they would be a belt?"

"It's hot out."

"You're telling me."

"I'm not enjoying myself in this relationship. It's causing me more distress than pleasure."

"That's an excellent reason to break up. So before you abandon me, let me play you one last song on my upright."

"Is that some kind of obscene remark?"

"That's cute, but no I really did mean upright piano."

"No. I have to go."

"Tell you what," he said, backing away from the door. "I'll just be over here playing the piano. Ideally you would be sitting on my lap during this, but you can stay right here on the deck or even climb into your car and drive away while I'm playing if you prefer, which will allow you not to see me have the five shots of scotch I'm going to have if you do."

Still with the joking tone. This she had not expected. Petulance she understood and could cope with. Sextus Mann had been petulant when she said she didn't want to have sex with him any more. Depression she understood and could cope with. When she told him she was leaving, Bernard Schwartz had lain on his back on the bed in their bedroom and covered his eyes with his right hand, his left hand thrust or tossed out to the side as far as it would go, no expression on his face, no movement in his limbs, no sound emanating from any part of him, the look and feel of a dead man, a memorable snapshot that left her consciousness for no longer than a week at a time even now and would no doubt be the substance of her last thought on earth. But at least she'd succeeded in breaking up with Bernie, at least she could count that moment as a success in terms of irrevocable departure. How could you leave someone who walked away from you and started playing the piano?

Being an ass, Moe Danmeyer played a song called "No Greater Love." He had big, thick, long-fingered hands that seemed to be everywhere at once on the keyboard. He had a kickback deal with the best piano tuner in all of central California and consequently, for his amateurish attack and pedalwork, he was rewarded with the most richly textured possible tone. He didn't so much play the melody of "No Greater Love" as play big fat rhythmically lazy chords that seemed to have twelve and fifteen notes in them and alluded to the melody, pointed mockingly at the melody while lagging distantly behind it and also somehow under it. Just like his whole approach to her breakup, his whole approach to "No Greater Love" was a joke. It wasn't "No Greater Love," it was "No Greater Love, eh Baby?" When Moe was done with the song, Lila was standing in the doorway, leaning on the doorjamb, tapping her foot not in time with the song, but because she was angry.

"Give me a damn scotch," she said, "and make it a small one because I'm getting in my car in about five minutes. And after you give me the scotch, don't you dare go back and sit at the piano."

"Where would you like me to sit?" he said, pouring her the scotch.

"Somewhere regular. A chair or couch."

"Where you gonna sit?"

"I'm not. I'm going to stand here and sip this thing—thank you—and have a short discussion about why I have to break up with you, in which I would like you to participate."

"You could sit on my lap and do this."

"Stop making jokes! Can't you see I'm upset?"

"All right. Sorry. I don't want you to break up with me."

"Don't you even want to probe my reasons for breaking up with you? Don't you want to find out what it is I'm dissatisfied with in this relationship and vow to work on it and make it better?"

"Not really. I'd rather you stay with me and be miserable."

"I said stop it!"

"Hey, girlie, sorry, but you don't get to break up with me *and* order me around."

"Why won't you have a discussion with me?"

"Like I said, I'm a hundred and fifty years old and I'm a man and I live in El Cuerpo, California. We're one town away from the state capital. You want a relationship discussion you've got to drive out to the coast. You've got to be in a convertible with a guy half my age overlooking the Pacific Ocean, for a relationship discussion. For the kind of discussion you want, you've got to be talking to someone born after 1960 and you've got to be down in Heart Valley or one of your coastal cities where they do that sort of thing. Where we are right now, this is practically the Midwest, in terms of that kind of discussion. I thought you said you were over forty. You didn't tell me you were gonna start acting like a fifteen-year-old. You don't like the commute? You don't like my beer belly? Bad breath? Dumb jokes? Go ahead and get out of here and keep dreaming. I don't want to be with a fifteen-year-old. That's called statutory rape."

Lila didn't answer for a while. She cried. She took a sip of scotch. "You've just insulted me."

"Yes."

"You do have bad breath."

"I know."

"It's from all that scotch you drink."

"No doubt."

"Use mouthwash."

"Okay."

"Brush regularly."

"Okay."

"I will sit on your lap now."

"Okay."

She did. The couch they were sitting on was right next to the piano. He reached out and played a couple of bass chords with his left hand while feeling under her dark red tanktop with his right hand.

"You're an absurd man," she said. "I wouldn't trust me if I were you."

They had a nice time on the couch until the sun went down.

49

Three hours before summer arrived in California, it arrived in Connecticut. While her mother was driving north to break up with her father's neurologist's father, Cathy was urinating on a fucking home pregnancy kit. Cathy had changed a lot since she'd begun attending Mass and having sex. She was looser, in just about every way you could think of. She was out in the yard now, waiting for that wonder of medical science and pharmaceutical target marketing to yield its result. One of the ways she was looser was morally. Fuck morality, was her attitude as of two minutes ago. The little indicator was in the upstairs bathroom and Cathy was out in the yard. She was practically in a state of nature, leaning against the white birch tree that her father, unbeknownst to her, had wanted to call Cathy, but which, on the advice of his son, he had called Phyllis, after no one in particular, demonstrating his capacity for abstract thought. It was a hot June twentieth and Cathy pressed her face against the rough papery bark of Phyllis. She was having a moment of unprecedented intimacy with nature, not counting the time the Pacific Ocean had almost killed her, nor the dozen times she and Frank Dial had fucked so intensely that she didn't know where she was while it was happening or just after it had happened. But this was a nice quiet moment with a tree while she waited to find out if she was pregnant.

She walked up the stairs to the upstairs bathroom. "The upstairs bathroom" now seemed to her like a lie. The very stairs on which she was now putting her whole weight seemed like a lie. This whole business of "a house in the suburbs" seemed like a lie, or somebody's idea of a joke; not God's idea of a joke, but man's big joke on himself; man, with his bottomless supply of unintentional humor.

Half an hour later, she raged up Frank's short driveway on her purple bicycle. She wasn't looking forward to this. Here was another of man's jokes: speech as a form of communication. Cathy picked up her purple bicycle and threw it against the side of Frank's one-story house. Frank's mother, Renata, was on the other side of the house tending to her garden in loose, comfortable sweatpants and a flowered t-shirt, and didn't hear the sound of the purple bicycle colliding with the pale umber bricks of her house. Renata Dial didn't know what was about to hit her. Frank didn't know what was about to hit him. Chris didn't know what was about to hit him. Cathy knew what had hit her, but she didn't know what it meant.

While Cathy was outside remorsefully picking up her bike, Frank and Chris were inside, sitting face to face, listening to a folk song. They had dragged the smaller of the two couches across the floor of Frank's mother's living room to face the larger of the two. Frank was on the larger, Chris was on the smaller—more of a loveseat, really. In between them was a coffee table and on the coffee table was Frank's portable cassette player with its little portable speakers. Chris and Frank were hunched down over the coffee table, staring at the machine, listening to the same song at the same time, whispering interpretive remarks. They had no idea that in about ten seconds Cathy was going to burst in on their tiny two-man totality and, with the announcement of her news, blow their brains out.

Chris said, "Are they saying 'Sea Lion Woman' or are they saying 'See the Lyin' Woman'?"

Frank said, "I hate listening to African-American folk music with you."

Cathy came in. Frank and Chris looked at her face. Chris left the room as fast as he could. After she told him the news, Frank looked back over the many weeks and years leading up to the moment when she told him the news as a time when fewer than fifty percent of the stuff in his life was wrong. Now and for the rest of his life, it seemed to him, greater than fifty percent of the stuff in his life was and would be wrong. With her news, Cathy had managed to divide the whole of time as Frank knew it into two discontinuous segments separated by a gulf that could be crossed in one direction only. Not that he blamed Cathy for this. He knew that what split time in two wasn't the news but the ten or so minutes of inadvertently successful procreative fucking of which the news was merely the inevitable result. What happened in the several seconds after she told him was that he threw his small handheld portable cassette player violently to the ground. The two of them watched in amazement as pieces of it shot out in a surprising number of directions and sailed through the dark air of the living room in long arcs. Cathy waited to see what Frank would do next. This was an intriguing moment in Cathy's life, something verging on fun.

If you were Chris Schwartz in this situation you somehow found yourself in Frank Dial's kitchen for a minute not knowing exactly what was going on in the living room but having a pretty good idea, and you were baffled and stunned and not fully cognizant of your actions which, quite bizarrely, just as you heard something hard hit the floor of the living room and shatter, consisted of walking out the back door and trying to engage Frank Dial's terrifying mother in a conversation.

Would it be such an overstatement to say that when it came to women, Chris was cursed? "Hi Renata," he said, for reasons only God could comprehend.

Renata, who was kneeling and, as far as Chris was concerned, doing one of those mysterious things women do to the earth when they garden, snapped her head up to look at Chris, and lowered it slowly back toward the dirt.

"Sorry Mrs. Dial, I didn't meant to call you Renata, but I'm a little distracted, or, how do you say, loopy, or off-kilter, due to this weird thing that's happening inside your house between your son and my sister that I'm not exactly sure what it is." Would it be so untruthful to say that Chris was *most profoundly himself* when he took this approach to a conversation with a woman—usually an older woman—which might be described as racing higgledy-piggledy into the conversation, relinquishing conscious control over his mouth, performing a gutty kind of free jazz improvisation around the concept of "conversation"?

"Chris, I'm gardening," Renata Dial said, brutally. Chris thought that if he had been the son of Renata Dial, he would long ago have fallen to his death in the attempt to scale the icy walls of the fortress of her correctness. It may never be known whence came his balls to persist in speaking to her.

"What are you planting? Gladiolas? Forsythias? Chrysanthemums? Tulips? Roses? Daisies? Lilacs? Lilies? Marigolds? Freesia? Milk of Magnesia? I love gardening. Been doing it for years. I'm a gardening expert. What can I do to help out? Say the word."

"Go away."

Chris stood there silently above Renata Dial, his noisiest retort yet.

"Why are you still here?" she said.

"I'm thinking."

"Do us all a favor," she said.

"What's the favor?"

She snapped her head up a second time and lowered it slowly.

"I'm thinking," Chris said. Whatever Renata was doing—weeding, Chris guessed—she now did more vigorously. "It's a sort of fire-back-into-the-frying-pan thought process," he continued, "vis-à-vis me leaving you and returning to the inside of your house where if I'm not mistaken there's some crazy shit going on that I don't even know what it is."

Renata shot up to a standing position and faced Chris. "You are driving me insane! I am beginning to understand why your father had the stroke."

"At least I don't have a mean little bitch for a mother."

Renata, a foot shorter than Chris, dropped her metal weeding claw and cuffed him in the head. Chris laughed. She cuffed him again harder. He did a balletic 360-degree spin and ended with a hands-out-to-the-side Broadway flourish. "We're really dancing now, Ginger!" he said, coping with unbearable fear and rage by imitating Fred Astaire. She stamped her foot. He stamped his foot and did another hand flourish. She shoved him out of the way and walked inside. He cried.

Frank picked up most of the pieces of the portable cassette player he'd dashed to the ground. There were some that he saw that he didn't feel like picking up. Cathy saw him see them and picked them up herself, annoyed at Frank for not having done so. The whole post-cassette-destruction sequence, which Cathy looked upon as a sign of how she and Frank would cope with the pregnancy together, was not a good sign, but it was not a bad sign.

Frank Dial returned to the main or dominant couch he had been sitting on, while Cathy sat on the smaller, lower, less comfortable, subsidiary couch opposite Frank, as if he were interviewing her for a job. They were debating the separation of church and state, neither knew why. It had something to do with abortion rights and may also have had something to do with Frank's use of the phrase "my decision-making process" in the same sentence as the phrase "your uterus." Unlike the Catholic church, Cathy was pro-choice. Still, she found it not so much unimaginable as freakishly disturbing that the fetus could be hoovered from her loins. She really used the phrase "hoovered from my loins," because this was the new, loose Cathy, recently touched by God and sex. She'd ceased to use that fake girlie style of politeness as a substitute for genuine piety. Central to the predicament of being one of God's creatures was being a creature, she had decided sometime in the last couple of months, and that idiot politeness, which represented her in all situations as a person who had no desires, was an attempt to deny the creature in herself. And now that she literally *had a creature in herself*, the violent and mechanized removal of the creature from inside of her soft red belly was something she would not allow to happen.

Frank was thinking the home pregnancy test was unreliable. He thought Cathy should visit a doctor, or better yet, she should move to a town far away and stay out of touch with him for years to come.

Before all this was over, everybody involved would change their minds numerous times, often within the course of a minute. Cathy, foreseeing this, decided right there on the smaller and less comfortable couch that the only person whose decision mattered was her own. On this point too she would change her mind numerous times.

Renata Dial entered the living room in a rage. She had just come from punching Chris Schwartz in the head. "Who moved the couch?" she asked.

"I did, Mother."

"Why?"

"Because Chris and I wanted to sit across from each other."

"Your friend Chris is no longer allowed in my house," Renata said. "So move it back."

"But wait, there's more," Frank said, because this afternoon everyone wanted to push the envelope of polite talk. I want to leave the couch where it is so I can spend as much time as possible looking at Catherine Schwartz, because I am in love with her."

Renata Dial knew that when boys reached a certain age they would say anything to shock their mothers. Boys would exploit any opportunity, boys would involve any bystander, they would even play fast and loose with the hearts of their strange little girlfriends if it meant being able to put their mothers into a state of shock for even five seconds, no matter how carefully their mothers had raised them to be polite to their mothers above all.

"Catherine Schwartz is pregnant with my child," Frank said.

"Catherine, is this true?"

"Yes, Mrs. Dial. I'm pregnant, and I'm going to keep the baby."

"Let me get you some fruit juice," Renata said, and got out of there as fast as she could. She found herself standing in the middle of her own kitchen, regretting that she hadn't known what to say, and still didn't. What on earth could she say to these two *children*, one of them her son and the other the peculiar little person into whose abdomen—out of all the abdomens no doubt available to this handsome and articulate black boy in a town that consisted almost entirely of wealthy and promiscuous white girls—he had inserted his penis and deposited his sperm?

Returning to the living room with two tall glasses of cranberry-apple juice, Renata said, "Are you certain?"

"Home pregnancy test," Frank said.

"You're coming to me with nothing but a home pregnancy test?"

"I'm also a month late. Anyway the home pregnancy test is 97 percent accurate, ma'am," Cathy said, having pulled that figure out of her ass in the new Cathy way of doing things.

Renata said, "If indeed you are pregnant, I will support any decision you and my son reach about this. But you must think carefully, and despite the flimsiness of your love for one another, which is only transient teenage affection after all, you must communicate as openly as possible about this until you've reached a decision that is satisfactory to both of you, and that decision will be not to have the baby."

"It's not flimsy. I love him and he loves me. I know he'll get a job to support the baby and when I'm old enough he'll marry me."

"Francis, is this what you and Cathy have decided?"

Frank nodded. He felt as if he were falling down a narrow cylindrical abyss, his hands and feet bound together behind him with faux-metallic duct tape.

Chris Schwartz entered the living room fearlessly. "What about college?" he said.

"Shut up," Renata said. She went to get him some juice. She barely remembered what had transpired between the two of them a moment ago in the yard. She came back, sat next to Cathy on the smaller of the two couches, and put her hand on Cathy's knee, a monumental gesture of support in the minimalist body language of Renata Dial. Chris Schwartz sat on the larger couch next to his difficult best friend, Frank Dial. They were all quiet. Chris thought of funny things to say either to cheer them up or annoy them. Renata wondered what became of the man who had impregnated *her*, a man she had excised from her life long before Frank was born. Frank and Cathy imagined various times they'd had sex. Chris said, "Behold, a virgin shall conceive." He was told to shut up.

50.

Meandering home from the Dials' on this muggy summer evening, Chris felt a surge of longing of the kind that worldly people often found ways to make use of. Chris wanted to be worldly, chiefly in his two weakest areas, money and women. He knew nothing about either. On the principle that one way to find out about a topic was to read a book about it, Chris sometimes tried to read books about money, or women, but the only thing that put him to sleep quicker than a book about money was a book about women. Books about men, or poverty, on the other hand, riled him up. After reading a book about men, or a book about poverty, Chris had more energy than he knew what to do with. Books about men *and* poverty he stayed away from, fearing they would create in him a state of such agitation that he'd commit an antisocial act.

He didn't like to do it, but when he got home he had a nice scotch. A nice scotch was one of the items he'd bought with the $75,000 his grandfather had bequeathed him. (Other items he'd bought so far: an American midsize automobile that he could not register because he did not have a driver's license and which therefore sat gleaming *sans* plates in the attached garage of his suburban home; a month's worth of comfortable socks.)

Things sucked. Everybody got to go through a major life change except Chris. Cathy got to be pregnant, Frank got to be a father at age eighteeen, Bernie got to be retarded, Lila got to be in love with this looming Jewish Sugar Crisp bear-type figure who also happened to be the father of hapless neurologist Lisa Danmeyer. Aha: there was someone whose life might be as static as Chris Schwartz's own: the hapless neurologist Lisa Danmeyer. He called her on the phone.

"Danmeyer."

"Who's this?"

"Schwartz."

"Schwartz who?"

"Ha ha, very funny. I'm calling to find out how your life is."

"You know, Schwartz, I resuscitate a dead man in the morning, I amputate a limb in the afternoon, and in the evening I replace the brain of a human with the brain of a pig: same old, same old."

"I knew it."

"Knew what?"

"Me too!"

"You too what?"

"My life is static."

Lisa sighed. In an incredibly stupid way, Chris Schwartz relaxed her. "How is your life static?" she asked.

"All these things happen around me and I remain the same schmuck I've always been. Do you want to have sex with me?"

"Oh, okay."

"Really?"

"No."

"Man, you are cruel."

"Tell you what, Schwartz, if either of us reaches the age of eighty and hasn't had sex yet, I'll let you have sex with me then."

"Neat."

Could it be that Danmeyer had all but succumbed to the seductive powers of Chris Schwartz, champion of woo? With a scotch and a half under his neck and La Danmeyer on his mind, Chris entertained a brief but heartfelt self-pollution, at the end of which he experienced .67 seconds of soul-crushing dread. Where soul-crushing dread is concerned, .67 seconds is practically an eternity. What to do with the accumulation of many such intervals has been the chief question of male adolescence since the dawn of time, to which all answers have been less than satisfactory.

Add to this universal predicament of youth the individual fluttery-mindedness of Chris Schwartz, and the result was ongoing confusion and paralysis punctuated by brief periods of frenzied activity that rarely amounted to anything. A bit drunk and rich in sweet dejection, he felt he had to try to do something to benefit the world. Sitting in his own little corner of his own little luxury bedroom in Bellwether, Connecticut, gazing languorously into the screen of his computer, with a sigh, Chris initiated a word processing document. Choosing a neutral font, he typed, "Preliminary Notes Toward a Proposal for the World's First Miscegenation Website: Submitted for the Approval of Francis Dial."

"In these troubled and troubling times," Chris wrote, and took another belt of scotch, "we have reached a moment when miscegenation—i.e., procreative love between two people of different 'races'—is not merely an activity to be engaged in by a few isolated couples on a whim-by-whim basis and blandly tolerated by the population at large. Why? Because through a reckless and blind devotion to the practical applications of science as a means of personal aggrandizement, we as a species have allowed ourselves to enhance our tradition of mistrust, hatred, and violence with a technology of destruction so efficient that it threatens to rid us of our own worst enemy: ourselves.

"Before I go further with this proposal I must admit that it's not my best work, for I am drunk, my head hurts from when your mother punched me in it twice this afternoon, plus, even as we speak, La Danmeyer may be falling in love with me. I would also like to take this moment to acknowledge that I always somehow manage to do less than my best work, and that all excuses are inadequate.

"The state of affairs that I was talking about in the first paragraph before I interrupted myself to talk about how shoddy the first paragraph was leaves us with no choice but to embrace miscegenation as a principle, to systematically deploy miscegenation as a method of population enhancement, to promulgate and inculcate its virtues in world culture, and to create a miscegenation incentive package in all world markets.

"Within my limited capabilities as both a scotch-drinker and a miscegenation mouthpiece, I feel I have answered the question 'Why now?' Be that as it may, and allowing sleeping dogs to remain

in a state of rest, there remains the pressing question, 'Why miscegenation?' The answer is quite simple, and becomes complicated
and confusing only when expressed by me: strife among men occurs
as the result of a false distinction human communities have made
throughout history between two groups which I shall call, for the
time being, 'us' and 'them.' This distinction is arbitrary and based
on superficial physical characteristics such as skin color, and will
only be broken down when it becomes impossible to tell one person
apart from another. This is where the creation of a single undifferentiated race of mulattos will come in handy.

"Miscegenation for World Peace—both as a principle and as a
website—is likely to make many enemies. But if the history of
American race relations has proven anything, it has proven that even
or perhaps especially the staunchest white racist knows at least one
black person he would really like to have sex with. Therefore, one of
the chief interactive features of the miscegenation website will be
the Make-a-Wish-List feature, whereby anyone who visits the site
may submit a list of up to twenty people of a race different from
their own whom they would like to have sex with, and one of our
miscegenation researchers will supply the visitor with an address
and phone number for each name on that list, in exchange for a
modest cost-covering fee of $500 per name.

"In addition, the site will be a clearinghouse for a worldwide
network of local support groups for mixed-race couples and their
offspring.

"Nobody is saying the Miscegenation Website will be an
overnight success. The investor looking for a quick fix should probably look elsewhere than www.miscegenation.org. The investor
looking for a high-risk, long-term tax shelter that will also assuage
his social conscience, however, would do well to leap at the opportunity to participate in this groundbreaking event in the world miscegenation movement.

"N.B.: Frank: this is all I have so far: what do you think?
Love: Chris:"

Chris cut and pasted his tipsy little proposal into an e-mail document and fired it off to Frank Dial. Then, lying facedown on his bed, he slept.

51

"How's that boy treating you?" Connie Hyde said to Cathy Schwartz in a Port Town diner.

"Did I tell you about Francis?"

"You didn't have to. You were wearing him on your face. That's his name? Francis? How come the violent ones always have the gentle names? My guy's named Gary." Connie Hyde was speaking in a stage whisper because Gary was due to arrive any minute. Cathy was interested to meet Gary, a genuine woman-batterer. The diner was in a bad part of Port Town. Cathy thought the best part of Port Town was still worse than the worst part of Bellwether, whatever that meant. Cathy was often the lonely and embittered audience for her own foolish thoughts, many of which long predated the pregnancy and therefore couldn't be blamed on the cocktail of hormones the bartender of her glands poured into the oblong highball glass of her veins, or wherever the hell the hormones were in her body. (She found the word *hell* surged up into her brain more than ever before, as if Satan himself were extending a personal invitation through his most reliable medium of communication, that ultimate insignia of loneliness, impure thought.)

"What do you mean I'm wearing him on my face?"

"I've been meaning to ask you how come you haven't been to any more meetings after that one you went to."

"Sister Terry told me I couldn't go because I wasn't, you know, battered."

"She believed that bullshit from you?"

"It's not bullshit. No one's ever hit me in my life."

"You had a black eye and a cut on your forehead."

"I ran into a stop sign."

"You've got to be kidding me."

"No I don't."

Connie looked annoyed. Cathy thought that having been fre-
quently punched had not diminished the sensitivity of Connie's face
as an instrument for registering her emotions. On the contrary: this
face was a tightly stretched canvas of ever-changing colors, and
while it did not have much elasticity, it offered as complete a variety of expressions as possible within a spectrum whose one end was
virulent outrage and whose other was sorrowful ecstasy.

"I'm pregnant," Cathy said, as if in response to something.

Connie's face cycled through several expressions and settled on
gossipy compassion. "What are you going to do?"

"I'm going to have the baby and raise it, and if Frank wants to
help me, I want him to."

"I think the money will make it easier for you to do this."

"Well, there isn't much money."

"How can you afford a big house in the suburbs?"

"I didn't say it was big."

"Won't your parents support you?"

"My dad's still getting over his coma. He probably won't ever be
able to work again except at McDonald's or something." A wave of
twitches crossed Connie's mouth in response to Cathy's derogation
of McDonald's. "I'm not going to ask my mother for money. Her
dad left me a bunch of money but I—"

The waitress interrupted Cathy to ask for her order. While she
was giving it, a man said, "Hello ladies, and hello to you too,
Connie." The waitress said hello and Connie blushed. A big gray-
haired man slid into the booth next to Connie. "I'll have two eggs
over you— I mean over easy," he said to the waitress. "Bacon, three
pancakes, home fries, white toast, coffee, orange juice." The man
had long, pointed sideburns, a big rough happy face, and rectangu-
lar white teeth.

"Cathy, this is Gary Hyde," Connie said.

Cathy said, "Nice to meet you. What an excellent sense of
humor you have."

A little sadness entered Gary's face and left it. He extended his enormous dry hand to Cathy. She shook it, noticed it was as smooth as her own, disliked Gary intuitively and wholly. The waitress finished their orders and left.

"Where's my kid?" Gary asked Connie.

"He's at Harbor of Life until we're done eating."

"Oh, you mean *the shelter*," Gary said.

"Just till we're done eating."

"Connie can't eat and be a mother at the same time."

"What things can't you do at the same time?" Cathy asked Gary.

"Two things I *can* do at the same time are talk to a schoolgirl and grab my wife's ass."

Connie said, "Gary!"

Gary smiled.

Cathy said, "Are those your real teeth or did you have to replace them with fake teeth after someone punched them out?"

"Who the hell is this kid? I don't have to put up with this."

"Ow!" Connie said. "Don't grab me like that. I mean it. This kid is whoever I want to hang around with. You be polite or shut up."

Time went by during which the three people in the booth didn't know what to say or where to look.

Connie said to Cathy, "So you were saying about the money."

"What money?"

"Your mother's father left you money."

"No he didn't."

"You just said he did. God damn it, what is going on here? Everything is ruined." She looked at Gary.

"What the hell are you looking at me for?"

Cathy, afraid she would become a pretext for Gary to administer a beating to Connie, said, "No, no, it's my fault. I did say my grandfather left me money. I was raised—perhaps wrongly—to consider it impolite to talk about money."

"Cathy's pregnant," Connie said.

Gary said, "Hey, congratulations. Sorry I was rude. I was raised—perhaps wrongly—to be impolite."

"You do have an excellent sense of humor in many ways," Cathy said.

"Cathy's going to have the baby and raise it whether the father helps her or not. She's going to use her inheritance to raise the baby. She's already got the nice house in Bellwether to do that in, plus an invalid father. Cathy, is the mortgage on that house paid already?"

"Yes."

"Does your father have health insurance to cover his illness?"

"Yes."

"So the money's free and clear."

"How much money is it anyway?" Gary said.

"Gary!"

"No that's all right, Connie. I like Gary's honesty and inquisitiveness. Gary, my grandfather left me one hundred billion dollars." Cathy was weirdly a little more like Chris since she got pregnant and was convinced she was carrying a boy. Words surged up into her brain, as if language were a hormone.

The waitress arrived with the food. People ate for a while and asked to have things passed to them. Cathy glanced at Gary's face, which was substantially bigger than the face of anyone she knew, and more varied in texture. He looked at her unabashedly with something she recognized as appetite, though whether it was lust or greed or murderousness or hunger she did not know.

At the end of breakfast Gary said, "I'm sorry I asked straight out about your money. It's really your business."

"It's okay. I gave mixed signals about it," Cathy said. Cathy felt they were talking about something other than money. "Should we go over to the battered women's shelter and pick up Charlie?" she said, and then, "Oh, sorry, I didn't mean to call it that. I mean, that's what it is, but I didn't mean to, I don't know, imply anything about anyone."

"You mean about me beating Cathy?" Gary said.

Connie elbowed him in the ribs.

"Ow!"

"Did you hear what you just said?"

"What? It's true."

"You just said 'me beating Cathy.' You said *Cathy*."

"What are you talking about?"

"You accidentally said her name instead of mine."

"I did?"

"Yes, idiot."

"I meant you." Gary turned to Cathy. "I meant I used to beat Connie but I've been taking classes. Now she breaks my ribs and I just sit here, because I love her, and because of taking deep breaths and counting to ten and things."

The waitress brought the check and Cathy handed her cash.

"No, I'm picking this up," Gary said.

"Well, I already paid her. Why don't you get it next time."

"Listen, you may be rich and live in Bellwether and be pregnant and have a rich grandfather, but a schoolgirl does not pay for the meal. A man pays for the meal."

"Then which one of us should pay for this meal?" Cathy said, and actually thought of telling Chris she'd said it, when she got home.

"Aw-haw-haw," Gary muttered, wagging his head in a kind of mock or possibly non-mock you're-cruisin'-for-a-bruisin' gesture.

They wandered down the street in the crap part of Port Town and picked up the little one from the shelter. The first person he hugged was Cathy. He pawed lovingly at his mother's thigh and shook hands with his father, who seemed hurt by the formality. "I taught him to greet me that way," he said.

"What a marvelous trick," Cathy said,

"Hey listen I'm really not liking being insulted by you," Gary said to Cathy. "What'd you have me meet her for anyway?" he asked his wife.

"Because she's interesting. Because she's an interesting person who's someone different for us to meet. She's a Jewish girl who's learning about Catholicism and I like her." There was some private communication going on between her and Gary that they were not doing a great job of concealing.

"I guess I'll go now," Cathy said. "Supposed to take my father to the park."

"Hey listen," Gary said, "I don't know what's the matter with me. I've been I guess pretty rude to you, which I apologize about. Please accept my apology, okay?"

"Okay, sure, I've been pretty rude myself," Cathy said, "although you deserved most of it." She punched him on the arm in fun. A wacky pregnant gal!

"Hey, how about we throw your bicycle in the back of the station wagon and give you a lift home."

"Okay," Cathy said, realizing she was making some kind of mistake, but not realizing which kind.

Gary drove up Cathy's driveway, got out, and opened the back door of his station wagon. He didn't help Cathy remove her purple bike. While she was holding it, however, he did lean across it and kiss her on the cheek, banging his knee on one of the pedals.

"Ow."

He got back in the car. He and Connie and little Charlie watched as Cathy walked the bike up to the front door and leaned it against the side of the house. Cathy could see them continue to watch her from the semivisible darkness of the inside of their car. She removed the keys from her backpack and let herself in.

part
five

52

Chris and his father, Bernard, were in the kitchen whipping up a couple dozen poor man's banana cream pies for the impending family brunch. Chris had hired a cleaning service to scrape away the multiple sediments of sticky dust and/or grime and/or mildew that had accrued over every one of their home's plants and inanimate surfaces, to which months ago Chris and Cathy had passively and silently agreed not to be the domestic slave. The house now gave off an aroma that combined bleach, ammonia, and pine-fresh mopping soap, with a double top note of b.o. and the patchouli incense Cathy had insisted on lighting that morning at the house's "critical smell sites" in some vague and misguided secular homage to the rites of the Catholic church.

Lila Munroe and Morris and Lisa Danmeyer were at this very moment driving toward the house in a midsize rental car. Cathy Schwartz and Francis Dial were in one of the rooms of the house; Chris could not bear to think of which room, nor what they were doing in it. Lately, in fact, Chris could not bear to think, but think he did. Without letup, his mind produced one thought after another for its own consumption—thought; thought; thought; thought, at a rate of one per second—as if this were not the most excruciating form of torture designed by anyone anywhere in the world at any time for any purpose. Not the Grand Inquisitor, not Pol Pot, not the Director of Central Intelligence himself could have devised a more relentless or seemingly unsystematic program of pain, terror, and confusion, the main difference between Chris's mind and the entire world history of inflicting anguish for political gain being that the former was unmotivated, purposeless, and—like breathing or talking—involuntary.

Chris tried to occupy his mind with the two tasks at hand: 1. making mass quantities of poor man's banana cream pies; 2. ensuring that his father did not coat the kitchen in whipped unsalted butter. Butter was one of the poor man's banana cream pie's three ingredients, the other two being bananas and machine-sliced white bread—no baking required. The poor man's banana cream pie was not only Chris's most delicious recipe, it was also his only recipe, and was part of a project Chris had had on the back burner for some time: a book of recipes that was also a book of social satire. So there was poor man's banana cream pie and also wage slave's banana cream pie (a crust of bread), homeless man's banana cream pie (a banana peel), and dead man's banana cream pie (a mouthful of dirt).

The double threat of Danmeyer *père* and Munroe *mère* had flown in together from the coast and were on their way over to the early August Sunday brunch in that gleaming ordinariness machine, the midsize rental car. Danmeyer *fille* was riding in the faux-leather back seat, and seeing the prematurely stodgy neurologist was the only event Chris Schwartz imagined he would enjoy that day.

Chris looked at his father, the tip of whose tongue protruded obscenely from between his lips as he focused on applying a dollop of butter to a slice of bread. Bernie was wearing a tight, silvery, synthetic short-sleeved button-down shirt and a pair of baggy hip-hop pants Chris had picked out for him. Chris giggled. "Nice bread-buttering job, Dad."

"Thanks, son."

"Ooh, Dad, is that sarcasm?"

"Well you don't have to treat me like a six-year-old."

"I'm having fun making this meal here with you so screw me if my enthusiasm comes out sounding like sarcasm."

Bernie's face turned red because he couldn't understand what Chris had just said to him. Chris sensed his father was about to have one of the fits that marked this period of his life. Bernie threw down the butter knife and stamped his left foot, his right foot being unstampable as a result of the stroke. Chris hugged his father.

"Don't hug me now."

"What's the matter, Dad?"

"I know I seem like an idiot, but in here," Bernie said in slow-motion without indicating where *in here* was, "I am a full-grown divorced man. My ex-wife is coming over today with her new lover. My son mocks me at every opp– every opp– chance. This, this— what do you call it?—educating me is, is a *farce*. You are making me into your pet—*monkey*. I think you are not a nice boy. You are a mean boy. I raised you to be a mean boy and now you are raising me to be a, a *fool*, a, a *laughingstock*."

Now Chris blushed, having understood what his father said to him. The doorbell rang.

"How do I look?" Bernie said.

"I guess you do look pretty stupid," Chris said, and walked out of the kitchen.

While his father cowered in the kitchen, regarding his clothes and body with hyperadolescent discomfort and rage, Chris answered the door. Moe Danmeyer and Lila Munroe stood blocking the view. They looked oppressively summery. Lila was tanned and had natural sun-induced highlights in her thick, golden, curly hair. She wore a sundress with a turquoise and red outsized flower print. Reflecting sunlight, the tiny blond hairs on her thighs shimmered. Chris was revolted, and wished to curl up in her lap. She hugged him and kissed him and mussed his hair and greeted him more warmly than she had in more than twenty years. And here came Moe Danmeyer with his expansive chest cavity. He grazed Chris's cheek with his fist and said, "Hey you precocious little bastard, how the hell are you?"

Chris said, "Hey you big fat bald hair blue collar mother-fucking jerk, don't get fresh with me."

Moe felt sad and old, while Lila, oblivious to what her son had just said, examined with curiosity the physical changes that had occurred in the house she'd once lived in for ten years. Or rather, she felt the difference of the house without being able to remember anything about what it had looked like when she lived there.

The grown-ups having been dispatched to the living room, that dreamy vision of loveliness and competence—La Danmeyer herself—entered Chris's home. She looked sullen and wan, reflecting, Chris felt, his own inner state. She wore a gray T-shirt, loose jeans, and sandals of a color it was impossible for Chris to determine, so taken was he with the natural wonders that were her toes. They were like little prehistoric mountain organisms: bony, long, crooked, blistered and gray, except for the cracked and marled nails, which were a turgid yellow. "Holy shit," Chris said.

"I was just thinking the same thing," Lisa said, and kissed his cheek. Chris was getting a big boner. He had promised himself to behave like an adult with her and struggled to renew his promise each moment she was before him. He took the hand of the fabulous La D and guided her toward the kitchen. "Come," he said, letting the word linger in the air no longer than a gentleman would, "with me to the kitchen and let me show you my food preparation scheme aka recipe aka gourmet sex joke aka brunch aka poor man's banana cream pie, plus, moreover, your former patient and my best confection, Bernard Schwartz. Oh La D, this is the finest hour of my life."

"It isn't the finest hour of mine."

"Your sullenness is my inspiration."

"You're the silliest person I know."

Chris's young heart was bursting with joy and full of the ineffable sad mystery of existence.

They found a motionless Bernard Schwartz standing in the middle of the kitchen, staring at the wall, his lumpy torso straining against the shiny silver fabric of his shirt.

"Bernard, how are you?"

"I don't know you."

"I am the doctor who took care of you at the hospital."

"In that case please explain: how did this happen to me? How did this happen to me?"

"You combined two incompatible kinds of medication, and the side effects were severe. You had a stroke."

"*How did this happen to me?*" Bernie was shaking. He picked up one of the buttered-bread-and-banana things and threw it against the wall. He picked them up one after another as fast as he could and threw them against the wall.

Lisa Danmeyer restrained him by hugging him from behind. "All right, Bernard, you have had a terrible setback in your life. Is there anything I can do for you right now that will help you? Tell me what I can do for you."

"I can't stand these clothes. I am being made to look like a—fool. I would like to wear clothes that are, are, right. It takes me an hour to dress myself. I would like you to help me dress in clothes that are, that are, right."

"I can do that, Bernard." Lisa scowled at Chris and beckoned him to assist her in helping his father up the stairs to his bedroom.

Cathy, Frank, Lila, and Moe were assembled in the living room. "I can get water or orange juice for anyone," Cathy offered. The others jumped at the chance to drink orange juice. While Cathy was gone, people said things like "How was your flight?" and "Fine." She came back and all sipped contemplatively for a time.

"What have you been up to?" Lila said, looking at Cathy and Frank.

"Well, Frank got me pregnant, if that's what you mean."

Moe laughed—he thought Cathy was joking. Lila asked if she was joking.

"Have you ever known me to joke about anything, Lila?"

"I'd prefer to be called Mom."

"*Mom*?"

Lila cried a little. "Honey, when did you find out you're pregnant?"

"What does it matter when I found out?"

"I think I mean how many months pregnant are you?"

"Three."

"So. Three. So that means— So does that mean— ?" Lila was in a chair across the room from her daughter. She leaned forward as far as she could: she was not so much sitting in the chair as squatting in front of it.

"I have another week to decide but I think I want to have the baby."

Lila got up and hugged her daughter's neck. Cathy didn't get up. Their torsos were at ninety degree angles. The tiny soft pink wet Dial-Schwartz fetus lay on its back in Cathy's womb, not conscious of a thing that anyone knew about. Lila wouldn't let go of the back of her daughter's neck.

"Mom, why don't you sit on the couch next to me. Frank, maybe you can go talk to my mother's boyfriend while I talk to my mother about our baby."

Francis got up. The women whispered on the couch about the baby. Cathy let her mother touch her arm and put her warm hand on her belly, and even liked it. Lila was more kind and excited and interested in the baby than Cathy had expected her to be.

"You know my daughter?" Moe said to Frank.

"I've met her."

"I was twenty-five when my wife gave birth to her. I was twenty when we had her older sister who died as a teenager of a drug overdose and a car accident."

"Wow."

"What do you mean, 'wow'?"

"I'm thinking of how I used to think that all black people had bad luck, and only some white people had back luck. Now I think everybody has bad luck."

"What bad luck have you had?"

"The racial thing I already mentioned."

"What else?"

"My dad left before I was born."

"What else?"

"That's not enough?"

"How about the kid?"

"What kid?"

"The one your girl is gonna give birth to this winter."

"What about it?"

"Is that bad luck to you?"

"I'm not sure."

"If it is, you better tell her."

"You don't even know me."

"I don't have to."

"Another thing I've noticed about life lately is that people who are around your age always act like they know so much more than people my age and they feel like the day's work is not done until they have passed on their amazing wisdom to people my age. But if you think about it in terms of geological time, people your age should shut up more often."

"HEY!" Moe yelled, startling everyone. He stood up. "I'm tired of being shown disrespect by all the snotnosed little shits in this house. There's rules in this world, and one of them is you don't say anything the hell you want to a stranger who's older than you. One of them's politeness. You want rude, you little shit, just say the word. I got rude in me that'd have you crawling out the door wishing you hadn't woken up today. So just tell me right now if rude is the direction you want things to go."

Bernie Schwartz came in wearing a suit. About who the big man yelling in his living room might be, Bernie was uncertain.

"Bernard Schwartz, Morris Danmeyer," Lila Munroe said.

Chris shoved his father deeper into the living room.

"Dad, what are you shouting about?" Lisa Danmeyer said, edging in around Chris and his father.

"Lack of decorum," Moe said.

"That's rich," Lisa said.

Bernie shook Moe's hand. "Who are you, exactly?"

Moe hated that he was being asked who he was. He hated that he had said "Lack of decorum," thus opening himself to the sarcastic remark of his child. He knew he wasn't wrong to have yelled. He knew he was good at being polite and easygoing despite the rude and anxious company he might find himself in at any moment. For the first time in the months he'd known her, he wondered if he hadn't made a mistake in choosing Lila Munroe as a lady friend.

As if there were a fixed cumulative total amount of ambivalence that had to exist in the combined minds of the two people in the relationship at any moment, Lila now felt unmitigated love for her man Moe. She thought how unbearable this family event would have been without him. She thought how appropriate and necessary his outburst was; in fact she didn't even think of it as an outburst, she thought of it as a disciplining of the unruly polity. She looked at him lovingly and tried to misread the look of fear and annoyance with which he returned her look.

Chris Schwartz, dadlike, convinced everyone to sit down. Lila and Cathy were still together on the loveseat. Moe was back in the comfy chair, but Chris had inserted Bernie on a wooden chair between Moe and Frank. He and Lisa pulled up two additional chairs. The asymmetrical group set about the work of pre-brunch chat. Lila Munroe's opening attempt was, "Who here doesn't know that my daughter is pregnant by Frank Dial and is almost certainly going to keep the baby?"

Bernie raised his hand. Lisa Danmeyer said, "What? Are you crazy?" Cathy slapped her mother's face. Lila took the slap. She was glad she'd said what she did, and glad somebody asked Cathy if she was crazy.

Cathy said to Lisa, "Who are you to tell me I'm crazy? As far as I'm concerned, you've failed our family." She indicated the befuddled Bernard with her head, knowing she was saying something false out of spite. "You're twice as old as I am and it's clear you've chosen your dubious medical career over intimacy and love and family. So you're basically judging me by your own standards of sanity which are irrelevant to me and my life."

Frank said, "Okay now I'm wondering if I exist here. Where was the word *Frank* anywhere in anything you've been saying? Are you ever gonna even just look at me?"

Cathy and her mother looked at Frank as if he were a flea.

"Would anyone like a poor man's banana cream pie?" Chris said. "Bet you can't eat just one."

"Bet you can't eat any," Bernie said.

"My man Bernie is really sticking it to me today. I'd call that progress, wouldn't you, Dr. Danmeyer?"

Cathy said, "Shut up Chris, we're talking about this."

Chris said, "Would anyone like a mimosa?"

Moe, Lila, and Frank raised their hands. Chris left the room. Cathy stood up to leave as well, but Lila grabbed her arm and pulled her back down to the couch. Cathy wished her mother had always done this sort of thing.

"Cathy, would you prefer to drop this topic?" Lila said.

"I would prefer if everyone acknowledged that I am sane and capable of making a decision about this. And yes, Frank, you asshole, I would like to discuss this with you and involve you in the decision, but so far the way you participate in our discussions is you brood silently or you become totally hysterical so I'm saying please help me deal with this pregnancy by getting a goddamn grip, my love."

When Cathy said *my love*, Frank decided to do whatever she wanted, and the mood in the living room lifted slightly.

"Bernie, what's going on with you, sweetheart?" Lila said, thinking the utterance of another endearment would bring the living room mood up to twice the level it had been brought up to after the first endearment was uttered.

"Don't call me sweetheart," Bernie said. "You abandoned me and broke my heart and now you've brought your boyfriend into my living room. You've done what you needed to, but don't call me sweetheart."

"Dude," said Chris, standing in the doorway holding a giant pitcher-sized mimosa in one hand and a platter of poor man's banana cream pies in the other. "You never used to say things like that. I like the new open hostility, my man."

Bernie said, "Shut up, Chris."

Chris was stung.

"Sorry, Chris," Bernie said. A tear ran down his cheek. Moe leaned over and put a hand on Bernie's shoulder. Bernie gently slapped it away. Cathy stood up and sat in her father's lap and embraced him. She caressed his head and looked in wonder at his face which, betraying his distress, was beautiful. Frank stood and put his hands on his pregnant girlfriend's shoulders. Lisa reached out and squeezed Chris's hand and motioned him toward Bernie, Cathy, and Frank. Chris took one of his father's hands and held it. Tears continued to run down Bernie's cheeks. Lisa held her two hands close to her face in a gesture that resembled prayer. Moe and Lila poured mimosas for one another.

There followed a quiet, relaxed discussion in which no one strove against anyone and no one tried to accomplish anything. Lisa Danmeyer looked at her watch, sighed, announced she had to go to work, and the brunch ended.

Frank and Cathy retired to Cathy's room and made love. Chris and Bernie sat across from one another. They watched the poor man's banana cream pies go stale and they watched the mimosas go flat. They watched light retreat from the living room and shadow encroach upon it.

Sitting in the overstuffed chairs in the room of their Bellwether bed and breakfast, Moe Danmeyer and Lila Munroe assessed the brunch. "This was some kind of test for us," she said.

He replied, "I think we did okay. We'll be all right."

53

Not long after the brunch broke apart, another family brunch
slouched toward the Schwartz home with unhappy implacability.

Gary, the violent husband of Connie Hyde, drove his boxy old
tan station wagon across the border of Bellwether, Connecticut,
feeling focused and purposeful, with an overlay of annoyance
regarding his wife and son. Connie Hyde sat next to him in the
front seat with a care. Their boy, Charlie, sat in the back seat playing with a superhero doll. The rich prig bitch idiot Cathy Schwartz
had somehow succeeded in moving Connie with her weird seriousness about charity and Catholicism. Connie didn't think this girl in
particular deserved what she was about to get. Connie was trying to
reconcile what she was going to do with what she would do if she
were a total instrument of Christian love, but the problem was she
didn't know what she was supposed to do to be an instrument. Or
maybe she did know what she was supposed to do and it galled her.
She was supposed to be one of the poor and meek. She was supposed to wait around faithfully in her humbled and screwed-up circumstances until the end of her life, at which time she would be
exalted. But it seemed to her that some people not only got to be
exalted in heaven, they also got to be exalted on earth. Jesus was a
perfect example. The Son of Man. King of the Jews. People wor-
shipped Jesus on earth, and the ones who didn't worship Him hated
Him with the kind of intense hatred that was an acknowledgment
of his power. And if you really looked at it, Jesus was mean to his
family. There was that time when he was talking to a whole group
of people and his mom and brothers were waiting to see him and he
said, "Who is my mother and who are my brothers?" How nice is
that? And another person who had it way better than Connie on

earth and also was going to go to heaven—and so when you tallied everything up had an overall better existence than Connie—was the pious Cathy Schwartz. Cathy got to live in her comfortable house with her caring parents and soft pillows and her thousand different types of skin moisturizer right here on earth. And frankly, Connie bet that once they all got up to heaven, she—Connie—would be assigned the job of washing the feet of people like Cathy, and by then she would probably be so stupid with angelic bliss that she wouldn't even care any more.

If you really stripped away the couple of layers of New Testament teaching that Connie was serious about, what you would discover was an Old Testament mind. A Job mind, to be precise. Connie wasn't an instrument of Christian teaching, she was an instrument that God could use to test the faith of people like Cathy who professed to love God and worship Him but who were happy and had every little creature comfort taken care of, so they really knew only one-tenth of what God was about. People like Cathy didn't have to deal with God when God was blood, or fire, or cockroaches, or crab lice, or syphilis, or dog meat, or a dead fetus. People like Cathy were not having the complete religious experience. But Cathy in particular was about to have her eyes opened, thanks to Connie Hyde. So maybe Connie wasn't the most exalted person on earth, but she had her little job to do, she was God's dirty little worker. And probably if she really believed that was true she would go straight to heaven, but she didn't believe it was true. She just wanted her own life to be maybe a tiny bit easier, so she'd take a little something from Cathy, who frankly was handed everything on a goddamn platter and didn't have the sense or the decency to be happy about it. Plus, if she didn't go along with him, Gary would kill Connie, or worse: he'd leave her.

Charlie Hyde, the eight-year-old son of Connie and Gary, sat in the back seat, not wearing a seatbelt just like Mom and Dad, immersed in a fantasy world he had constructed around a flexible plastic doll. The doll—a young man with a tight colorful uniform and special powers—was flying over the suburban home of Cathy

Schwartz. With his X-ray vision, he could see Cathy in the kitchen with her nice mother and father, baking chocolate chip cookies. The doll, using his extrasensory perception, predicted that trouble was coming to this nice family, though he could not predict exactly what kind of trouble it was going to be, and therefore could not use any of his special powers to ward off the trouble. All the superhero doll could do now was wait. In his life of fighting crime and rescuing decent folk from dangerous situations, waiting was the most difficult thing the doll had to do.

"I've got an Egg McMuffin here," Connie said. "Who ordered that?" No one said anything. "Did anybody in this car order an Egg McMuffin?" Silence. "So I just made it up, is that it? I just hallucinated that someone wanted this. I went up to the counter and asked for something that no one actually said they wanted, and then I paid for it from my paycheck which I worked for all week and nobody ordered it and nobody wants it."

"Will you shut the fuck up?" Gary asked.

"Please don't say that in front of him, for the millionth time."

Charlie emerged from his fantasy world to say, "Maybe Cathy will want to eat the Egg McMuffin."

"Yes, Gary, let's bring it as a gift for her," Connie said pointedly.

Through a plastic straw, Gary took a long contemplative haul on his Sprite, and felt the gas rising in his throat. "Are you with me on this? I can't do this if you're not with me. I need cooperation. We discussed this many times and you agreed we would do this, and now we're on our way to do it so we can start a new life in New Mexico and you're sitting here right next to me talking about 'I worked for my paycheck all week' on a job you just quit and 'Let's bring Cathy the Egg McFucking Muffin,' so I'm really wondering very late in the game here if you're going to be one hundred and ten percent with me because that's what I'll need if this is going to work."

"Sure. I'm one hundred and ten percent behind your excellent, foolproof plan."

"COME ON!"

Gary's loud voice brought Charlie out of his fantasy world. He looked out the window, sighed, and went back into it. His super-hero doll said to himself, "There is so much evil in this world and alas, I am only one man."

54

While the tan station wagon moved toward the house, Bernard Schwartz sat on the grass in the house's yard, leaning against the tree he had not long ago named Phyllis. Phyllis was a comfort to him. He enjoyed the rough, striated, gray-brown bark of Phyllis against his back, and he liked her dull, hopeful smell. He looked at the grass. As part of an ongoing experiment or secret training, he made an effort to see how many individual leaves of grass he could hold in his mind at once. This was far different from the authorized kind of training in which he was required to describe a picture of a woman standing at a kitchen sink, or make a pretend phone call to a travel agent, or read a recipe and then purchase its ingredients in a grocery store. Holding a miniature version of a leaf of grass in his mind made his thought supple, but for nothing. It was a mode of cognition that had no use but pleasure.

He looked up and saw two clouds above. There was a small cloud and a big cloud. The small one moved toward the big one. This didn't remind him of anything. He looked at the fence that separated the grass from the road. He looked at a black bird sitting on the fence. It looked at him. It cocked its head. It seemed to have a quizzical expression on its face, or on its whole shiny black body. Bernie was excited by the vibrancy of the bird, a creature that seemed to be made of alertness. As an experiment in thought, Bernie held the bird in his mind, or rather, he held the bird's mind in his mind. The bird hopped several times along the fence, flew straight up into the air, and so, in a sense, did Bernie. He saw "his" human body, seated on the ground by the tree, becoming smaller. He rose up past the second story windows of the house. In one window he saw two naked people lying still on a bed. One of them was his daughter, a girl he liked so much, Cathy. The other was her boyfriend, Francis. Their legs were touching, her pale pink leg and his dark brown one, and that pleased the bird mind of Bernie. In another second story window he saw that sweet and funny-looking boy, his own son, Chris Schwartz. Chris was standing before a mirror, gazing at his own reflection, making faces. He made the same three faces again and again. The first face looked like the face of someone who was sad, the second like the face of someone who was happy, the third like the face of an angry, even hateful person. He held each pose for several seconds before moving on to the next. He turned away from the mirror, looked out the window, and saw a small black bird hovering oddly there. "Hey Dad," he said, looked back to the mirror, and sped up the sequence of faces: sorrow mirth rage, sorrow mirth rage, sorrow mirth rage, sorrow mirth rage: all the feelings of all the people in the world throughout time, condensed, codified and contained in the flat square that hung on the wall of the room of one small boy in Bellwether, Connecticut.

Bernie, as the black bird, flew out over the yard of the house, over the road next to the yard, over the modest green forest on the other side of the road, and back over the yard, where his own body was resting against the tree with eyes glazed and half-shut. He saw Frank walk out the door of the house, pause to look at the human body of Bernie, and continue across the yard.

Bernie let go of the mind of the bird and returned to his own mind, satisfied and tired. He looked around and tried to imagine that any of what he saw was his. From the old life to the new, he had carried with him but a shred of the concept of possession. Insofar as he understood it, possession seemed to him false. Nothing belonged to him—not the house, not the people in it, not the clothes he was wearing, not the words he was sometimes able to produce with "his" mouth, or somewhere inside of "his" body; not "his" body, nor the life that animated it. No, not the life that animated his body, and certainly not, he had finally discovered, those other things people meant when they talked about his life, or anyone's: the sum total of all he'd done and all that had happened to him, or of anything anyone thought when they thought of "Bernard Schwartz." Even his own hopes he did not own, though they were dear to him. He hoped that he would always be near that boy, Chris, and that girl, Cathy. He fell asleep.

55

Upon hearing the doorbell, Cathy raced down the stairs thinking Francis had come back to kiss her one more time before going home to help his mother make dinner. Though she did not yet consider herself one of the true faithful, even the partial acceptance of God into her life that she had managed so far caused in Cathy a marked relaxation as she moved through her house. Late this Sunday afternoon, it made sense to her that God and the Dial zygote had taken root inside her at more or less the same time. This wasn't a blasphemous thought—she did not believe she was carrying the new messiah in her womb—but only a notion that earthly love and heavenly love resembled one another, enabled one another, maybe even were linked to one another, for better or worse, till death rent them asunder.

Connie Hyde's tense and terrified face was what Cathy saw first when she opened the door. It shocked her. What Connie saw was a rosy beatific smile turning to a pale frown, which produced in her all the hurt she needed to participate in Gary's plan not only dutifully but with bitchy vigor. "Hey girlfriend," she said, saccharinely.

"Connie?"

"You remember Gary and Charlie?"

"Come on in."

"Thank you."

"What are you doing here? No I'm sorry, that came out wrong. I mean did you come here to see me, or are you just . . . ?"

Connie stepped aside to reveal the gun that Gary held in his right hand, down by his thigh. Cathy gasped. Gary said, "Sh, sh, sh. Let's do this fast and quiet." He was speaking nonchalantly, cheerfully. "Who's in the house besides you?"

"I don't know what you're going to do," Cathy said, "but it's appalling that you brought your son along. Charlie, what do you think of your father's gun? Do you know what he's going to do with it?"

Cathy was watching Charlie squirm and shrug behind his mother's leg and therefore didn't notice what Gary was doing until she found that the cool, hard barrel of his handgun was pushing against her teeth and upper gums and then scraping her palate toward the back of her mouth. She gagged and threw up and Gary nearly pulled the trigger and shot her brains to mush. He moved the gun down to his waist and aimed it at Cathy. "Just so you know," Gary said in a chatty melody, "I'll fucking kill you. So back to my question which is who's in the house besides you?"

"Nobody."

"If there's people in here and you don't tell me about them, they're gonna die."

"I think my brother's upstairs."

"Call him."

Chris had stopped making faces in the mirror, and was now lying on his bed passively involved in his favorite and least favorite activity, thinking. He heard Cathy call his name from the bottom of the stairs, and because she hadn't done that before in her life, he knew something was weird. Later, he would curse himself for not having pursued the meaning of the weirdness of her call before responding to it; he would wonder what the use of all this thinking was; not much, he would think.

He stood at the top of the carpeted stairs with his hand on the smooth mahogany banister. "Chris," Cathy said. "This man is going to shoot me with his gun if you don't come down here now. I'm sorry."

"Who are these people?"

"This is Connie Hyde from the battered women's shelter. This is her husband, Gary, the one who beats her. This is their son, Charlie, whom they decided to bring along to do whatever they're going to do with that gun, maybe rob and murder us."

Chris saw the gun now and thought of saving himself by diving down the hallway to his father's room, locking the door, and calling 911. Cathy would probably die, but it was tempting, but he didn't do it. Instead, he said, "Out of curiosity what kind of gun is that? I'm quite a gun enthusiast myself despite my complete ignorance and terror. I have a subscription to *Soldier of Fortune* magazine back in my bedroom that maybe you'd like to look at with me before you slaughter our whole family. I just love a big hairy sociopath with a gun. My sister here is pregnant and perhaps you'd enjoy beginning your massacre by giving her a bullet-wound abortion."

Gary fired his gun and Cathy fell to the floor. Gary pointed the gun at Chris. "Come down the stairs," he said. Chris stumbled down the stairs. Cathy stood up, trembling. Gary hadn't shot her, he'd shot the wall behind her.

Chris was trembling too, and richly, verbally excited. "Are you here to rob us? We're having a special this afternoon on gunpowder-seared flesh, bone splinters, and bloody destroyed organs. What's your pleasure, you decent brave person you?"

The five people in the house were all standing in the small space between the front door and the stairs. "What's going to happen," Gary said, "is I'm going to stand here with this gun pointed at you two and Connie here is going to go around your house and get all your valuable stuff and put it in the car."

Chris said, "What, you're not going to put the child to work? Seems a shame to waste all that time and energetic child labor."

Gary jabbed Chris in the mouth with his big left fist. Chris's head snapped back. Blood trickled and then flowed from his top lip and upper gum. He touched his front upper incisors with his tongue, found that one of them was loose, that it hurt a lot to wiggle it, and thereafter kept his tongue away from it as much as possible, except when he talked.

"So how much money is in the house?" Gary said to Cathy.

"Not much."

"How much?"

"I have fifty dollars. How much do you have, Chris?"

"Hundred. Would you like it, *Gary*? I'd love for you to have it."

"You have hundreds of thousands of dollars and you keep fifty bucks on you? What kind of shit is that?"

"I don't have hundreds of thousands."

"The other day you told me you had a lot of money. Now if you're lying to me I'm going to kill you."

"Well, I had less than a hundred thousand to begin with, and I gave it all to the shelter. But, you know, do what you want. You're already going to hell."

Connie looked perplexed, then angry. "You really gave all your money to Sister Terry and that piece of crap place that doesn't help anybody? Wow, you rich little sheltered idiot. That's the stupidest thing I ever heard in my life."

"It figures that a cunt like you would be totally unable to understand my sister's generosity," Chris said, finding a justifiable if not exactly a useful outlet for his misogyny.

"Oh my God, I can't believe it," Gary said. "I thought you had a lot of money. This stinks. All right, all right, just start collecting things and bringing them to the car, Con. You people better have some decent stuff here." Connie left the room and Charlie followed her. Gary remained in the entrance foyer of the house pointing the gun at Chris and Cathy. "You two sit on the stairs," he said. "This really stinks. I'm so disappointed."

Neither of them moved.

"Sit on the stairs!"

They sat. There was a period in which the three of them were quiet and listened to Connie rummage around in the living room. She came back out holding a stack of stereo equipment.

"This is great," Connie said. "I'm the woman and I'm carrying the stuff."

"Could I trust you to hold the gun on these people? No."

"How am I gonna get the door open?"

"Charlie, open the door for your mother."

Charlie opened it and walked out to the car with Connie.

"This is an interesting child-rearing technique," Chris said, bleeding from the mouth. "What are your hopes for your son's future?"

"That he doesn't turn into a soft pussy dickbrain like yourself."

"Soft pussy dickbrain. Hm, if he's lucky, he'll inherit his father's eloquence."

Cathy snorted. She kissed her brother's cheek and took his hand in hers and held it.

Out on the lawn, sitting under the tree, Bernie had seen Connie leave his house with the stack of stereo equipment in the slant light of early evening. Now he saw her return to the house, and though he could not hear what she was saying, he judged by her gestures that she was speaking harshly to the little boy who was with her.

Connie walked through the door and Cathy hissed at her, "The Catholic church killed Edith Stein, Saint Teresa Benedicta of the Cross!"

"I have no idea what you're saying to me."

"She was that Jewish woman who became the Catholic saint that I was telling you about."

"So?"

"The Nazis couldn't have killed her without the Catholic church. The heads of the church didn't lift a finger to save a woman who'd devoted her whole life to them. Some grand organization you're a part of."

"So? Who cares?"

"So then why'd you bring me to church?" Connie said nothing. "Why? Why did you bring me to church? So you could come here and rob me? You brought me to God. And now you bring a gun into my house and point it at me. What do you really care about? Anything? Your son? You're a fine woman, Connie. You're one of the best people I know."

"Shut up. You don't know anything. You have your easy little life in Bellwether. Oh sure, your parents split up, boo hoo. Your father's sick, boo hoo. Nothing really bad has ever happened to you. You've never had to make a hard choice about anything. Don't you get on your high horse with me, you little bitch."

Bernie walked through the open front door. Chris yelled "Dad!"

Gary turned his head to look at Bernie. Chris jumped up and reached for Gary's gun. Gary turned back around and Chris saw the quicksilver movement of the gunhand of Gary and heard a loud bang, after which he did not hear anything.

56

The tiny tan station wagon came to a stop in a dank patch of asphalt next to that long industrial gash in the east coast of America, Interstate 95. One of God's unhappy children, Gary Hyde, had had to stop the car because he could not continue to drive while his wife was punching the side of his head. He stilled and silenced her with a hard right to her ear, or maybe *through* the ear would be a better way to put it, Gary having aimed his fist at the passenger side door beyond the far side of her head in the way he'd been taught to do as a boy.

Connie could not speak or move for a minute. The robbery was a carelessly planned, unmitigated disaster. After he did what he did to Chris Schwartz, Gary had panicked, grabbed Connie and the kid, and left the house. They had succeeded in taking $1000 worth of stereo equipment, hardly the sort of treasure with which to start a new life in a new city, especially if you were being hunted by the police for murder. Connie wept quietly now. "You made me betray her, and then you botched the job," she said. Gary, ashamed, feinted another punch at her head. Connie didn't flinch. "Hit me," she said. "Hit me, hit me, *hit me!* Charlie, watch your Daddy *hit my head as hard as he can with his fist.*" Gary put the car in drive. Connie grabbed his right arm and said, "Stop!" Gary put the car in park. Connie opened the passenger side door, got out, opened the back door, took Charlie's hand, and pulled him out of the car. To Gary she said, "You're on your own now." She and Charlie walked away from the car holding hands. She had eight dollars in her pocket. He had his superhero doll in his. She lifted Charlie into her arms and carried him fifteen paces before he got too heavy and she put him down. On an otherwise deserted street, they walked past the edge of the light given off by an open, empty gas station. Connie wasn't sure which town they were in.

"Where are we going?" Charlie said.

"I don't know."

"What's Daddy going to do?"

Connie walked faster, slowed down, stopped. She looked at Charlie. She swung him around and walked him back in the direction they had come from. Five minutes after they had left it, they arrived at the car, which hadn't moved. Connie opened the rear passenger door and helped Charlie into the backseat. She climbed into the front next to her husband, but didn't look at him. Using the same powerful hand he'd hit her with, he grabbed her sleeve and pulled her toward him and hugged her. He took his other hand off the wheel pivoted in his seat, and gave her a full hug. As soon as he released her she scooted over to the edge of the seat furthest from him and looked out the side window. Gary started the car, eased it up the entrance ramp, and joined the hundred thousand others who, by means of the interstate, were driving west.

57

In the hospital, in her first spare moment after it happened, Cathy looked for God again. The first place she looked was within her own heart. He wasn't there. The second place was within the heart of Frank. Instead of finding God there, she quarreled viciously with him, cried in full view of him. And now she was wandering hallways that smelled of ammonia, talc, and urine, each smell put on the earth by God for a purpose that would remain beyond Cathy's understanding for years to come. She walked the hallways looking for the hospital chapel and thinking how she had put her brother in harm's way. She was a sheltered naive rich idiot girl, as one of the Hydes had said of her recently, or maybe she had said it of herself.

Cathy found the church, the chapel—the house of God within the house of illness, injury, and death. She opened the door. It was dim, carpeted. Sound was muffled by a low hum immanent in the perfumed air of the room. Cathy stood just inside the doorway. The door, on the most patient hinge in the world, continued to close behind her. No one was in the room. Cathy went no further. There was a curtain next to the door and she stepped behind it. It covered her from head to toe. She covered her eyes with her hands and felt the thrill of being hidden.

The door to the chapel clicked shut and opened again. Cathy's father, Bernard, stood in the doorway, bewildered. Cathy stepped from behind the curtain and startled him. "What were you doing?" he asked.

"Nothing. I was going to pray but I changed my mind."

"What is that?"

"What is praying?"

"Yes, what is praying?"

"Talking to God."

"In words?"

"Yes."

"I couldn't– do that."

"There are other ways."

"Like– what?"

"I don't know."

"Does God talk too?"

"I don't think you can expect him to."

"Do you ask– God for– things?"

"Sometimes."

"Does he give them?"

"No."

"Then why do you pray?"

"To let Him know I care." Cathy accidentally guffawed at what she had said. Bernie frowned.

"What were you going to pray for?"

"For God to take care of Chris."

"You're a nice girl."

"No, I'm not."

"Show me how to pray?"

"What?"

"Show me how to pray?"

The problems in Cathy's life today were not the same as the problems of a year ago: the failure of love, the failure of decency, violence done to her own family, the human body's principle of self-destruction; sending a child out into this.

Her father looked at her beseechingly. She took him by the hand and led him up the aisle toward the altar. She stopped, entered a pew, and drew him in behind her. She knelt down and helped him do the same. She positioned his hands in front of his face.

"I'm scared," he said.

"Say what I say. Our Father."

"Our Father."

"Who art in Heaven."

"Who art in He– He– "

"Heaven."

"Heaven."

"Hallowed be Thy name."

"Hallowed be Thy name."

"Thy Kingdom come."

"Thy Kingdom come."

"Thy will be done on earth as it is in Heaven."

"Thy will be done on earth as it is in Heaven."

"Give us this day our daily bread."

"Give us this day our daily bread."

"And forgive us our trespasses."

"And forgive us our trespasses."

"As we forgive those who– "

"As we forgive those who– "

"As we forgive– "

"As we forgive– "

"As– "

"As– "

58

Mistakenly, someone had put a second body into Chris Schwartz's coffin along with his own body. Or maybe the coffin was not "his," but belonged to the body that was in it with him. Some gentlemen who were employed by the graveyard might now, by means of pulleys, be lowering the coffin into a hole not dug for Chris. The unhappy men and women looking on in black clothes might be that person's people.

One fact Chris was eager to ascertain was if the other person in the coffin was a man or a woman. Being sightless and immobilized due to his death, he couldn't tell for sure. Chris hoped the body in the coffin with his own until the end of time was that of a woman, preferably a beautiful young woman cut down in the prime of her life in a nondisfiguring way. Knowing his luck, Chris steeled himself to accept that it was a man. If it was a man, best case scenario was it was Frank Dial; best case scenario for Chris, that is. Best case scenario for Frank was it was someone Frank hated, like Gary, the guy who'd killed Chris. Yes, the same luck that brought Chris death at seventeen might also have brought him eternal slumber in a confined space with his own murderer.

He felt something on his hand. The other person in his coffin had moved. For Chris it now came down to this: which was worse, a dead woman or a living man?

A light came on.

"Chris?" said a voice he'd know even in death: that of lady neurologist Lisa Danmeyer. She was the person lying next to him in the coffin. Such joy Chris felt, followed by such remorse that Danmeyer should also have died, or been buried alive.

"Chris," Lisa said. "You're not dead. You're in the hospital. You have a concussion. You've been pistol-whipped."

"Pussy-whipped?"

"Pistol."

"Why are you lying next to me?"

"Because you are my patient."

"Do you do this with all the patients?"

"No. You are my special patient. You are my favorite patient."

"Oh Dr. Danmeyer, you are the best doctor."

Chris lay on his back and Lisa lay on her side, facing him and pressing against him. She was naked.

Chris said, "This is very healing."

Lisa caressed Chris's face, chest, and arms. She massaged his legs and stroked his penis gently and continuously for a time. Then she put her moist, soft lips around it.

Chris said, "I love being pistol-whipped."

Lisa laughed her rich melodic laugh, which was somewhat muffled by Chris's penis. Chris sighed and shivered. A lovely amount of warm semen jumped out of his body and into the mouth of his doctor. To put it another way: Chris told a joke to the woman he loved, the woman laughed, and Chris came, and while in the English language these must be described as three separate events in chronological sequence, in reality they were a single event, an orgasm as much spiritual as physical, the punch line of a happy cosmic joke.

Chris opened his eyes. He was in a hospital room. Someone said, "Must have been some dream." That was Frank Dial, standing above him. Lisa Danmeyer stood next to Frank. Cathy Schwartz stood next to Lisa. His father and mother were there, as was Moe Danmeyer. Same lot as at the brunch, now incorporating a concussion and postorgasmic melancholy.

Lisa, who was wearing her white neurologist's outfit, asked Chris, "Do you know where you are?"

"Heaven?"

The right side of his head felt as if it were made of jagged rock, while the rest of his body felt like that of a baby chicken. A policeman came in and asked him a dozen questions. He fell asleep and woke up again.

Francis Dial and Cathy Schwartz stood side by side holding hands next to Chris's hospital bed. "This is it," Cathy said.

"This is what?"

"We're getting married."

A priest, who had been standing behind them, stepped forward, as did La Danmeyer. The priest in his flowing black gown and La Danmeyer in her tailored white neurology suit constituted a kind of anti-bride-and-groom. The priest uttered the usual litany, sickness and health, so forth. "If anyone knows any reason why this union should not go forward, speak now or forever hold your peace."

Chris said, "Yeah, I've got a reason: so they don't turn into zombies of love. So they don't get drafted into the worldwide army of married couples, that gigantic ragtag militia of the living dead, roaming the earth with their arms out in front of them looking for innocent people they can pair off into more couple zombies. First they put them through the indefinite period of excruciating torture known as courtship, and then, with the crude implement of marriage, they murder their souls. The new couple joins the international army of dead-eyed zombies walking the land catatonically looking for fresh young blood. And when they're not doing that they're off somewhere in some bed humping mechanically in the missionary position. Not like La Danmeyer and me. Ours is a special love that transcends sex, but just barely."

The priest ignored Chris's objections. Lisa Danmeyer removed two red rings from Chris's IV stand and gave one each to Cathy and Frank, who put them on each other's fingers. The priest pronounced them wedded.

Frank said, "I forgive you for that time you let me die."

Chris said, "Why?"

Frank said, "Because during the robbery, you died for the mother of my baby."

Chris said, "That's disgusting."

59.

Chris was not now half awake or fake awake. This was the Tuesday after the Sunday of the latest head trauma to be suffered by a Schwartz family member, which also happened to be Chris's eighteenth birthday. He was legal, whatever that meant. The pistol whip was like the bar mitzvah he never had. He was a man. It was all clear to him. Hello, he wanted a drink. He knew a little skank bar by the hospital, just a lovely stroll away from Port Town General in the soft purple air of a summer night. It was late and nobody was around except Chris Schwartz and his cartoon-looking white head bandage. If he could get out of bed everything would be perfect. Nice sparsely populated bar next to the hospital. Give me a bourbon. Make it a double. Here you go—whoa there, Mac, that's a hundred-dollar bill. Keep 'em coming. Clipped manly sentences spoken man to man in the bar. Nice head bandage. Thanks.

In the hospital room, Chris stood atop his tiny feet in the thin polyester one-piece garment whose main feature was Chris's pimply teenage ass hanging out the back of it. He was dizzy as fuck, just as no doubt in some parallel universe, fuck was dizzy as Chris. He put on his pants one leg at a time. He put on his same old Chris Schwartz nerd shoes of countless humiliations gone by, tough luck you big crybaby. Shirtless, going on gut, he climbed into the pale blue lightweight windbreaker with the blood stain on the right shoulder. Looking good. Feeling crappy. He was on the elevator. He was off the elevator. Nobody looked at him. Nobody cared about him. He was out on the street in the soft summer night air, just like he pictured it in his hospital room a minute ago. When you become a man, your life is an uninterrupted series of fulfilled wishes.

He was in the dark bar gagging on day-old cigarette smoke. A few people here and there were playing pool or kissing—things of that nature. Chris approached the bar and ordered his double bourbon with slurred speech. The bartender looked at the long strip of white gauze wrapped many times around Chris's noggin—the halo of the head trauma victim—and gave him what he wanted. Chris had no money. "I have no money," he said.

"Great."

Chris forced himself to drink the bourbon in three gulps in honor of his eighteenth birthday. He rested the upper half of his body on the dark shiny wooden bar. The blood oozed out of his head, and the hard, mineral-rich toxic sweat wedged open his pores and burst out all over the surface of his skin. Not bad, asshole. He stood up, a man's job. He made a phone call. He walked out of the bar and wandered down a side lane.

It was 3 A.M. His birthday was over. Chris had a feeling that could be summarized with the phrase "It's all over now."

He fell into a ditch. Just a damp hole by the side of a thin Port Town side lane. It made sense to him that a ditch should figure in his life at this time. He was relaxed, despite the unbearable pain in his head. Having received an incoherent phone call from his son in a Port Town bar, Chris's father, Bernard Schwartz, back in Bellwether, got behind the wheel of a car for the first time since his own cerebral incident of almost a year before. In his mind's eye, Bernie saw Chris lying in the ditch, and, though he did not know how to drive, he drove off to rescue him. Back in the ditch, Chris was losing consciousness. He wondered how stupid he would be when he woke up, if he woke up. He'd wake up. And when he did, his barely competent father would be present to care for him. And sometime after that, but long before Chris didn't need his father's care, an accident would befall Bernie, whom Chris would care for all over again. Later still, Chris would be the one in need of succor, and Bernie would supply it.

Lying in the ditch, fading from conscious thought, Chris had this vision: him and his father trading comas in a brain damage round-robin: coma, rehab, coma, rehab, coma, rehab, father and son, on and on, in that finite loop of breakdown and consolation known as the future.

Acknowledgments

Thank you, Carles Allende, Michele Araujo, Nick Balaban,
Gabriel Brownstein, Shanna Compton, Leslie Falk, Celia Farber,
Arthur Gibbons, Tom Hopkins, David Janik, Tennessee Jones,
Roland Kelts, Ann Lauterbach, Neil Levi, David McCormick,
Brian McLendon, Bruce Morrow, Richard Nash, Sarah Palermo,
Ellen Salpeter, Sergio Santos, Carole Sharpe, Susanna Sharpe,
Adam Simon, Bob "Robert" Sullivan, Lynne Tillman,
Colm Toíbín, Leslie Woodard, Kevin Yao, Alan Ziegler.

Matthew Sharpe is the author of the novel *Nothing Is Terrible* (2000) and the short-story collection *Stories from the Tube* (1998). He teaches creative writing at Columbia University, Bard College, and in New York City public schools. His stories and essays have appeared in *Harper's, Zoetrope, BOMB, American Letters & Commentary, Southwest Review,* and *Teachers & Writers* magazine.

Printed in the United States
by Baker & Taylor Publisher Services